P9-DWO-225

RANSOMED

CALGARY PUBLIC LIBRARY

NOV - - 2010

RANSOMED

A NOVEL

ELS VAN HIERDEN

© 2009 by Els Van Hierden. All rights reserved.

WinePress Publishing (PO Box 428, Enumclaw, WA 98022) functions only as book publisher. As such, the ultimate design, content, editorial accuracy, and views expressed or implied in this work are those of the author.

No part of this publication may be reproduced, stored in a retrieval system, or transmitted in any way by any means—electronic, mechanical, photocopy, recording, or otherwise—without the prior permission of the copyright holder, except as provided by USA copyright law.

ISBN 13: 978-1-57921-961-1
ISBN 10: 1-57921-961-6
Library of Congress Catalog Card Number: 2008923593

This book is dedicated to my husband Edward, and my children Julian, Chelsia, Bethany, Elise, and Mark. Thank you for all your encouragement. You are an incredible gift from God.

AUTHOR'S MESSAGE

There are times in our lives when we connect with someone appointed by God to fulfill a great task, and our lives are not the same because of that encounter. Such was the case with us when we connected with Ray Wieler of Children's Camps International, a small but extremely effective organization based in Winkler, Manitoba.

My husband Edward and I have been involved with various children's organizations in the past, but found that many are top heavy and very little of the donations reach the children. When we heard about the incredible impact CCI is making on hundreds of thousands of children around the world, and saw the truth of this first hand in India, our hearts were touched in a deep way.

CCI partners with indigenous churches in India, Nepal, Kenya, Belize, and Cambodia, equipping them to reach their communities with ongoing ministry, and facilitating fundraising opportunities in their native country. Because CCI trains in-country leaders who will in turn train other leaders, the ministry has grown in enormous proportions. Local children attend camp for a week, receive the Gospel and a warm meal daily, as well as year-round instruction which continues to build the children's faith, and raises a new generation to fulfill the Great Commission.

I strongly encourage you to get involved with this ministry, either through a monthly village sponsorship, or in some other way. For more information please visit www.ccicamps.com

Thank you for purchasing my book. As we partner together, the world can be transformed, one child at a time. May *you* be blessed!

—**Els Van Hierden**

PROLOGUE

February 2003

Perm, Russia

Sofia Ivanova crouched down on the rutted sidewalk. Shivering, she huddled deeper into her frayed winter coat. A sharp northern wind blew shreds of garbage along the barren street toward the frozen river.

The bottle she clutched in her numb fingers was almost empty. With a sigh, she lifted the translucent flask to her lips and downed the remainder of the vodka. Like the mid-winter ice on the Kama, the alcohol froze her pain and deadened her senses. She loosened her grip on the bottle. With a sharp thud it cascaded onto the sidewalk, splintering into razor-sharp fragments.

"Watch out, woman!" Scowling, a tall man dodged the shards of glass at his feet. Bewildered, Sofia glanced up.

The dimly lit street teemed with people. Groups of men, dressed in black wool coats and mink fur hats, congregated on street corners, their cigarettes dangling loosely from the corners of their mouths. Lovers dashed by, hand in hand, oblivious to the disheveled woman on the sidewalk. Liquor kiosks flourished in the crisp winter night.

Sofia hoisted herself to her feet, her stiff hands groping along the wall of the ramshackle building. A mouthful of vomit hit her palate.

Bending over, she heaved her stomach contents onto the street, splattering her boots and the hem of her coat. She wiped the spit off her mouth and shuffled forward. She had no choice. She could stay here and freeze, or face Igor. Perhaps she could offer herself to him one more time. Forty rubles. Enough for a bus ticket to her grandmother's home in Kutchino.

She trudged along, her toes numb. When she reached Igor's small apartment, she found the concrete building unlocked. Gathering her courage, she knocked. Maybe, just maybe, he would listen.

Igor met her at the door, his gaze dark and penetrating. He crossed his arms and leaned against the door jamb. "Did you take care of it?"

Sofia shook her head. "No . . . I . . ." She hadn't been able to screw up enough courage to go through with the procedure.

"Why not? I told you not to come back until you got an abortion."

Two years ago Sophia had given in to his demands. She would not go there again, not even if her life depended on it. She would never forget the filthy room, the wretched screams of other women behind the fabric dividers, the clanking of the steel pail as the assistant threw the contents into the dumpster.

"Igor, I need forty rubles."

Ignoring her, he walked back into the apartment and dropped onto the old couch in front of the TV.

"Please. I'll do anything for you," she pleaded as she shuffled into the living room.

Igor's head snapped up, eyes flashing. "Get out of here. Your stench reeks up the whole place."

God, I've sinned. I guess I deserve this. She turned back toward the doorway, knowing the consequences if she pushed Igor's patience too far. Last week, when she told him about her pregnancy, his blows had rained down on her head and body.

"Get out," he'd hollered as he tossed her out of the apartment. *"And don't come back until you fix the problem."*

That night she almost lost the baby. Part of her had wished she would so she could go back to him. Back to the only stability she'd ever known.

Why had she fooled herself into thinking he would accept her back? She stumbled out into the night. Where could she go? Aimless, she wandered through the streets. Her feet became numb with the cold. Exhausted, she leaned against a street-light.

A small white truck pulled up along the curb. A tall man stepped out and approached her. She held up her hands in defense. "Please, no . . . ."

"Do you need help, Ma'am?" The man smiled at her. His breath formed a frosty-white cloud in the air.

She stood in wary silence as he came close.

"It's all right," he said gently. "I'm Pastor David. I can take you to a warm place with a bed and food."

Sofia hesitated, and then followed the man to the truck. After all, what did she have to lose?

CHAPTER ONE

November 2003

Perm, Russia

Karina Svetlana laid down her pen on the paper-strewn desk in her small office and gazed out the foggy window. Dusk had crept in stealthily, shrouding the ancient village of Kungur in a blue-gray hue. Rusty cars on the rutted road puffed exhaust in billowy clouds, like the delicate spray of a harbor porpoise that she'd watched in the Baltic Sea many years ago. Back in the days when life was uncomplicated and she still believed her dad loved her and that people were good and kind.

Her father, a successful lawyer during the Brezhnev era, had been among the privileged few in the former Soviet Union. Their family enjoyed the good things few people could afford. Until the demon of alcohol took over.

Turning away from the window, she pushed a wisp of hair behind her ear as she straightened the stacks of paper on her desk. Russia's stiff bureaucracy ruled with an iron fist, even in the outlying villages. The tight scrutiny meant that every detail had to be recorded, and orphanages were not exempt. As director of the Kungur Baby House, Djetskii Dom Number Two, Karina carefully managed every area, from rationing the meager food and clothing supplies to chronic staff shortages. She felt like a tight-rope walker without a safety net.

Karina swiveled the squeaky chair and stood up. She didn't really have anything to complain about. Her employment provided her with all she needed and even a little to spare. That was a lot more than many Russians could claim after the fall of communism. With the security of housing and jobs swept out from under people's feet, more kids than ever ended up on the streets. Thankfully, state orphanages were available. Kungur Baby House provided a valuable service to the community.

Squaring her shoulders, she marched down the hall to the infirmary and opened the door. The babies and toddlers lay wide eyed but silent in their small steel cribs, staring at her as she entered. Some rocked their heads from side to side in constant repetition, while others sucked their thumbs or fingers. Karina stopped by the crib of a little boy, about two years old. Placing her hand on his feverish forehead, she looked at the caregiver on the other side of the room. "How is he doing?"

"A little worse than this morning."

A fit of gurgling coughs wracked the infant's tiny frame. Karina took a damp cloth from the basin on the nightstand and wiped his forehead. "Has he had his medicine this afternoon? And did you apply the mustard plaster poultice?"

The young girl nodded. "I've done all that, but his fever continues to go up. It just doesn't want to go down."

Karina put the washcloth down on the edge of the basin. "Keep him as comfortable as possible. There isn't anything else we can do right now. Perhaps the fever will break tomorrow." She turned away from the little bed. The disease probably would not diminish, but one could always hope.

Heading down the hallway, she grabbed her coat and scarf off the hook. The faded linoleum creaked beneath her high-heeled boots. She shrugged into the long wool coat and tossed the knit scarf around her neck.

"I am going now, Ina," she called upstairs to the other caregiver.

"OK." The elderly woman peered around the railing of the stairs. "See you tomorrow."

Crisp winter air flooded into Karina's nostrils as she stepped onto the cracked concrete step. She looked forward to a relaxing evening at home, perhaps with an old movie on the only TV channel. As she dug in her pocket for a cigarette, her eyes fell on a tiny package on the ground. A faint whimper reached her ear. Bending down, she touched the rags. Her breath quickened at the realization of the contents.

Not again!

Her heart pounded as she scooped the bundle off the ground and dashed back into the orphanage.

"Ina!" Her voice echoed through the quiet orphanage. Placing the infant on the table in the main nursery, she pulled the strips of cloth off the little body. The faint cry grew stronger as the layers came off.

Karina recoiled from the sticky blood covering the baby's body and face. The boy was no older than a few hours. The umbilical cord, wet and slimy, dangled against his shivering blue-gray belly.

"I need a warm-water bath," Karina called over her shoulder as Ina hurried down the stairs, wheezing. Karina rubbed the bluish limbs to stimulate circulation while her coworker filled the steel sink.

"Don't make it too warm," She cautioned through clenched teeth.

Please, little baby, live. The desperate plea of her heart circled up through the water-stained ceiling as the infant lay motionless, his mewling cries silent. His hands hung flaccidly on the table, tiny toothpick fingers spread slightly apart. A tuft of blond hair lay flat beneath the caked blood.

Karina lifted the baby off the table and immersed him in the tepid water, which instantly turned crimson.

"Warm up some milk, Ina. Not too hot. Just a dropper full." She had dealt with these situations before. Too often, in fact. Babies were regularly left on the steps of the orphanage. But none had been this close to the cold hand of death.

The temperature outside had reached close to minus fifteen degrees Celsius. Who had left him there? Did they not realize that death for a newborn in this weather was certain in a very short time? Rage flared in her heart.

The baby's eyes were closed, the eyelids virtually translucent. Ina dripped a tiny amount of milk between his anoxic lips while Karina supported his head.

"He ain't gonna make it." Ina glanced at Karina, a concerned look on her face. "Too far gone, this one. They should've brought him in to us, not left him outside in the cold. People are so stupid." Her voice trembled.

The baby's breath grew shallower, his color a dark shade of purple. Karina lifted him out of the water into the warm towel that Ina had pulled out of the gas dryer. A soft, rasping gurgle escaped out of the baby's throat as his head fell against Karina's chest.

"He's leaving us." Ina dipped her fingers in the basin of water and reverently touched his forehead.

A final puff of air escaped from the baby's lungs. A slight quiver traveled over his frame. For a moment, Karina held the lifeless baby against her breast, her breath ragged. The clock in the background ticked loudly. Hands shaking, she handed the towel-wrapped baby to Ina.

"We did all we could. I'll be back in the morning to prepare the necessary papers." Karina turned to the sink and washed her hands. The smell of death cloyed her nostrils. A wave of nausea washed over her. She hurried out the door, away from the strangling odor.

The refreshing evening air settled her stomach but did nothing to ease the unrest in her mind. She hurried across the street to her apartment. Her footsteps echoed on the cement stairs as she climbed to the second floor of the concrete building. She pulled a large metal key out of her trouser pocket to unlock the door. The old lock squeaked stubbornly as she turned the key.

A single light bulb glowed dimly in the dreary room, casting eerie shadows on the walls. Unzipping her black boots, she lined them up by the water heater, and threw her coat on the two-pronged hook. She stumbled through the hallway to the living area. Halting by the window, she dropped her forehead against the cold glass and fumbled in her pocket for a cigarette. The flame of the lighter threw a faint ray of light into the semi-dark room. Karina inhaled deeply as the soothing smoke flowed into her lungs.

I am sorry, little one. I wish I could have done more for you, but now it's too late.

A gasp escaped through her clenched lips. Turning from the window, she collapsed onto the mustard-yellow sofa. Demons of guilt plagued her as she pulled her knees against her chest. Rocking her body back and forth, a low tide of muffled sobs rolled into a tsunami-like wave of grief.

———— ⌀⌀⌀ ————

Pastor David heaved a fifty-pound bag of potatoes onto the already bulky load of his '73 Toyota pickup. The weight pushed the box down onto its axles, leaving the tires only half visible.

"Gotta do it again, old boy," he told the creaking truck as a bag of onions followed the potatoes. "The children out there depend on us. You and I have to keep going." He opened the rusty door and jumped onto the driver's seat.

Just as David turned the key in the ignition, Jake, his assistant at the shelter, crossed the parking lot.

"Are you sure you should be going to the orphanages today?" He bent down, leaning his arm on the rolled down window. "Stefan has been terrified since his gang boss showed up from Moscow yesterday."

David nodded. "I know, but there's nothing I can do even if I stay here. He'll be safe inside. Tell him not to leave the building."

"You're probably right. I'll tell him to stay put for a while." Jake straightened his back. "When will you return?"

"I'm going to Kungur, so I'll be late. I'll see you later." David rolled up his window and shifted the truck into gear.

The city of Perm twisted along the river Kama like a long emaciated snake for more than sixty kilometers, though only a few kilometers wide from downtown to the edge of the city. Before long, David left the city behind him and headed southeast on the highway to Siberia, the Ural Mountains directly ahead. The sun rose like a huge blood-red ball over the snowy white hills, enveloping the countryside in a golden glow.

"The sun does rise in Siberia," he had told his friends in the United States. "And so will the true Sun. As long as His children are faithful."

For twelve years he had worked among these people whose rulers had asked God to leave, perpetrating the lie that God existed only as a crutch for weaklings and imbeciles. Twelve difficult years, every one of them. Spiritual warfare abounded on all sides. Every day he worked among people who succumbed to alcoholism and poverty.

Life had been different back in America. His MBA provided rapid advancement on the corporate ladder. The spacious new house on the edge of town, with its solid oak floors and marble countertops, was the showcase of his success. With his stocks and saving bonds in place and his children in a private school, the future had seemed secure.

Foolish pride.

On the day the school bus overturned in front of a semi truck south of the Denver turnpike, his reason for being had ceased. With the loss of his two children, the American Dream lay shattered at his feet. The empty, silent house thundered his folly every time he stepped through the double front door with its stained-glass Renaissance windows.

His wife remained equally mute. Their resentment against each other gradually reached the height of Mount Everest. The painful silence grew thicker and thicker until Sheila found a sounding board in his best friend, Andrew.

His relationship with Sheila had been skeletal at best, almost from the start of their marriage. Similar to the stick family that his five-year-old daughter had drawn for him on her first day of kindergarten. It hung above his desk like a prophetic message, although he hadn't understood then. "Mom and Dad" read the caption underneath the tallest two emaciated figures.

Sheila blamed him for his continual absences as he traveled across the country for Imperial Mutuals. Yet she craved the lifestyle his career provided. Glamorous trips to the Bahamas and Hawaii, Alaskan cruises with black-tie events, lucrative Christmas bonuses. She reveled in his role as elder on the board of the prestigious Mid-West Community Church. With its multi-million-dollar campus, it was the gem of Denver's centers of worship. Sheila immersed herself into a variety of programs, leading women's Bible studies and organizing charitable events.

He had not expected the affair from her or from Andrew. After all, he and Andrew had been friends since they were kids, growing up in the same neighborhood and attending Colorado State University together. They joined the same church and often got together for prayer and Bible study. For five years the two of them met weekly as account-

CHAPTER ONE

ability partners through Promise Keepers. Obviously, Andrew was not as accountable to him as he'd perceived.

If he still had Danae and Geoff, he could've coped with Andrew and Sheila's betrayal, but the two little graves in Grace-Mount Memorial sucked him into a vacuum that threatened to consume his life.

So in 1991 he'd left the States to find his purpose and to give himself to a greater goal than capital increase and self-fulfillment. He'd ended up on the streets of Perm, using his saving bonds to fill the hungry and his love for God to feed their souls.

David's truck rolled to a stop in front of the first orphanage on his list: Konava Baby House.

"*Dobroe Utroe,* Pastor David!" The heavyset orphanage director met him at the door and greeted him warmly, a smile on her otherwise stern features. "How are you?"

"I am doing very well, Maya, thank you. What are you in need of today?"

"You're such a blessing! Just yesterday we ran out of potatoes. I prayed to St. Paul that you would come today."

"God must have heard your prayers." He swung the bag of potatoes over his shoulder and followed her into the orphanage, the smell of dirty diapers pungent in the air. A few shy and shabbily dressed children peered around the door of their room, their faces lighting up at the sight of David in the hallway.

"Hello," he boomed with his deepest voice. "Come here, you little cookie monsters!" Lowering the potatoes to the floor, he crouched down to the children's level, his muscular arms extended. A flurry of scrawny bodies flew into his outstretched arms. Digging into his pocket, David pulled out a bag of store-bought cookies. The children thronged around him.

"For all your hungry tummies!" He doled out the cookies, making sure no one was missed. "OK, off you go now." As the munching children returned to their room, he picked up the bag of potatoes again.

Maya watched intently, fleshy arms folded across her corpulent bosom. "God bless you, Pastor David. He'll repay your efforts."

"Don't mention it. The children's joy is my reward." He followed her to the kitchen, a song of praise in his heart.

CHAPTER TWO

"Come in," Karina replied to the knock on the door without look-ing up from filling out the death certificate on her desk. She quickly signed her name on the "Attending Physician" line and then glanced up at her visitor.

"Hello, Mr. Valensky." Her disdainful eyes met Pastor David's then fell back to the papers on her desk.

"How are you today?"

She raised her penciled eyebrows, ignoring his question. "Can I help you?"

"I'm here with vegetables for the children." He leaned against the door.

"We don't need your food, Mr. Valensky. I told you that last time." Her fingers impatiently tapped her pen in an uneven rhythm on the paper.

He ambled to the straight-backed chair in front of her desk. "May I?" Without waiting for her reply he sat down, his hands resting on his knees. He leaned forward, his intense blue eyes capturing hers.

"Ina told me that you're almost out of potatoes and you have no other vegetables left. Winter has only just begun."

Karina watched him warily, anger churning in her heart. Who did he think he was? A hero in a Hollywood movie who waltzed in to save the poor little Russian orphans from starvation? Yet the truth of his words rang ominously in her ears.

"I contacted the Ministry of Health this morning, and they have promised ample supplies." She thrust out her chin and straightened her back.

"The food supplies I have with me will help get you through until the government rations arrive," David answered gently.

Considering his words for a moment, Karina laid her pen on the desk. "OK, I will take the food. Provided you accept fair compensation."

"As you wish. I have the receipts with me." David pulled the slips of paper out of his shirt pocket. "I'll deliver the goods to Ina. She can give you the inventory for payment. I'll collect next time I'm in the city."

"No," Karina answered quickly. "Send Ina up when you have unloaded the truck, and I will see to it that you receive your money immediately." *Even if I have to pay for it myself.* She would not receive a hand-out from an American. Never.

———◦◦◦———

David rose from the chair and made his way to the door. Why was this woman so obstinate? He'd made the journey to Kungur many times in the last few months, but today was the first time he'd made it into her office—by arriving unannounced—but that was besides the point.

In the doorway, he halted. "I also have a bottle of penicillin in the truck. Purchased it this morning before I left Perm. Clean needles and syringes, too. Do you need any?" His hand rested on the rusty doorknob, his back to Karina.

David had no idea why he had purchased the penicillin. Kind of a crazy thing to do at five hundred rubles for a 100-cc. bottle of perishable medicine. Enough money to feed several children for a month. But his walk with God had taught him that when the request seemed ridiculous, God was probably the master of it.

Karina remained mute for so long that David began to wonder if she had heard his question.

Looking at her over his shoulder, he saw the rapid rising and falling of her chest as she stared at the papers on her desk. "Ms. Svetlana?"

She lifted her head and dropped her hands onto her lap, her face once again smooth and controlled. "Yes, I do need the penicillin." Her lips formed a tight line. "How much will it cost?"

"How about a hundred rubles?"

"Don't try to give me a deal." She angrily tossed her head. "I will pay the full amount."

"As you wish."

"Can I pay you next time?"

He saw her wince as she asked for the extension. "Sure. I'll deliver it to Ina."

David left the office and joined the older woman in the orphanage kitchen.

"I am glad she changed her mind about accepting the food." Ina grinned broadly, revealing several large gaps between her yellow-brown teeth. She wiped her work-worn hands on the red apron that encased her rotund frame like a big roll of Kielbasa sausage as she traipsed behind him to his truck.

David lifted the last box of cabbage out of the box of the pickup and followed her to the root cellar under the orphanage. A few cans of vegetables and half a box of potatoes stood on one of the shelves.

Ina leaned toward him. "Never saw anyone as stubborn as that woman. But she does care for the kids. Found a little one abandoned on the steps last night. Just a few hours old." She took the box out of his hands and set it on the bottom shelf. "He died shortly after she brought him inside. Karina takes that sort of thing real hard." She trundled back up the steps.

David followed in silence, stunned by Ina's story. So much loss. If only they could make a greater difference . . . .

"Little Oleg is real sick. He's had a high fever for several days. He's supposed to go home with some people from the States next week. Don't know if he'll make it." Worry clouded her wrinkled face.

David touched the old woman's arm. "I'll be praying for him. Jesus cares for the little children. He can make Oleg well again."

"Thank you so much!" She fingered the cross around her fleshy neck.

With a broad smile and a hearty wave, David jumped in the truck and roared off. Once again God had spoken to him, given him a message that morning regarding the penicillin. A child's life had probably been saved through it. He was glad that he'd been obedient.

———∞∞∞———

Karina stood behind the lacy curtains and watched David drive the Toyota out of the muddy courtyard.

Why did he happen to have penicillin today? Maybe he always carried it with him. Highly unlikely. Not at that price. *Why does he keep coming back?*

After picking up the bottle, she hurried down the corridor to the children's quarters. The silent babies in the steel cribs along the wall stared at her as she walked by, but her eyes were fixed on Oleg, the sick little boy. Listless, he lay in his crib.

"Is he doing any better?" Bending over the bed, Karina touched the skinny infant's feverish forehead.

"Not much." The young blonde girl wrung out a faded washcloth above the basin and wiped the boy's puffy red face. "He needs medicine from Perm."

"I bought some today." Karina set the bottle on the cabinet by the crib. She cracked open a needle-and-syringe case and drew up a few cc's of the antibiotic, flicking the air out of the top of the syringe with her fingernail.

Lifting the baby's white nightshirt, she injected the small amount of precious white fluid into his tiny gluteal muscle. The baby cried plaintively as the needle penetrated.

"I'll be back tonight to check on him." She withdrew the needle and laid the syringe on the nightstand. Oleg's situation had been serious, but she felt much relieved. Mr. Valensky's bottle of medicine had come just at the right time.

———∞∞∞———

David's cell phone rang as he reached the outskirts of Kungur. Russia remained an enigma to him: babies died from lack of penicillin, yet cell phone service reached the remotest regions. He pulled the truck over to the edge of the road. As he answered, he heard Jake's agitated voice on the other end.

"David, it's Jake. We have a terrible situation here at the shelter. Stefan committed suicide."

David sat in stunned silence. Stefan had been like a son to him. His hand shook as he held the phone. Jake had warned him that morning, but he hadn't listened. Now it was too late.

"You were right. I shouldn't have left today. What happened?"

"The other teens here at the shelter found him upstairs in his room, a needle still sticking out of his arm. We're waiting for the police to arrive."

"I'll get back there as soon as possible. Keep me posted if you find out something else." David closed the phone and slid it into his coat pocket. He dropped his forehead onto the steering wheel as tears coursed down his cheeks. His shoulders shook with the sobs that wracked his body.

Stefan had arrived at the shelter a few years previous, emaciated, severely abused from his life in a street gang, and hooked on cocaine. After coming clean, he became David and Jake's right-hand helper, tackling the never-ending workload with ceaseless energy. A bright boy and eager to learn, Stefan enjoyed the online courses in which David had enrolled him to further his education.

But now Stefan was dead.

Overwhelmed with pain and grief, David's mind wandered back to January 21, 1991, a date he would never forget.

Traffic on the I-19 south of the Denver turnpike came to a standstill with cars bumper to bumper in both lanes. Soft flakes of snow cascaded onto the asphalt. David tuned in to Rock AM 105 for a traffic update.

"Serious accident on the I-19. School bus has collided with a semi-truck. We'll give further updates as available."

David glanced at his watch. Four thirty. Sheila said she'd pick the kids up from school after her ladies' group at church. They should be home by now.

The stalled traffic merged into one lane. He inched past the accident scene. The bus was too mangled to decipher the name of the school. On the side of the road lay several small, lumpy forms under blue tarps. David prayed for all the families who would soon be trapped in the relentless claws of death and grief.

With his thoughts still on the accident, he exited the I-19 and turned onto the quiet street where he lived. As he pulled into the driveway, he spotted a police cruiser parked along the curb by his house. Sweating profusely, he parked on the concrete pad in front of the garage. He forced himself out of the car and robotically made his way up the path to the front door.

Sheila sat alone on the velour sofa, eyes red and swollen, a box of Kleenex beside her. A constable rose from the living room chair when David stepped inside. "I'm so sorry, Mr. Valensky."

David's hands gripped the stair railing as scenes from the accident flashed in his mind. The mangled bus, the small bodies under the blue tarps.

The officer moved over to him and laid his hand on David's shoulder. "Both of your children died instantly. A semi-truck hit their school bus."

"You were supposed to pick them up," David blurted out, glaring at Sheila. Without waiting for a reply, he turned around and stormed out of the house.

———— ⌘ ————

David lifted his head off the steering wheel and stared out over the Russian landscape. Despite the passing of the years, the pain remained fresh, the wounds easily opened once again.

David shifted into first gear and pulled onto the highway. He needed to get to the shelter as soon as possible. He had been through different crises in the shelter over the years but never one of this magnitude. The other teens would be shaken up beyond belief.

God, give us strength. Without You, we fail.

Jake met him in the hallway as David entered the building.

"The police just left with Stefan's body." Jake raked his hand through his disheveled sandy-brown hair. His usually crisp white shirt hung wrinkled on his lean frame.

"What happened?" David threw his coat on the rack and searched Jake's ashen face.

"Let's go into the office so we don't get interrupted." Jake led David to one of the small offices along the hallway. After stepping inside, he closed the door and collapsed in a chair.

"Stefan didn't show up for lunch today, so Alik and a few others went upstairs to look for him. They found him on his bed. They immediately called me. His body was still warm when I got there. He couldn't have been dead very long. Overdosed himself on drugs." Jake shook his head. "I just can't believe it."

David closed his eyes. "I shouldn't have left him," he whispered hoarsely. "As far as I know, the gang boss didn't get in touch with Stefan, but perhaps sheer fear drove him to this. But where did he get the drugs from?"

Jake shifted his tall frame in the chair. "We'll probably never know that. Teens have different connections all over the city."

"Yeah, we'll never know. Unless the other teens can tell us, but it's unlikely that they will." David methodically moved toward the office door. "I'm going up to Stefan's room."

Jake followed David out of the room. "The police collected fingerprints and hair. They also took the syringe."

"Where are the teens?"

"In the living area. I've kept them away from the second floor."

With a heavy heart, David climbed the stairs and opened the door to Stefan's room. The blankets on the bed were rumpled with a small blood stain on the bottom sheet. Stefan's Bible lay open on the nightstand. David's eyes fell on the highlighted portion of John 3, Stefan's favorite passage.

"For God so loved the world that He gave His one and only son, that whoever believes in Him shall not perish but have eternal life," David read out loud.

Tears coursed down David's cheeks. He didn't bother to wipe them away. *Why, Stefan? Did you feel you had no other choice? Or did someone force you to this?*

Turning around, he left the room. He descended the stairs and crossed the hallway to the dining room. About twenty kids sat hunched around the wood stove, their faces somber. David helped himself to a bowl of thick borscht from a pan on the wood stove. He hunkered down on a three-legged stool and reluctantly ate. His stomach repulsed the food, but he had to set an example for the kids. If he didn't eat, neither would they.

They sat in silence, at a loss for words. Death was a common occurrence on the streets of Perm with gang fighting and drugs rampant, but the kids who lived in the shelter had left that life behind.

David rose from the stool and lifted the worn Bible off the shelf. What could he say to these kids to fill the holes in their hearts? The pain was deep. God would need to bring healing in His time. He joined the circle of kids around the wood stove and looked at the sad, discouraged faces.

"Tonight we are devastated by the loss of Stefan. We are sad, angry, and we don't understand. But one thing we do know: God's Word never changes."

He opened the Bible to Romans chapter 8. "Who shall separate us from the love of Christ? Shall trouble or hardship or persecution or famine or nakedness or danger or sword? No, in all these things we are more than conquerors through Him who loved us. For I am convinced that neither death nor life, nor angels nor demons, neither the present nor the future, nor any powers, nor height nor depth, nor anything else in all creation will be able to separate us from the love of God that is in Christ Jesus our Lord."

He looked around the group. These were rough kids. Street smart and mean. Most of the guys had been involved in the drug trade and the girls in prostitution. They were all orphanage "graduates" or runaway kids for whom the state hadn't been able to provide housing and jobs.

David loved them with every fiber of his being. These were the kids he'd come to Russia for. He knew God had called him to this place.

"God is in control, and we will continue to trust Him in life and in death." He closed the Bible.

Sixteen-year-old Alik wiped the sleeve of his stained cotton shirt across his eyes. Sasha snorted and blew his nose. The others sat motionless, lost in thought.

David slipped off the stool and knelt on the rough plank floor. Every boy and girl in the smoky room followed his example. Together they offered up their anguished cries to the Father.

***

The following morning, David drove to the downtown police station. Perhaps they'd release Stefan's body for a proper burial.

"No, you cannot have the body." The burly officer behind the counter folded his arms across his chest. "You're not a relative and you have no rights." He stared coldly at David from behind bulletproof glass in the former KGB headquarters.

David checked his anger. Arguing with a Russian policeman was as futile as singing to a deaf man. He pulled a hundred rubles out of his pocket. "Where's the boy's body?"

For a moment, the policeman greedily eyed the money. Then his face became vacant again, the gray eyes emotionless. "I don't know where he is. The Ministry of Education looks after bums."

David pulled another hundred rubles out of his pocket.

"My final offer. Take it or leave it." Holding the money in his hand, he turned toward the door.

"Wait. Maybe I can find out for you." The officer disappeared through the narrow door at the back of the room.

David despised this game which some called "changing their minds from *nyet* to *da*." It was, however, the only way to get things accomplished at times. Bribery was part of life here. Usually he refused to feed their lust for money and extortion. But today he just wanted to get the job done.

His fingers drummed on the scuffed counter. He hated waiting in this frozen place where people meant nothing, and the authorities preferred the street kids dead rather than alive.

The agent sauntered back to the glass window. "Sorry. The authorities will not release any information." His eyes remained fixed on the money in David's hand.

David threw fifty rubles on the counter. "Thanks for the trouble." Who knew when he might need help again? It made sense to keep friends in the police force.

"Spasiba. Thanks." The officer pocketed the money.

Dejected, David left the police station. Not that he should've expected results. When it came to the homeless, the police had never been cooperative.

He remembered the winter of '91 when he'd first arrived in Perm. Vladimir, his co-pastor at the small evangelical church, and he had gone to the Open Market to feed the street kids. A crowd of children gathered around them as they doled out thick sandwiches of hard Russian sourdough bread with butter and sausage. Dozens of dirty hands clawed at the food, devouring it in huge, animal-like gulps.

The police arrived with gummy clubs, scattering the children without mercy. One of the officers stood with his face inches from David's, his breath tainted with vodka. "Why are you feeding these vermin? The sooner they're dead, the better."

It was a good thing that Vladimir hadn't translated for David until after the police left.

After that experience, the two men decided to feed the kids away from the public. At first, they hunted through the city's extensive sewer system, the only warm dwelling for street kids in the dead of winter. David eventually got used to the stench, the filthy clothes, and the frightened faces. Like rats, they emerged from the dark crevices and scampered after the team to the shelter. Word spread fast through their internal network, and the number of emaciated kids who showed up at the shelter increased daily. Despite their help, violence raged hard, the young brains intoxicated by glue or gasoline sniffing habits. Stabbings were frequent, deaths not uncommon.

David had created strict rules for the shelter. Anyone intoxicated was not welcome inside, but would be fed on the street. For the main overnight shelter, their organization, Living Hope, required full-time school attendance and a clear record for three months. Desire for a better life lifted some of the kids above their addictions, but others could not shake their habits.

For some, like Stefan, the power of Jesus had been the true source of healing. David had had high hopes for the boy with his contagious love for the Lord and his buoyant spirit. Stefan's death rocked David's world, the pain in his heart too deep for words.

CHAPTER THREE

November 19 2003

Ingrid Sorenson took a kettle of boiling water off the stove and looked at the pregnant girl sitting on the wooden chair by the table, her youthful features contorted with pain. The older woman poured the water in the metal basin on the table and hung a clean towel on the chair. The baby's arrival would not be long now.

Too bad Sofia's grandmother had died shortly after the girl's arrival in Kutchino. Now she had nowhere to stay and no support for the baby once it was born. If Ingrid hadn't decided to be in town until Christmas, Sofia wouldn't have had anyone to deliver the baby. Thankfully, the girl had enough common sense to give the baby up.

Ingrid remembered Sofia when she was a young child living with her grandmother, but then she'd left Kutchino for the big city. Her grandmother had mentioned her occasionally, usually with disdain. The old woman had told Ingrid that Sofia had ended up with bad friends and booze.

"I can't do this!" The young woman gripped the back of a chair as another contraction gripped her body. With a groan, she buckled over.

"Yes, you can." Ingrid rubbed her lower back. "You are strong. You can do it."

When the contraction ebbed away, Sophia looked at Ingrid with glassy eyes. "I'm dizzy. I need to lie down." Holding on to Ingrid's arm, she made her way to the single bed by the window and eased herself onto the straw-filled mattress covered with an old plastic sheet.

Another contraction, stronger than the previous one, rocked her body. She writhed in pain.

"Breathe, Sofia, breathe," Ingrid instructed. "In through your nose. Out through your mouth. That's it."

The girl sucked air into her cheeks and exhaled with concentrated effort. Ingrid wiped Sofia's forehead with a damp cloth.

"Let me check to see how close you are." Her hand slipped under the covers. "Almost there; just a few more hard contractions and you'll be ready to push. Then I'll break your water and the baby will come." She turned away from the bed and washed her hands in the basin on the table.

Sofia panted from exertion, her usually thin face was round and puffy with retained fluid.

Ingrid worried about the possibility of toxemia. The baby was eight weeks early, and Ingrid had no medical supplies on hand. The nearest hospital was an hour away by car, but no one could take her. She wished Sofia had stayed in Perm, but who could've anticipated the baby's early arrival?

"Ingrid!" Sofia sat up, her hands clawing at her bulging abdomen. Her eyes were dark and dilated.

Ingrid checked the girl once more. "OK, push now. As hard as you can."

Sofia nodded, her respiration shallow and labored.

The next contraction came within seconds of the previous one. With each contraction, Sofia pushed with all her strength, popping the miniscule blood vessels around her bulging eyes.

The baby's head appeared. A slight rotation, and his diminutive frame slipped onto the soggy plastic sheet.

With a deep groan, Sofia fell back onto the thin pillow. Her blonde hair lay plastered against her sweaty forehead.

Smiling, Ingrid lifted the crying baby onto Sofia's abdomen. "You have a son," she crooned. "A fighter. He'll be all right."

With tears in her eyes, Sofia pulled the baby closer. "As soon as I can get a ride for him, he'll have to go to Perm." She stroked the wispy blond hair on his little head.

Ingrid stood at the side of the bed, looking down on the newly delivered baby. Sofia was right. He had to go to Perm as soon as possible before Sofia could get attached to him. After all, the girl had no home or money to care for him. A shame she'd gotten pregnant. "He's a lovely baby," Ingrid said, resigned. "Do you have a name for him?"

"Alexander. Alexander Igorovich."

⁓⁓⁓

Exhausted and discouraged from the events of the last few days, David made the trek to Kutchino, a distance of about one hundred kilometers from Perm. The tiny village by Stalin's dreaded Perm-36 labor camp now housed only a handful of residents, most of them employed by the state to maintain the museum for tourists. David wondered why people would be interested in visiting the Gulag, the most severe labor camp for political dissidents and opponents of the Soviet regime. The barren, treeless area had a stench of death and destruction.

Ingrid Sorenson had called and asked him to pick up a baby born the previous night, to be placed in care of the Russian State. The cycle of life and death continued in a ceaseless flow.

He pulled up in front of Ingrid's shabby log cabin. The door hung haphazardly on rusty hinges, the window frames collapsing inward. The roof had shagged around the old chimney. A plume of smoke curled upward.

"Hello?" he called, rattling the worn doorknob.

"*Dubroe Utroe*, Pastor David. Come in. I just brewed some coffee. Please join us." Ingrid opened the narrow door.

David ducked underneath the low beam and entered the gloomy dwelling. As his eyes adjusted to the faint light, he saw a frail form propped upright in the bed against the wall. Coming closer to the bed, he recognized Sofia, the girl he'd found half-frozen on the street that previous winter. She'd stayed at the shelter for a while after being kicked out of her boyfriend's apartment in the dead of winter. But she hadn't told him that she was pregnant. Then, one day, she suddenly had disappeared. The other teens told him that she'd planned to go back to her grandmother's place, but he'd never heard from her again.

He crossed the small room to the bed. "Sofia! What a pleasant surprise."

The girl scarcely lifted her eyes to his face, her cheeks sallow and her lips drawn together. "Hello, Pastor David."

He glanced at the baby who slept in the crook of her arm. "And look at this little man." Kneeling by the cot, he touched the baby's rosy cheek. "A healthy young lad. Ingrid told me you need to give him up."

She nodded, swallowing hard.

"That must be tough." He touched her cheek in the same manner he'd touched the baby's. A tear rolled down her face and fell onto the threadbare quilt.

"I'll be praying for you and for the baby too. Whenever you're in Perm, feel free to stop by the center. You're always welcome." David stood up from his position by the bed.

"Spasiba. I appreciate all your help," she whispered, eyes downcast.

"The coffee is ready." Ingrid placed two chipped ceramic cups on the table. "Milk or sugar?"

"Please."

"Have a seat." Ingrid pointed to the two wooden chairs by the table.

David had met Ingrid several years before through the orphanage ministry. She'd delivered many babies in the outlying areas, some of whom he'd transported to Perm to be placed for adoption. He hadn't realized she was still around until she'd called him last night.

"You've been keeping well, David?"

"Yes." He lifted the cup to his lips and sipped the lukewarm coffee.

"And how are things at the shelter?"

"There are always difficulties to work through." He wasn't interested in discussing them with her, though.

"I imagine there are." Ingrid seated herself across from him and picked up her cup. "I appreciate that you could make it out today to pick up the baby. He's small, and I think that he may need medical attention."

David raised his eyebrows. "It's unlikely that they'll do anything for him." Not to mention Sofia's heavy use of alcohol during her pregnancy. Surely the baby had to have some effects from that. He downed the last of the coffee and set his empty cup on the table.

"I'll warm some milk and get the baby ready for the trip." Ingrid stood up from the chair and walked over to the crude, wooden kitchen counter. She took an old glass bottle from one of the cupboards and lifted a small pan off the woodstove. Scooping the thick skin off the lukewarm milk, she poured the milk into the bottle, screwed on the nipple, and handed it to David.

Sofia clung to the baby as Ingrid approached, covering his tiny face with kisses. "Good-bye, Alexander."

Ingrid pried the baby from her grasp, changed his diaper, and wrapped him securely in an old blanket. "Ready to go," she announced. Holding the baby in the crook of her arm, she followed David out to the truck.

He opened the passenger door, and Ingrid placed the baby against the back of the passenger seat, supported by a rolled-up towel. "Sorry that I don't have a car-seat," David apologized. "But it should work."

Ingrid handed him an envelope. "This letter explains the circumstances of the child's birth. It has my name and address so the authorities can contact us with the necessary paperwork for Sofia to sign for the adoption."

"And the father?"

Ingrid shrugged. "She hasn't mentioned his name. I don't think she has any contact with him. After all, he kicked her out when he found out she was pregnant."

David closed the passenger door and walked around to the driver's side. "Thanks for what you've done for Sofia and the baby."

Ingrid dismissed his comment with a wave of her hand. She wiped away the tears that flowed down her weathered cheeks and straightened her shoulders.

As David drove down the rutted driveway, he noticed Sofia standing at the window, her hand raised in a final salute, her face contorted with raw emotion.

⸎

The pediatric hospital rose stark and dreary against Perm's polluted gray sky. The barred windows and gated entrance reminded David of a prison rather than a place of healing.

Cradling the baby in his arms, he climbed the crumbling steps. The newborn whimpered like a kitten.

The nurse at the desk sized him up with scornful eyes. She placed her portly hands on her hips as David explained the purpose of his visit.

"You cannot leave the baby here. We're full. The doctor won't see you."

David knew they had room. They just didn't want another newborn to look after. He handed her Ingrid's letter. "The baby isn't mine," he said with a clipped tone. "I'm only the chauffeur." He placed the howling child on the desk in front of the blustery woman and turned to leave.

"Hey, Mister," her panicking voice called him back. "We need some more information. Could you please wait?"

He halted at the door, then turned back, restraining his impatience. "I don't know much about the child's history."

The nurse scooped up the baby and disappeared behind the cracked glass door. David lowered himself into an old chair against the wall. Closing his eyes, he tipped his head back and slowly inhaled. Corporate meetings used to be the only event that pushed him to the edge. Unbending executives, who only thought of stuffing their own pockets with greenbacks, plowing over the backs of their employees. That was before he worked in a country where people plowed over the backs of innocent children.

"Abstinence is the kindest gift you can give yourself and others," he always told the teens at the shelter. *"It shows that you respect yourself and your friends, and it prevents a generation of kids born into poverty."*

They usually looked at him as if he had arrived from another planet. Yet he knew he was right. The flood of rejected children had to stop, and it was not through abortion. God have mercy on this country. And on America, too.

"The doctor wants you to come in." The nurse motioned to him. David rose and followed her down the hall to a small room where a bearded doctor examined the naked baby on a rickety table covered with a stained plastic sheet. The baby cried sadly, flailing his tiny arms when the cold stethoscope touched his ribbed chest.

The doctor glanced up when David entered, but then turned his attention back to the baby. "Hyper excitability syndrome with perinatal encephalopathy. Congestion in the lungs and heart murmur," he told the attending nurse who scribbled notes on a sheet of paper in a manila folder.

David had seen files like this in orphanage offices. A single page of writing summed up a life sentence of rejection. Not healthy enough. Not rich enough. Not loved enough. Property of the State of Russia. To be caged in institutions until age eighteen. After that, kicked onto the street with crime and prostitution as a profession.

David gritted his teeth. *Lord, I need Your grace. I can't do the work on my own. Send more laborers into this enormous harvest.*

When the doctor finished his exam, David signed a document stating that all known information regarding the infant had been released.

"You can go now," the nurse told him without another glance.

David's heavy boots echoed in the empty corridor. One hundred babies existed in this prison-like facility, yet an eerie silence pervaded the air. He wondered whether the babies knew their cries would not be answered. Were they resigned to their lot in life already?

The door thudded shut behind him as he stepped into the crisp winter air. Fresh snow crunched under his boots as he walked to the truck. Perm appeared lovely and serene in this weather. A rotten peach underneath a soft, inviting peel. Stepping into his truck, he called Jake at the shelter to see if there'd been news regarding Stefan.

"The authorities won't release Stefan's body," Jake told him. "We're not his legal guardians so we don't have any rights. They said he was buried this morning."

David felt saddened. "It won't matter much to Stefan, but I think the funeral would've brought closure for the other teens."

"Yes, it would've. Where are you right now?"

"I just dropped the baby off at the hospital. I'll be back at the shelter in a few hours."

After he hung up, David navigated the Toyota through the dense traffic toward the sprawling graveyard on the edge of town. He parked along the rusty fence that surrounded the cemetery. Simple wooden crosses stretched on in seemingly endless rows.

David trudged across the vast terrain, his eyes scanning the pristine blanket of snow in search of a dark patch of dirt. From previous experience he'd learned where the authorities buried the homeless.

His breath formed tiny ice crystals on the thick scarf over his face and froze in small clusters onto his eyelashes. He thrust his gloved hands deeper into the pockets of his thick parka. A chilling north wind howled through the old spruce trees, stirring the fluffy snow into powdery clouds.

After about twenty minutes, he rested his eyes on a rough wooden cross bearing the inscription "Stefan Vitalovich, 1985–2003." He sank onto the frozen ground. The cold earth sapped the warmth from his body. He thought back to his son, Geoff. How proud he'd been when Geoff made his entrance into the world. He'd held him in his arms, his son's downy head barely visible above the white wraps. As he nuzzled the soft peach fuzz, he'd told Sheila what a great hunter and fisherman Geoff would be.

"Think of all the camping we'll do as a family," he'd told Sheila as she sat in the hospital bed. His heart swelled in his bosom. She'd smiled at him with tired eyes, weary from labor.

Every summer for six years, they'd camped and fished. Geoff never became the fisherman or hunter David had dreamed he'd be. There simply hadn't been enough time.

With a stifled cry, David's gloved hands groped the crumbling soil.

I know You haven't forsaken me, Jesus, but I hurt so much. Even after all these years. The pain never ends. Help me have that sweet joy and peace of knowing You so I can help others.

Most of the time he felt that serenity, but today his heart was heavy with the fresh sense of loss. For a few moments he remained bent down, the icy wind howling around him through the dead grass. Then he pushed himself onto his haunches, his knees and hands stiff, and trudged past the rows of crosses.

CHAPTER THREE

By the time he made it back to the shelter, the sun had set behind the distant hills. The windows of the shelter welcomed him with their cheerful glow through the closed blinds. David pulled around to the back of the building and parked in the courtyard. He felt a surge of gratitude as he looked at the old, spacious complex that had served their organization so well for more than a decade.

Stepping out of the truck, David hauled himself up the walkway to the back door. As he entered the living area, the teens riveted their eyes on him. As their leader, he was undoubtedly expected to offer some hope, or at least an answer, but he had none. Russia had outwitted him again.

CHAPTER FOUR

Her hands trembled in her lap as Karina stared at the government documents on her desk. She licked her dry lips and swiveled her chair toward the frosted window. How could she possibly comply with this request to inspect the orphanage for children with lesser mental capabilities? But how could she resist? Although the regime had officially collapsed, the old Soviet machine ground on, pulverizing its citizens under its brutal force. The same communists who once ruled remained in control of many government positions.

What could she do to stop the authorities from coming in and checking the children to see which ones should be put in institutions for children deemed imbeciles? She was responsible for the children under her care. How would she stand by if the government took some of them away? Four-year-old Tosya and three-year-old Edik came to her mind. They were born with severe Fetal Alcohol Syndrome, and the government would certainly move them to another place. She had to think of a way to stall the inspection.

Karina breathed on the window and scratched some frost off the pane with her long fingernails. Russian winters made her feel like a prisoner. The raging cold controlled her every move, much like the governing authorities.

The Toyota pulled into the courtyard. She quickly swiveled back to her desk, lips pressed together. Why did *he* have to show up just now?

Thanks to Mr. Valensky and his penicillin, little Oleg had pulled through that serious bout of pneumonia, but that didn't mean she was happy to see him. In fact, she was never happy to see an American man. Especially a *single* American man. She'd learned that lesson the hard way. Bending over the papers on her desk, she pretended to concentrate. Steadying her hands, she organized the papers into file folders.

After a few minutes she peered out the window again. He was no longer in the truck. She organized more papers until they were all filed away, and then stood up from her chair. The hallway was empty and silent before her. Where could he be? She hurried to the children's living quarters.

The faint sound of a man's deep laughter greeted her when she reached the stairwell. Anger bubbled up in her as she bounded up the stairs. Who did he think he was? No one was allowed into the children's rooms without her permission!

Stepping into the room, she saw him sitting on the floor, surrounded by a group of toddlers. She looked down on him with disdain. "Well, hello, Mr. Valensky."

The children scattered at the sound of her voice.

She shoved her hands in her pockets and planted her feet a little apart. "You can't come in here without my permission."

David lithely jumped to his feet, towering a good foot above her. "I was merely playing with the kids. They love the attention. I meant no offense. How's Oleg?"

"Better," she scowled. Ina must have passed that information on to him. She wagged her tongue like a dog his tail.

"I'm sorry if I did something wrong. I play with the children in other orphanages I visit," he apologized.

"At Kungur Baby House we maintain strict control over our children."

"I see that." He looked around the empty room.

Anger rose in her chest. "Why do you insist on coming here?"

"I've often wondered the same thing. It's obvious you don't want me here." A muscle jerked in his cheek.

Karina's arms dropped against her sides. "What do you want?"

"To help you."

She pursed her lips and narrowed her eyes. "I don't want your help." —

David grabbed his coat off the chair by the door. "Have it your way. I won't come back again. I have plenty of work elsewhere." He pushed past her into the hallway, marched to the outside door, jerked on his snow-boots, and gripped the doorknob.

Karina stood mutely in the doorway.

"I'm sorry." David let out a deep breath. "I shouldn't have—"

"I accept your apology." She lifted her chin slightly and met his gaze. "Good-bye." Her high heels clacked on the faded linoleum as she strutted down the hall.

<hr>

David watched Karina disappear into her office. The woman obviously didn't care about the kids. Never had he seen her in the children's rooms. She was cold and heartless. Opening the door, he left the pungent diaper smell for the refreshing winter air. With large strides, he crossed the courtyard.

Go back.

No! She obviously doesn't want me here. Stubborn woman!

Go back.

No way!

Go back.

He stepped into his truck and turned the key in the ignition.

This is not about you.

He hung his head. He didn't want to go back in there. He didn't want to see that woman again. In fact, he never wanted to come back here. But deep inside he sensed a nudging that was greater than his anger. *You'll have to go with me then, Lord. I'll go back, but only in obedience to Your will.*

CHAPTER FOUR

Karina observed David through the small opening in the frost on the window. Her heart pounded as the truck door opened and David crossed the parking area to the entrance. She hurried over to her desk and sat down, pretending to work. Why would he be coming back?

In response to the loud knock, she made her way to the door, her legs rubbery. "Come in, Mr. Valensky."

She closed the door behind him, tension coursing through her body. "Have a seat." She pointed to the chair and then sat down behind her desk. Karina noticed the creases around the corners of the man's mouth and the tired look in his deep blue eyes. For a moment sympathy flickered in her heart but she immediately suppressed it. Americans could not be trusted.

David leaned forward. "I apologize that I broke your rules and came in without permission. But I really want to help you."

"You Americans think you're God's gift to the world. But in reality you couldn't care less. You just want to look good. The saviors of the world. Isn't that it?"

"I come here because of the children, Ms. Svetlana. I've been doing orphanage ministry for years. If I didn't care, do you really think I would do this?"

"Why did you come back just now?"

"God told me to offer you help once more."

Karina eyed him suspiciously. God did not usually enter the equation in her world. Could he be trusted? Was he any different from the other American she had known? Could this man truly help her? She hesitated, then spoke.

"I have two children here at the orphanage, a boy and a girl, who cannot be adopted out. No one wants them because they have Fetal Alcohol Syndrome. The authorities are coming in a few days to do an inspection. They will undoubtedly deport these two children to another facility. They will be treated like imbeciles, locked in cribs without human stimulus. Have you ever seen one of those facilities?"

"I have. So how can I help you?"

The empathy on his face gave her courage. "I need to place these two children in a family. If I have signed adoption proposal papers, they will not be taken away."

"How old are they?"

"Three and four."

He observed her in silence for a few minutes. "I'll do my best to find a solution."

"Thank you, Mr. Valensky."

"Call me David."

After David left, Karina stood at the window and watched the Toyota disappear from the courtyard. Perhaps she'd misjudged him. Maybe he was not like Frank after all.

Brusquely she turned back to her desk. No, experience had taught her that Americans could not be trusted.

The drive back to Perm gave David time to think about his options. There weren't many. He couldn't think of anyone in their church who would be up to the challenge of raising two children with Fetal Alcohol Syndrome. Yet he had said he wanted to help.

Lord, You'll need to intervene supernaturally to save these kids.

David shivered as he thought of Russia's most dreaded but carefully hidden orphanages. He'd been in one of those institutions a few years ago, an experience that had shaken him to the core of his being. The older children had stood in the courtyard as the food convoy drove in. Dressed only in underwear, they shivered violently in the frigid Russian winter air. Inside the building, the babies lay in their cribs, covered in their own excrement, their eyes staring blankly into space.

He pressed his hand against his forehead. The fate of two children's lives lay heavily upon him. He couldn't think of anyone in his church community who would be able to take the children. He dialed Vladimir's number. Perhaps his co-pastor would have some ideas. Most people that he knew were stretched to the max to provide for their own families, but Vladimir had many connections elsewhere.

The phone rang but no one picked up. Vladimir was probably still at work. Dejected, he threw the phone down on the seat beside him.

———◦◦◦———

Karina sat across from her friend Tanya over a cup of steaming coffee at the small café down the street from the orphanage. "This guy is driving me crazy! He never leaves me alone. Today he waltzed into the children's quarters without permission." With shaking fingers, she lit another cigarette. She inhaled deeply and then exhaled the gray fumes, watching the cloud circle to the ceiling where it mixed with a blue sea of cigarette smoke.

"It sounds to me like he wants to help you with the children. What's wrong with that?" Tanya held the coffee cup between her delicate fingers, her fingernails painted bright red. Her blonde tresses playfully framed her oval face, and long, silver earrings dangled softly against her cheeks.

"I can run the orphanage without him."

"No one said you couldn't. But everyone can use a little help." Tanya sipped the dark, murky brew. "He only comes occasionally. What's the big deal?"

"He's an American."

"He's not Frank."

"Leave Frank out of this!" Karina set her cup onto the vinyl tablecloth with so much force that the coffee sloshed out.

"Be honest with yourself. Frank is still controlling your life."

Heat rose in Karina's cheeks. "I thought you were my friend." She smashed the cigarette into the ashtray and grabbed her purse.

"Stop running from the truth! You need to deal with this thing once and for all."

Karina hurried out of the coffee shop without saying good-bye. She rushed down the street toward her apartment. Deal with it once and for all? If only it was that easy. Frank had used her and dumped her. He had led her to believe he loved her and would be there for her, but when the hard times hit, he deserted her. How could she forget that? If it wasn't for his betrayal, she'd still have her son.

She climbed the stairs to her small apartment and opened the squeaky door. Obviously Tanya didn't understand what Frank had put her through. She punched the play button on her tape player on the floor. Loud Tchaikovsky music grated her nerves. Irritated, she shut the player off again.

Karina walked to the kitchen, and poured herself a glass of vodka which she downed in one swig. Then she filled her glass again. She'd end up with a headache tomorrow if she continued drinking, but right now she didn't care. The liquid warmed her insides and soothed her frazzled thoughts.

She walked back into the living room and sank down onto the couch. As she closed her eyes, Frank's face drifted into her mind.

"Anna Karenina," he joked with a sparkle in his deep blue eyes, his body muscular, and his smile irresistible. At six foot four, Frank Olafson resembled a polished Viking god. He made her laugh at the silliest things and made her feel special and loved.

He had moved to Russia from the States to study Russian history at the University of Moscow where she had just finished her first year of medical studies. From the moment she met him in sociology class, his presence captivated her. The girls thronged around him. Frank drew crowds, entertaining them with his gregarious stories and boisterous laughter. He could've had any woman he desired. Yet he chose her. Why, she couldn't understand. She was shy and plain. A wallflower.

"Someday, Karina," he'd promised, "I'll take you to the States. We'll see New York and the Statue of Liberty. I'll show you Madison Avenue, and we'll go to the top of the World Trade Center."

His enthusiasm was contagious. He painted America as the land of milk and honey, freedom and love. And she believed his every word.

Together they explored Moscow—sometimes on foot, other times by tram or bus. Frank bought her beautiful gifts of perfume, chocolate, and flowers. Their romance flourished. Expensive vodka and wine flowed freely at the parties they attended and organized. Suddenly popular and in the thick of the university's social life, twenty-year-old Karina reveled in the limelight.

Frank kissed her like no one had ever kissed her before, his arms encircling her with a passion and tenderness that drove her wild. That spring he moved into her apartment on Grosnov Street. And by summer she was pregnant.

Karina buried her face in her hands and wept until she had no tears left and the vodka bottle stood empty on the table.

CHAPTER FIVE

David's cell phone rang, jolting him out of sleep. Rolling over in bed, he reached for the phone on the nightstand.

"David, this is Karina Svetlana. I just received news from the authorities."

David rubbed his hand through his disheveled hair. "Look, I haven't had a chance to contact anyone yet. Things like this don't get solved overnight."

"I need an answer now. The authorities will be here today."

"I'm sorry, but I can't do anything on such short notice."

The phone abruptly beeped in his ear. She'd disconnected. As he tossed the phone on the nightstand, it bounced onto the floor. Mumbling under his breath, he crawled out of bed and picked it up.

Wide awake now and frustrated, he trudged through the hallway to the bathroom to shower. The warm water soothed his ill humor. Why did that woman always manage to get on his nerves? Or rather, why did he allow her to get on his nerves? Of course, he wanted to help her find a solution, but he needed time. Couldn't she understand that? He hadn't even had a chance to discuss it with Vladimir.

Why didn't she just adopt them herself?

Why don't you adopt them?

Now, that was a crazy idea! Adopt a couple of toddlers? He laughed out loud.

He'd read statistics on the Internet about orphans in Russia. Fifteen thousand children were released from state orphanages every year. Within a year of their release, fifteen hundred had committed suicide, six thousand became homeless, three thousand turned to crime, and the rest were unemployed. Not a bright outlook on life. Such a fate was exactly what he tried to prevent at the shelter. But to take on two little kids himself was ludicrous.

He stepped out of the shower, dried his short-cropped blonde hair with a terry-cloth towel, and lathered his face with shaving cream. The razor scraped the old stubble off his cheeks. After rinsing the dirty foam off the blade, he dug into his closet for a clean pair of jeans and a freshly pressed shirt.

Guilt pricked his heart as he thought of the rude way he'd spoken to Karina when she called that morning. He picked up his cell phone and dialed her number.

———

Karina washed down a bite of sourdough bread and cheese with a sip of coffee and then answered her phone.

"Ms. Svetlana, David here. I'm sorry about my shortness with you earlier. How long can you put off the authorities?"

"I told you not to worry about the situation, Mr. Valensky." She couldn't hide the irritation in her voice.

"Look, I want to help, but I need some time."

"I don't have time. I told you that already."

"Then I'm going to pray that the authorities miss the children completely when they arrive for their inspection today."

"That's highly unlikely."

"God is above all, Ms. Svetlana. But if they do see the children, tell them that they have adoptive families waiting for them. On my word of honor, I'll have someone visit them in the next two weeks."

"Who do you have in mind?" She didn't believe him.

"I'm still praying about it, but if I can't find anyone, I'll take them myself."

The phone nearly dropped out of Karina's hand. "These are special needs kids. And you haven't even met them."

"I'll be up with more supplies next week. I can visit them then."

"Mr. Valensky, you are absolutely out of your mind!"

"Probably. Anyway, call if you need anything. Otherwise I'll be by on Monday or Tuesday."

"Spasiba. Thank you." Astounded, she placed the phone back in the cradle. *Maybe you were right after all, Tanya. Maybe, just maybe, he's different.*

⸎

As the call disconnected, David shook his head. Had he lost his mind? How could he commit himself to such a crazy thing? If this wasn't of God, he was in trouble!

Jesus, please let the authorities miss those children. And if not, show me the way. My life is in Your hands, and I am prepared to do Your will.

After breakfast in the dining room, David met with Jake in his office.

"The director at Kungur Baby House has two children with Fetal Alcohol Syndrome. If the authorities find them, they'll demand they be moved to one of those dreadful facilities unless they can be adopted immediately." He dropped into the worn faux leather chair behind his desk. "I promised I'd take them if no one else does."

Jake's eyebrows shot up. "Why would you even consider such an outlandish proposal?"

"I'm just trying to follow God's will."

"I hardly think this could be God's will for your life. Not when the kids here at the shelter need you."

David shrugged. "I want to make this a matter of prayer. Certainly God can make the authorities overlook these kids."

"Believe me, I'll be praying." With a grim face, Jake left the office.

David pulled his worn Bible off the shelf and flipped to the first chapter of James. His Bible had a crease in that page. He had read the book of James many times, but today he needed it more than anything.

CHAPTER FIVE

"Consider it pure joy, my brothers, whenever you face trials of many kinds, because you know that the testing of your faith develops perseverance. Perseverance must finish its work so that you may be mature and complete, not lacking anything."

Give me perseverance, Lord. Give me faith and patience. I've been through a lot the last few days, but nothing compared to what Your Son did for us on the cross. David closed the Bible and stood, resolved to carry on regardless of what God had in store for him.

Karina called David on his cell phone during his afternoon coffee break at the shelter. "They completely missed them! Can you believe it?"

"That's wonderful! I told you God answers prayer." David had never heard her voice so excited before.

"I should be going," she replied uneasily. "Just thought I'd let you know."

"Thanks so much. I'll stop by as soon as possible."

After the call ended, David remained motionless for several seconds, clutching the cell phone.

Thank You, Lord, for showing Karina that You are real and in control. And thank You for taking care of this for me. Feeling greatly relieved, he poured a cup of coffee from the pot.

"The lady from the orphanage?" Jake looked up from his newspaper on the table.

"Yes. The inspectors missed the kids."

"Good. That situation's been on my mind all day. I couldn't believe you offered in the first place."

"God obviously had a plan all along to show her the power of prayer."

"Maybe so, but I'm glad you aren't involved with this anymore." Jake folded the newspaper and tossed it aside.

Not involved anymore? An inexplicable feeling filled David that he was more involved with Kungur Baby House than ever before.

CHAPTER SIX

July 14, 1998

Calgary, Canada

Vanessa!"

A concerned voice echoed through the fog, faint and distant. A wave of intense pain followed by nausea hit Vanessa as she tried to sit up. Quivering, her hands groped across the bed as she steadied herself on the metal railing. Jared's face shimmered before her eyes, and a pounding headache settled across her forehead. Moaning, she sank back into the pillows.

A hand touched her shoulder. "Take it easy. There's no need to rush." A cool cloth was spread across her brow. She recognized the voice as Jared's, her husband. Relaxing under his tender touch, she took a deep breath.

"Water," she mumbled through cracked lips, mustering her strength.

Jared placed his right hand under her head and lifted her slightly to bring the cup to her lips. She sipped the cool liquid, her throat thick and swollen.

"Where am I?"

"In the recovery room. You have a few complications from the birth."

Complications? She remembered delivering the baby, but there was no recollection of anything past that. "What kind?"

"You've had surgery. You need to rest now."

She drifted back into an anesthetic-induced sleep.

When she woke up again, her mind was more focused. Jared still sat in the chair beside her bed, his hands folded in his lap. He leaned forward to kiss her on her forehead.

"I'm tired." She didn't have the strength to sit up.

"You've delivered a baby."

"I feel sick." Dread settled over Vanessa. "Where's the baby?"

"She's in the neonatal unit until you're strong enough to take care of her."

"What happened to me?"

He chewed on the corner of his lip. "After the delivery, you began to hemorrhage. The doctors couldn't stop the bleeding, so they had to remove your uterus."

The concrete block on her chest seemed to go right through her body, ripping out her heart on the way. "No," she whispered, as the tears spilled out of her eyes and coursed down her cheeks. "No!"

Jared wiped the tears off her face. "We've got a beautiful baby," he consoled her, his voice choking with emotion. "And I've got you, alive and well. What more could I ask for?" He stroked her hair. "It's OK, babe. Don't fight it."

Breaking down in his arms, Vanessa Williams mourned for the children she'd never have.

September 10, 2004

Vanessa cradled the cordless phone in the palm of her hand. The phone call had finally come! Dazed, she punched in Jared's number.

"We have an adoption proposal," she announced when she heard her husband's voice on the other end of the line. "Leah from Loving Hearts just called. She says there's a nine-month-old baby in Perm,

Russia. The agency wants us to travel there in two weeks for our first visit."

A long silence followed on the other end of the line. "Wow," Jared finally said. "We've been waiting for three years. This is amazing!"

"Leah is going to send us the information on the child," Vanessa explained. "It should be here today."

Vanessa hovered around her computer until the e-mail arrived. When it appeared in the inbox, she sank into the chair and read with eager anticipation. Alexander Igorovich, born on November 19, 2003, at thirty-two weeks gestation. Small oval window of the heart, hyper-excitability syndrome, and perinatal encephalopathy. Nothing to worry about. A common Russian diagnosis.

She raised her eyebrows. She'd give Leah at "Loving Hearts" a call and find out what it exactly meant.

"Don't worry, Mrs. Williams," Leah assured her. "Once the baby is older, this diagnosis will be lifted, should everything be fine. In all the years we've brought babies from Russia to Canada, we've never had serious problems after their arrival."

As Vanessa hung up the phone, six year old Annie tugged on her sleeve. "When is my little brother coming, Mommy?"

Vanessa stroked the girl's blonde head of hair. "Very soon now, sweetie."

"Good. I want somebody to play with me." Satisfied, she ambled over to the toy box in the living room.

That night during supper, Vanessa handed Jared a printed copy of the proposal.

He frowned. "Doesn't sound very encouraging."

"I called Leah about it today. She says that all children in Russia receive a similar diagnosis at birth, as they feel birth is a very traumatic experience. But I'll do some research myself as well."

Jared stood up from his chair and poured himself a cup of coffee from the pot on the kitchen counter. "That's good. I'm sure you'll get the facts straight." He placed his cup on the table and sat down.

"Leah said that if we apply for the Russian visas immediately, we should be ready to travel within the next ten days for our first visit with Alexander," Vanessa told him.

"And then one more trip after that one to pick up the child. Still sounds like a lot of work to me," Jared replied.

Vanessa leaned across the table and kissed Jared on the cheek. "Russia demands two trips. You knew that when we started. But it'll all be worth it. You'll see."

"Yes, we'll wait and see." Jared didn't sound reassured.

∽∘∽

The following two weeks passed in a flurry of activity. Vanessa arranged for her parents to look after Annie in their absence, ordered rubles at the local bank, and applied for the visas.

Finally, the day of departure arrived. Vanessa packed a few last-minute items, including toys and new clothes for Alexander, just purchased the previous day. It had been ten days since Leah had called with the proposal. Today they had to leave for Russia, but she didn't feel entirely prepared.

"Vanessa!" Jared called from the bottom of the stairs. "It's time to go."

Her eyes swept around the brightly painted baby room. A large giraffe, two elephants, and a hippo were painted on the wall behind the crib and changing table. Rainbow-colored curtains hung in front of the large window. Alexander could be sleeping in this room before Christmas. She closed the door behind her and hastened down the stairs to the honking SUV.

"What took you so long?" Jared grabbed the bag out of her hand and threw it into the back of the Jeep. He backed the vehicle off the concrete garage pad and turned down the driveway.

Vanessa glanced at her watch. "Our flight isn't for three hours. We've got plenty of time."

"Mom and Dad are meeting us at the airport to pick up Annie, and we don't want to make them wait."

"Yes, Jared." She wasn't about to disagree. Jared was short-tempered when under pressure.

They drove the rest of the distance in silence, each lost in their own thoughts. Even Annie remained silent in the back seat, thumb in her mouth. She held her old teddy bear close to her chest.

Once inside the airport, Vanessa's mom and dad met them by the check-in counter.

"All ready to go?" her mother hugged Vanessa warmly.

"Yes. As ready as we'll ever be."

Vanessa hugged and kissed Annie repeatedly. "We'll be back in a few weeks. Take good care of Grandma."

"I love you, Mommy." Annie wrapped her arms tightly around her waist. "I'll pray for you every night."

Jared lifted the suitcases onto the conveyor belt and turned to his in-laws. "Thanks for looking after everything while we're gone." He shook his father-in-law's hand and kissed his mother-in-law.

"We'll be praying for you." Vanessa's father squeezed Vanessa's shoulder.

She kissed his stubbly cheek. "I love you, Dad. We'll see you soon, with pictures of your new grandson."

CHAPTER SEVEN

September 2004

David's one-month leave of absence to the States had refreshed him immensely. Following the devastating loss of Stefan nine months before, he'd needed it. Whistling a praise chorus, he entered the department store on Main Street just south of the University of Perm to buy a new pair of jeans and winter coat.

At the Denver airport his seventy-nine-year-old mother had pressed three hundred dollars into his hand. His plane had been delayed, and they'd had half an hour of extra waiting time. He'd considered it a bonus. He didn't know how much time she had left on this earth, or if he would ever see her again this side of heaven.

"I don't want you to spend it on the shelter or the kids," she'd told him. "You need to look after yourself or you'll burn out. You're too thin." She'd wagged her bony finger in his face. "What you really need is a good woman."

He had laughed. He was always too thin in her opinion. He doubted that a woman would change that. Unless she could cook like his mother. "I have you. What more could a man want? Besides, keeping one woman happy is challenging enough!"

Her wrinkled face had grown serious. "I know that the divorce was hard on you. But I hope you'll find another wife. Someone who'll support you and take care of you. You've struggled enough on your own. No man should have to spend his life alone." She'd bent forward, a gleam in her eyes. "Are there no good single women in Perm, my boy?"

He hadn't answered, but now, standing in front of the perfume and ladies' wear sections across from the Tommy Hilfiger store, her words echoed in his mind. Natasha, a girl at church, had shown feelings for him during the last couple of months, but she didn't interest him. Besides, he suspected Jake had romantic feelings for her.

The shop's display window featured a poster of a seductive, heavily made-up woman in skin-tight jeans, her hip cocked to the side. No, there were no good women who held his interest. David turned away from the window and exited the mall. He headed to the open market where jeans cost ten bucks and his money helped feed Russia's poor vendors instead of American franchises.

A few hours later he returned to his apartment, a new pair of jeans and a winter coat in his hands. His footsteps sounded hollow in the stairwell of the day shelter, his new residence. The shelter closed at six o'clock every night, so the teens had meandered off to the main or south-side shelters, which were open at night, or to their hideouts in the sewer and heating system underneath the streets of Perm.

The renovations of the day shelter had gone well thanks to the long hours and significant sweat put in by the Youth With A Mission team that summer. The fifty-year-old building smelled like fresh paint, the walls colored cheerful yellow. The old linoleum had been ripped out and replaced, and they'd converted the attic into living quarters.

For the first time since coming to Perm, David had his own fully equipped apartment, complete with kitchen, living room, bathroom, and bedroom. It even had its own washer and dryer. He reveled in the peace that came with having some private space to call his own. After spending the day at both shelters, the serene room welcomed him into its silence, a luxury after all these busy, noisy years of living with teens.

He placed the new jeans on a shelf in his small closet and draped the winter coat on a hanger. The leftover money from his mother's gift went into an envelope in his bureau drawer. He regretted that she wouldn't let him use it for something else, for the shelter had several items on its wish list. But God would provide for that as He did for all their needs.

David placed a praise-and-worship CD into the hard-drive of the computer and opened his e-mail inbox. Ninety-five e-mails since he checked last night! He deleted the junk mail and scanned through the rest.

His eye fell on an e-mail from CNN News. A lady named Pamela Lowall requested an interview for CNN's "Without a Home" program, a TV show featuring street kids and orphans around the world, and the ministries working with them. She wanted to visit Perm to get a closer look at some of the shelters and orphanages.

David frowned. He didn't like being in the limelight, but he recognized the importance of public awareness for their program, especially in the United States. He invited her to visit Living Hope. After he hit the "send" button, he regretted replying so quickly. He should've prayed about it first.

<hr />

Karina leaned against the doorjamb of the children's living quarters, listening as David entertained the children with a Bible story.

"The soldiers came with swords and sticks, and they took Jesus along as if He had done some horrible thing." David's story held the wide-eyed children spellbound. They sat in a semicircle around him on the floor, watching him intently.

"The bad soldiers beat Jesus till he was bleeding. They made him carry a heavy cross all the way up a high hill. Then they hammered nails into his hands, like this." He pretended to hold a nail in one hand and pounded it with the other. "After that they lifted the cross so everyone could see Jesus hanging on those nails." David opened his arms wide.

"All the people laughed at Him and said they would believe that He was God if He came down off the cross. Do you think Jesus was angry?" He looked around the circle.

The children nodded solemnly. Some wiped away their tears.

"Oh, no." David shook his head. "He said, 'Father, forgive them, for they don't know what they are doing.' Do you know what forgiveness is?" He looked around the circle at their serious faces. "That means that if someone hurts you or says mean things about you, you won't hurt them back, but you'll do nice things for them."

Karina raised her eyebrows. *Forgive people who hurt you, and do nice things for them?* Did David actually believe that? She doubted it. He was a good storyteller, though. The children were captivated. And he showed a true interest in their lives. She loved the kids, too, but they didn't flock to her as they did to him.

"He's teaching religion, Karina." Ina moved in beside her.

She shrugged. "No one else teaches them anything, so I won't worry about it." In fact, she enjoyed his stories.

Adam and Eve in the garden. Samson, the derelict warrior. The romance of Boaz and Ruth. David and Bathsheba. Bitter stories with sweet endings.

"The disciples wrapped Jesus in strips of cloth and put him in a big cave," David went on. "They were very sad that Jesus was dead. Do you know what happened then?"

David paused, letting the suspense build. The children's eyes fixed on his face as they shook their heads. "Jesus didn't stay dead. He came out of the tomb, and all the people who followed Him saw Him alive. Jesus is alive today, too. If you believe that He is God, you'll go to heaven, a beautiful place where there are no tears or sadness. All you have to do is pray and tell Jesus that you're sorry for your sins. He will love you and take care of you. Would any of you like to go to heaven?"

All the children nodded.

David prayed that they would love and know Jesus and then go to heaven to be with Him when they died. After the prayer, he handed them crayons and a picture of a tomb with two angels seated on a big stone. A woman stood beside the tomb, weeping.

Karina ambled into the room, admiring the pictures as the children held them up for her to see.

"Thanks for spending time with them," she whispered to David. "They really look forward to this time. I'd say it's the highlight of their week." And hers as well, but that was none of anyone's business. Since his offer to adopt the two Fetal Alcohol Syndrome children, she'd softened her heart toward him.

The children scratched the crayons across the picture, obliterating Mary and the angels under a layer of color. David stepped toward the door. "I need to get back to Perm."

They walked through the hallway together.

"When will you make a commitment to Jesus?" He took his coat off the hook in the hallway and shrugged into it.

She took a step back, refusing to meet his gaze. "I believe in God."

"A personal relationship with Jesus Christ is much deeper than merely believing in the existence of God."

She gave a hollow laugh. "When I see this forgiveness stuff you talk about firsthand, I'll know Jesus is true."

David's voice grew soft. "Through Jesus it is possible to forgive everyone, regardless of what they do to you."

"You haven't experienced what I have."

"We all experience different things. I lost both my kids in one day. After that, my wife left me for my best friend. I had a lot of forgiving and healing to do. Forgiveness is difficult, but it sets you free. Without it you're captive to your past."

"I'm sorry." She shouldn't have judged him. He had gone through terrible hardships. Still, there was no way she could forgive her father for what he had done to her. And there was no way she would forgive Frank.

David's voice broke into her thoughts. "First you need to surrender to God. Only then can you forgive those around you." He zipped up his coat. "Why don't we talk about this again sometime? I'll be back next week. Maybe we could have lunch together?"

Karina gulped. "OK," she stuttered, too surprised to refuse.

The skin around David's eyes crinkled into a myriad of tiny lines. "Noon?"

She pushed her sweaty hands into her pockets and nodded.

"I'll be here then."

For a moment their eyes met. She noticed their deep-indigo color, speckled with grey flecks, and the rough stubble on his cheeks.

"God bless you, Karina. See you next week." With a quick wave he headed out the door.

Karina leaned against the wall, trying to catch her breath and regain her composure.

"Such a nice man."

She wheeled around and found Ina grinning.

"You're a lucky woman."

"Nothing is going on between us. And don't you go spreading stories!"

"I won't mention a word of it to anyone. On my heart of promise." Ina touched the wooden cross around her neck to back up her words. "But if nothing is going on, why are you making such a big deal about it?"

"I don't want stories to get started. You know how things get exaggerated."

"Where there's smoke, there's fire."

Karina marched down the hallway and slammed her office door behind her.

No man had taken her out since Frank left. She'd sworn she would never let herself get hurt again, that no man would ever get close enough to even have a chance. Now David had invited her to lunch. And she'd agreed.

He's not Frank, she reminded herself. She had to admit that Tanya had a good point. She had to stop being a captive to her past. But would she ever be able to?

Head pounding, she grabbed two aspirin out of the little vial in her purse and washed them down with cold coffee. She rubbed her temples and closed her eyes.

⸰⸰⸰

Karina's mother grimaced as she wiped her hands on the old gingham apron. "Your daddy's not feeling well. We must be very quiet." She stirred salt into the thick cream-of-cabbage soup. It seemed that was all they ate these days. Cabbage and potatoes mixed together in water and flour, with the occasional piece of sausage.

Little Karina jumped off her chair. "I want to go see him."

Her mother grabbed her arm. "No. You must not."

She tried to shake loose from her mother's tight grip. Intense pain shot through her shoulder and tears welled up in her eyes. "You are hurting me. Let me go!"

"Only if you promise you'll not go see him."

"OK, I promise."

Her mother let go. "Good girl." She soothed, taking a cookie from the jar. "Here, have a cookie. And don't talk to your father about what I said."

The sugarless cookie tasted bland and pasty, but Karina knew better than to complain. Her mother had had a short temper ever since her father had arrived from Moscow.

Her father didn't come out of his room for supper. Karina and her mother ate the bland cabbage concoction in silence.

Long after she went to bed that night, Karina woke up to a blood-curdling scream. Bolting upright in bed, she sat stock-still from fright. When the scream reoccurred, she dashed out of bed and peered down the hallway. The scream had come from her parents' room. She halted by their door, scared and cold.

"Be quiet," she heard her father say, his voice rough and demanding. "You'll wake Karina."

Her mother broke into muffled sobs. Too scared to move, Karina stood shaking by the door.

When her mother's crying finally subsided, Karina hurried back to bed, chilled to the bone. Teeth chattering, she jerked the thread-bare blanket over her head and waited for the first crack of morning light.

At breakfast, her mother's eye was purple-blue and almost swollen shut, her lips thick and crusted with blood on one corner. Her left arm dangled limply by her side.

"I fell down the root-cellar stairs last night," she explained in a monotone voice as she stirred the porridge. "I wasn't careful enough."

But Karina knew better.

From that moment on Karina hated her father with a dreadful passion. Not to mention what he put her through after her mother's death. That's when she learned to hate not only him, but other men as well. Only Frank had made his way into her heart. She should've known better.

Karina sat up in her chair. Picking up the phone, she tried to dial David's cell number, but her fingers lacked the strength to push the buttons. She had to pull herself together; one lunch hour did not equal a commitment. He probably just wanted to talk to her about his God anyway. He'd never let on that he was interested in anything else.

She placed the phone receiver in its cradle and turned her attention to assembling the health profile for Alexander, whose prospective adoptive parents would be arriving from Canada.

The road back to Perm had never seemed so long. David's mind wandered as he drove back to the city.

How did I get myself into this? He had no intentions of forming any type of relationship with Karina, and now he had weaseled himself into a date.

It's just lunch, he reminded himself. *Don't blow this out of proportion.*

He wanted to talk to her about Jesus, of course. But he also wanted to know more about her. Perhaps it would give him insight into her broodiness, her sarcasm, her hatred for Americans.

Once in Perm, David didn't go to the shelter for supper as he'd planned. He needed to sort some things out and spend time in quiet reflection.

After a pasta dinner at his favorite Italian restaurant, he drove to his apartment. It greeted him with palpable silence. The heater had been off all day, and a damp chill hung in the room. He flicked the switch on the small space heater and positioned his chair in front of it, sock-clad feet close to the glowing element. Feeling lonely, he trudged to the ill-stocked kitchen and filled the electric kettle to brew a strong cup of coffee.

He thought about Sheila, his ex-wife. The first few months after their marriage had been fun and exhilarating, the passion intoxicating. But things changed after the honeymoon phase. Their problems started long before Geoff and Danae passed away. But he hadn't seen the collapse coming. Absorbed in his career, he'd been away from home almost every week, so he and Sheila had drifted apart. By the time their battered relationship became evident, they both accepted it as "normal married life." He made the money; she took care of the kids, ran the household, and slept in his bed. Seemed like a fair deal at the time. Now he couldn't believe how self-absorbed he'd been.

Pouring hot water on the grounds in the filter, he watched the clear liquid become murky brown as it dripped into the mug. He walked back to the living room, set the mug on the small table, and then turned down the space heater. He settled in the old chair, the hot mug between his cold hands. With little puffs, he blew at the steaming liquid.

It had been a long time since he'd spent one-on-one time with a woman. He suddenly looked forward to the lunch date with Karina.

CHAPTER EIGHT

The Boeing 737 taxied off the tarmac to the terminal at Sheremetyevo International Airport. Vanessa stared out the tiny porthole at the gloomy building. The airport looked exactly as she had imagined: drab and gray. She rubbed her temples in a circular motion and swallowed again to unplug her ears.

The eleven-hour flight from Toronto had been long and tedious, without any in-flight entertainment. Now Jared and Vanessa faced an eight-hour layover in Moscow before their one A.M. flight to Perm.

As the plane rolled to a stop at the terminal, Jared put his Stephen Covey book into the black leather bag containing his laptop. "Smooth flight," he said with a yawn. "Rather boring, but I had a few good naps between meals."

Vanessa had managed to catch some sleep as well, in spite of her excitement.

The Russian passengers silently filed out of the plane, their faces somber and morose. Jared and Vanessa followed the throng into the terminal. Once inside, they saw long lines at the passport control booths. Jared pointed at several Russian passengers scribbling on documents. "Do you think we're supposed to fill out one of those cards?"

"I don't think so. It's probably for Russian citizens." She picked up one of them. "I can't even make out what it says. Let's see if the person at the booth can speak English."

They lined up behind what seemed the shortest queue, but it barely moved for the next hour. People continually pushed ahead of them without so much as a word of apology. Other passengers in the line quietly accepted the intruders.

"This is unfair," Jared seethed. "Why do people let them get away with this?"

"Ex-KGB mentality," Vanessa whispered. "Complain and you're put in the Gulag."

Jared pointed at the next line, which was slightly shorter. "I'm going over there. We'll get back together whenever one of us gets to the booth." He disappeared in the crowd. Vanessa made it to the booth while Jared was still stuck near the back of his line. She tried to catch his attention but the throng of people around her made it impossible for him to see her. The customs clerk behind the thick glass asked something in Russian.

"Do you speak English?" Vanessa asked.

The clerk shrugged and repeated her unintelligible request, an irritated look on her face.

Vanessa handed over her passport, but even that didn't satisfy the irate clerk.

"The immigration card?" a man behind her said in English with a thick Russian accent.

Turning around, Vanessa looked at the burly man dressed in black.

"You're supposed to have the immigration card filled out."

"I didn't know," she stammered, her eyes searching the crowd for Jared.

The man pushed one of the cards into her hand. "Name here, first and last. Address there. And sign here," he pointed.

The line behind the booth continued to increase. Vanessa quickly filled out the card and handed it to the clerk, who scanned it and put two official-looking red stamps on top.

"Thank you," she said to the man behind her, who grunted in return.

The clerk spoke sharply and motioned for her to move on.

Jared was nowhere to be seen. She hoped he'd been able to fill out the card and make it through customs.

Suitcases lay scattered around luggage belts, some wrapped tightly in cellophane, others with their contents spilled onto the floor. In a corner she spotted two of their suitcases, still intact. Picking them up, she whispered a silent prayer of thanksgiving. Just as she located suitcase number three, Jared appeared.

"That was confusing. It took me a while to figure out that I needed one of those cards." Jared picked the last suitcase off the ground. "Looks like you made it through all right."

"I guess we're learning as we go along."

"We need to get to the other airport to catch the flight to Perm. Let me go find out how to get there." Jared pointed to an information kiosk. Vanessa waited with the suitcases as he hurried across the terminal.

She stifled a yawn. They'd be very tired once they arrived in Perm. Hopefully, they'd be able to catch some sleep, either on the plane or once they arrived.

"The bus stop is across the road," Jared told her when he returned. "The bus comes every half hour, the lady said, and it's free."

A dozen taxi drivers approached them as soon as they stepped out the door. Some of the drivers offered their services in English and followed them to the bus stop like a pack of hyenas. "Only eight hundred rubles. Take you there fast. Bus may be gone."

Ignoring the taxi chauffeurs, they crossed the busy road to the bus stop. Within a short time the bus rolled to a halt at the curb. Jared lugged the suitcases onto the bus, and they dropped onto the hard plastic seats.

"So far, so good," Jared said cheerfully as the bus rattled across the rutted road to Sheremetyevo Two, the smaller national airport. Before they could enter the building, security personnel searched their suitcases and performed a thorough body check.

"It's very safe here." Jared grinned at Vanessa's dismayed look as the heavyset female security guard slid her hands over Vanessa's body.

Their luggage checked, they entered a small waiting room. Vanessa eyed the dirt-covered floor and grimy seats. "Cleanliness isn't high on their priority list."

"Let's sit over there." Jared pointed to a small table and two chairs in the small airport café. A few travelers hung around the bar, smoking cigarettes and drinking large glasses of cheap vodka and wine.

"Rather smoky in here." Vanessa coughed in the thick blue smoke. But it would be all worth it: just a few more hours and they'd see Alexander.

The last leg of the trip from Moscow to Perm was short and un-eventful. The small plane touched down on the tarmac at 4:30 A.M. Twenty-eight hours of straight travel; Vanessa was exhausted.

Jared rubbed his eyes. "I sure am looking forward to a good night's, or day's, sleep."

A well-dressed woman walked straight toward them in the terminal, smiling broadly. She identified herself as Maria Ivanova, the Russian coordinator of Loving Hearts. "I recognized you from pictures sent with the file from Loving Hearts. Welcome to Perm." She bustled ahead of them to the luggage area, protected by soldiers with machine guns slung over their shoulders, their faces dour.

"Follow me," Maria instructed once the suitcases had been located. She led the couple to a rusty minivan outside the terminal. A short, skinny man leaned against the van, a cigarette dangling from his fingers. When he saw Maria, he stood straight and smiled, revealing brown-stained teeth.

"This is Sergei," Maria said. "He does not speak English, but he is a good driver." She clambered into the front seat as Sergei loaded their suitcases in the back of the van.

Maria turned to face Vanessa and Jared. "I take you to hotel first. You have till eight thirty to clean up. Sergei and translator, Elena, take you to Ministry of Health to accept proposal. Then Sergei and Elena go to orphanage with you. I sure you will like the boy. The people at the orphanage say he is wonderful. Well behaved and sweet."

We're going straight to the orphanage? Vanessa wanted to ask if they could get some sleep first, but the words stuck in her throat. Maria seemed to have their entire day planned out.

At the Ural Hotel, they followed Maria to the front desk while Sergei unloaded their suitcases.

"Passports," the receptionist said in English without looking up.

Jared frowned and looked to Maria.

"You need to give passports to register with hotel. Standard procedure. You will get back tomorrow," Maria explained the strange request.

Concern crept into Vanessa's heart as she watched their passports disappear into a file. What if they didn't get them back again? She'd heard that happened all the time in Russia. But they didn't have a choice.

The rickety four-person elevator squeaked up to the third floor, where another lady sat behind a desk, looking bored.

"You need show your room key to her every time you come and go," Maria told them by the desk. "They want make sure you stay in hotel. All hotels do that here. Nothing to worry about."

Jared pulled the key out of his pocket.

If there was nothing to worry about, why was there so much security? Filled with trepidation, Vanessa followed Jared and Maria down the hall to their room. The runner in the middle of the linoleum floor was frayed, the colors faded. The edges curled away from the wall. The walls were yellowed, without any pictures.

Jared thanked Maria for her help, then opened the door of the cubicle-size room with two single beds. After placing her luggage against the wall, Vanessa dropped onto the sagging bed. They'd have to be ready to leave in an hour and a half. Barely enough time to shower and have breakfast. There was definitely no time to sleep. But Jared lay down on the bed beside hers and almost immediately started to snore.

<hr>

Yung's Café smelled of grease and deep-fried fish. The filthy floors had obviously not seen a mop in years, and bedraggled curtains hung limply in front of the mud-splattered windows. Chagrinned, David led Karina to a small table in the corner, away from the other patrons. He would've liked to take her to a better restaurant, but Karina had refused to go to the downtown cafe. There wasn't much choice of restaurants in the town.

CHAPTER EIGHT

Holding out Karina's chair for her, he waited until she was seated, then took the chair on the other side of the table.

The diminutive Chinese waitress did not speak much Russian, but smiled incessantly to make up for her linguistic handicap. She handed them a dog-eared menu and disappeared.

"What do you like to eat?" David wasn't sure anything in this place would be palatable.

"Whatever you are having." Karina stared at her menu.

When the waitress returned, David pointed to the Chinese titles above the Russian descriptions of two dishes. She responded with theatrical facial expressions and arm waving. It would have been comical had he been in the mood for it. Instead, the difficult communication heightened the tension that hung between Karina and himself.

"I can only stay for an hour," Karina said as the waitress disappeared through the swinging door to the kitchen. "A Canadian couple is coming by this afternoon to visit Alexander for an adoption proposal."

"That's wonderful."

"Indeed. He gets a home with love and lots of money. Not everyone is that lucky."

David took a sip from his cup of bitter coffee. "You're making a difference in kids' lives."

"Really?" She raised her eyebrows. "For most of them, it seems we're just providing a meager existence until they get put out onto the street."

"You're taking care of them until they can be placed in a home. The better care you provide, the more kids from your orphanage will be adopted out."

The waitress returned with two platters of steaming food, which consisted mainly of fried rice and cabbage with a few tiny shreds of chicken mixed in.

Karina picked up her fork and poked it into the cabbage mixture.

"Mind if I ask a blessing before we eat?"

She looked up. "A blessing?"

"Yeah, to thank God for the food."

"Oh. Sure, go ahead." She put down her fork and waited for him to proceed.

He bowed his head, folded his hands in his lap, and closed his eyes. "God, thank You for this day and for the good food You've provided for us. Thank You for our health and strength. And thank You for Karina. Bless her work at the orphanage. Show her that You love her and You have a plan for her life. In Jesus' name, amen."

Karina raised her eyebrows. "You take your religion seriously, don't you?"

"Why shouldn't I?"

"After all God's done to you, taking your kids and your wife, why should you?"

"When we get hurt, we tend to blame God. But He can always be trusted. He loves us and wants the best for us. The Bible says that all things work together for good for those who love God. I remember that, even in the middle of my pain."

"If He's that powerful, why doesn't He stop all the misery in this world?" Bitterness laced her words.

David washed down the first bland mouthful of food with lukewarm coffee. "Suffering comes because we live in a world full of sin. We can't hold God responsible for that."

"How can you trust a being who can stop pain but doesn't?"

He chewed his food before answering. "I can physically stop the kids at the shelter from making mistakes, but I allow them to make their own choices, even when those decisions may hurt them. That doesn't make me irresponsible or uncaring. Sometimes that's a loving choice."

"The orphans didn't choose to be abandoned by their families."

"Kids suffer because of their parents' mistakes. The decisions we make affect the people around us, also our kids."

A flash of irritation crossed her face as she doused the gelatinous mass of slimy cabbage in pepper.

"Sorry that I couldn't take you to a better place. If you come to Perm, I'll take you to this little Italian restaurant on Lenin Street. I eat there regularly. The food's great."

David could tell by the look on her face that she didn't care where he ate. Putting his fork down, he decided to change the topic. "Where did you grow up?"

"St. Petersburg."

"Did you go to school there?"

"No. University of Moscow."

"And then you came to Kungur?"

"Much later." She kept her eyes focused on her plate.

The kitchen door swung open, and the waitress burst into the room, whisking David's plate off the table.

"Not sure if I was done." He grimaced. "But I guess I am now."

"Sorry," Karina said as if it was her fault.

"No worries. I wasn't all that hungry anyway." Judging by the amount of food left on her plate, Karina wasn't either. "Are you finished?" His attempt at small talk had failed. There was no reason to stay in the restaurant any longer.

"Yes." She pushed back her plate.

He put twenty rubles on the table and stood.

They walked back to the small truck, which he had washed for the occasion. It wasn't likely that she'd take note of it, though. He opened the passenger door for her.

"Thank you." She slipped into the bucket seat.

David climbed into the driver's seat and turned the key in the ignition. Without another word, they drove across the bouncy road back to the orphanage.

When they reached their destination, Karina opened the door of the truck without waiting for him and stepped out. "Thanks for lunch."

"You're welcome. Have a good week." David didn't bother getting out of the truck. He slammed the truck into reverse and headed back to Perm. The lunch had been a fiasco. What had he expected? That she would immediately open up to him? He should've known better. He pressed his foot down on the accelerator. The Toyota skipped across the potholes like a deer over a rutted field.

He'd seen the pain in her eyes. Her callous front served as a cover-up for the hurt she carried. Could he reach her with the Word of Life? If she'd been a teen at the shelter, would he give up so easily? Would he have considered the lunch a failure or a first step in building a relationship of trust that could take months? He knew the answer. And he knew he would not give up on Karina.

⁂

While Jared caught a restful half-hour catnap, Vanessa lay in bed staring at the ceiling. Questions danced through her head like fireflies around a beam of light. What would their little boy be like? Would she feel an immediate bond with him? How would she respond to him? Was he as sweet as Maria led them to think?

Too restless to stay in bed any longer, she got up and woke Jared. "Time to get ready."

Grumbling and groggy, Jared crawled out of the twin bed and stretched. "That wasn't much of a rest."

"Be thankful that you caught some sleep." Opening the curtains, Vanessa got her first glimpse of the decrepit buildings and barren streets. Her stomach churned with an intense bout of nerves. She turned away from the window and dug through her suitcase for a fresh change of clothes.

Jared disappeared in the bathroom to take a last minute shower.

"We should head downstairs if we want to get some breakfast," she called to Jared when she'd finished dressing. They had twenty minutes until the driver would come to pick them up.

He stepped out of the bathroom, rubbing his wet hair with a faded green towel.

"Give me five minutes."

Vanessa glanced at her watch. "We don't have five minutes if we want to eat."

"OK, three then." He disappeared into the bathroom again.

"Please, hurry."

"OK, OK." Jared quickly pulled on a pair of blue jeans and a rugged sweater. Vanessa grabbed her handbag and the travel bag with toys for Alexander.

"Don't forget the camcorder," Jared reminded her.

"I've got it."

"Good. Let's go then."

They found a small dining room in the basement of the building. A rather odd place for a restaurant, Vanessa thought. But then, most things in Russia were rather odd for her.

Jared helped himself to the buffet of sausage, hard-boiled eggs, crusty sourdough bread, and Russian pastries. Vanessa placed a single slice of sourdough bread on her plate.

Jared popped a pastry into his mouth. "Food's good here."

Vanessa sipped her tea and nibbled on her bread and jam. She hadn't been able to sleep and now her appetite was gone. Glancing at her watch, she noticed it was almost eight thirty. "We really need to go upstairs. Sergei should be here in five minutes."

Jared stuffed the rest of the egg sandwich into his mouth, while Vanessa picked up their bags off the floor.

Sergei waited for them by the door of the foyer. "*Dubroe Utro*," he greeted them with a grin.

A thin lady with limp hair and dull blue eyes spoke with the reception-ist at the desk, and then approached them. "I am Elena, your translator for today. I will accompany you and Sergei to Kungur to meet with the child." Her English was concise and carefully pronounced with special emphasis on each word. "We will go to the Ministry of Health now for the adoption proposal." Turning around, she motioned for Jared and Vanessa to follow her to the van in front of the hotel.

After a short drive, they reached a large concrete building. Sergei swerved into the parking lot and brought the van to a halt.

Jared and Vanessa followed Elena into the colossal structure. The tiny windows and heavy doors reminded Vanessa more of a prison than a government building. The squeaky elevator, even older and slower than the one in the Ural Hotel, rattled up to the third floor. Tools and boxes of supplies lay scattered everywhere, covered by a thick layer of dust as if the renovation crew had suddenly aborted the project. Cubicle-sized offices lined the hallway.

Elena paused in front of one of the doors. "This office belongs to the Director of Child Welfare. She will give you the child's file. Then we will go to the orphanage." She knocked softly. Upon the reply from inside, she opened the door for Jared and Vanessa.

The office held a large wooden desk, behind which sat an austere lady. Her auburn hair was pulled back in a tight knot at the bottom of her neck, and her sharp eyes seemed to take in every detail. She assessed Jared and Vanessa with disdain as she motioned to the two chairs in front of the desk.

"Have a seat," Elena said. "This is Ms. Kochnova."

Ms. Kochnova rattled on in Russian and Elena translated. "She says to tell you that before you sign the proposal, you must know that all children up for adoption have health problems. There are no healthy children in the orphanages. Otherwise they would have been adopted by Russian citizens."

Vanessa blanched. The social worker in Canada had reassured them that the Russian diagnosis was simply misinformation. Vanessa remembered her saying that in all the years of adopting children out of Russia, they had experienced no serious problems.

The woman pulled a document out of a file folder and slid it across the desk toward Jared and Vanessa.

"If you still wish to visit Alexander, sign this document stating you understand what I have told you and you are willing to proceed with the adoption," Elena translated.

Picking up the pen, Jared signed the paper. Vanessa hesitated. Was it really true what the director had said?

"Sign here," Jared pointed to the paper, oblivious to her discomfort.

Vanessa picked up the pen and signed. They could always refuse the adoption should something be wrong with the child. . . . She pushed the paper across the desk toward the burly woman and followed Jared and Elena to the door.

Elena escorted them out of the building, back to the van. "Now we will go to Kungur."

Vanessa silently slipped into the back seat and stared out the window. Why had Leah led them to believe that this child would be healthy? She felt her tension rise. What if the child had serious health problems? Then what would they do?

Sergei swerved through the dense traffic, honking profusely. Vanessa gripped the back of the driver's seat to steady herself. Her stomach lurched with the sudden acceleration and deceleration. Soon the old van reached the Siberian highway, and the traffic diminished. Sergei pointed to a heavily fortified building in the distance and said something in Russian.

"Military installations," Elena translated. "Mainly nuclear weapons. Until fifteen years ago, Perm was closed to foreigners. The maps did not even show the road to Perm. Much has changed since then. We have food and clothes. Life is good here now."

Good? Vanessa looked at the ramshackle buildings along the road. If the economy was good now, what had it been like before?

"Have you ever been outside Russia?" Jared asked.

"Once, to Romania, before communism fell there."

Vanessa tried to see the culture through Elena's eyes. This was the only life most people here had ever known. She wondered how they survived.

Before long the ancient city of Kungur lay before them. A large concrete statue of a man with bent arms greeted them on the side of the road. The sign underneath the statue had Cyrillic writing, but Vanessa could only decipher one word: Kungur. The city looked like the other Russian cities Vanessa and Jared had seen: dilapidated and somber, with roads in dire need of repair.

Sergei pulled onto a small side road, swerving to miss the potholes, and then parked alongside a large, ramshackle building. "The orphanage," Elena explained, opening the door of the van.

Although run down, the building was not as bad as Vanessa had envisioned. Two double strollers parked in the courtyard were the only sign that any children occupied the place. An old tractor tire and two swings served as a playground.

Lord, please provide homes for all the kids who live here, Vanessa prayed, touched by the bleak scene.

"We will now go inside and meet the boy. Then the director will talk with you," Elena said. She made her way to the back entrance, where a series of crooked wooden steps led up to a small door.

"Watch your head," Elena warned as she ducked under a slanted beam above the narrow stairwell. She opened a door in the hallway and took them into a small, empty office. "Wait here. The boy will be brought to you. Then the director will come. She speaks English. I will be back in a while."

The office was unassuming but clean, with a desk and two chairs. A few scraggly plants bloomed in small clay pots on the window ledge. Water-stained, green-striped '70s wallpaper pulled off the wall along the baseboard. A big, threadbare rug covered the yellowish linoleum. A Macintosh computer and keyboard formed a stark modern contrast to the faded interior.

Vanessa sat down on the hard chair by the desk. The long journey and emotions of the day had left her exhausted. Jared retrieved his camcorder out of their travel bag and flicked the On button, poised to capture the first moment.

"For the people at home, and for later on, when Alexander grows up," he explained, removing the lens cap.

Vanessa had a hard time thinking that far ahead. Right now she just wanted to get their first meeting with Alexander over with. "I wish I had some water." She licked her dry lips as she took off her coat and laid it on the armrest of the chair. "I should've thought to bring a bottle from the hotel. The water here may not be safe for drinking."

"We can ask Elena when she returns," Jared suggested.

With a short knock, the door opened. A plump nurse, followed by Elena, entered the office carrying a pale, limp baby. The nurse grinned at Jared and Vanessa, revealing several missing teeth. "Ina," she said, pointing at herself. Chattering in Russian, the woman laid the infant on the rug on the floor and stripped off his little coat. His head dropped listlessly to the side. A trickle of drool dribbled out of the corner of his mouth. He showed no interest in his surroundings but stared into the distance. Ina lifted the baby onto Vanessa's lap, her lips moving in a constant flow of words.

"She says he's a very good baby," Elena said. "Everyone loves him here. He never cries."

Vanessa steadied the flaccid infant on her knee. His thick blue-and-white knitted sweater and jeans were neat and clean, and the soft layer of blond fuzz on his head had been pasted down with a bit of water. He refused to make eye contact with anyone in the room.

"All orphanage children have a hard time with strangers," Elena pointed out. "He will get accustomed to you soon. The babies do not get handled a lot. The workers are too busy with all the children to spend one-on-one time with them."

Vanessa stared at Alexander. At nine months old how could he possibly be *this* small? And his eyes seemed so empty and dull. She found it hard to imagine that it was simply shyness.

Elena moved toward the door. "I will leave you alone for a while with the baby. The director will come shortly. She speaks English."

Jared put the camcorder on the desk and pulled a toy out of their travel bag. He knelt on one knee before the baby on Vanessa's lap and cooed, squeezing the yellow plastic duck. A slight light dawned in the baby's eyes. He stretched out his thin arm to touch the toy.

"He can't weight more than twelve or fifteen pounds," Vanessa whispered.

"But he's quick," Jared remarked with a smile as Alexander touched the duck with his fist. "His eyes are smart and bright."

Vanessa gawked at Jared. Were they talking about the same baby? All she saw was an irresponsive child with empty eyes and drool running down his sweater. Was this how Fetal Alcohol Syndrome babies looked? Or did he perhaps have autism?

"Look at his smile. He's not afraid of us at all." Jared tickled his belly and made a funny face. Alexander chuckled. His little fist reached for Jared's nose. "He strikes me as a very intelligent boy, especially considering he's been in an orphanage since birth. I wonder if he can sit up by himself."

"Look at his size! There's no way he can."

"Why not? He's nine months old."

"We'll have to ask the director. Did Elena mention her name?"

"I don't think so, but they said she was coming shortly."

They didn't have to wait long. After a short knock, a dark-haired woman in a black skirt and cream-colored blouse entered the room. She was followed by a shorter lady, dressed in a wrinkled tan skirt and purple flowered blouse.

"I am Karina Svetlana, the director," the taller woman said in English with a slight smile. "This is Mrs. Volsky, the social worker." The director's voice was melodious and her grammar impeccable, despite a heavy Russian accent. "Welcome to Kungur Baby House. Alexander is a very sweet boy." She tickled his chin, then sat behind the desk and opened a thick blue folder.

"These are his medical papers. He was born at home at thirty-two weeks gestation, early birth due to maternal toxemia. After that he was taken to the neonatal hospital. Then he was transferred to a full-care hospital where he stayed until he came here three months ago."

Vanessa balanced Alexander on her lap. The child had barely moved since Ina had put him there except for the brief interaction with Jared. Did she dare question the director about his flaccid body and his general disinterest in his surroundings?

Karina flipped to the next section in the file. "He's had a few bouts of acute rhinitis—the common cold—he has slight rickets due to lack of sunlight. Otherwise, he is healthy and active. His initial diagnosis of perinatal encephalopathy was lifted at three months of age, as was the syndrome of hyper-excitability. He has been tested for AIDS, hepatitis, syphilis, and tuberculosis. All tests have come back negative. He has been vaccinated for all common childhood illnesses." Karina looked up at them. "Do you have any questions?"

"Does he have Fetal Alcohol Syndrome?" Vanessa asked. It seemed to be the only concern that had not been addressed.

"No, not based on his file. Anyone who drinks alcohol in excess in Russia gets registered with the State, and Alexander's mother is not on file. So I don't have any concerns about that."

Vanessa raised her eyebrows. How could the State possibly register all alcoholics?

"Any information on the mother?" Jared asked.

Karina glanced at the file. "Her name is Sofia. She is in her twenties and lives an hour south of Perm. She loves Alexander very much but is too poor to keep him."

"And the father?"

The director shrugged. "The mother has not released any information regarding him."

Vanessa rocked the baby. He observed her with sad, light blue eyes. Her heart ached for this little one, rejected at such a young age. But was she ready to take him home with her? Was he the right child for them?

CHAPTER EIGHT

"The doctor can come tomorrow and do an exam," Karina said, "You will need Dr. Petrovich's approval for the emigration. He will fill out the necessary paperwork to send to Moscow for Alexander's visa. Should you decide against the adoption of this child, Maria will find a new proposal for you. You must, however, let us know prior to the doctor's visit. He has to come from Perm and will only do so if you wish to proceed with the adoption."

Vanessa stared at her husband. The time had come to make a decision. She gave the baby to Jared. The child sat as quietly with Jared as he had with Vanessa, staring up at Jared's face.

"The babies seldom see men in the orphanage," the director said, "but it looks like Alexander is doing very well with you. Do you have other children?"

"One," Vanessa stated. "A five-year-old girl." She pulled a small photo album out of her purse and handed it to the director.

The director leafed through the pages, examining each shot carefully. "Such a beautiful child. So big and strong. You are a lucky woman." With a smile, she gave the album back to Vanessa.

Vanessa had never considered herself that lucky. After all, they hadn't been able to have more children after Annie. She slipped the album back into her purse. Her heart ached for her strong, healthy child even more now that she'd met emaciated little Alexander.

Elena peeked around the corner of the door. "I am ready to go whenever you are."

Jared handed the baby to Mrs. Volsky, the social worker. He pulled the gifts they'd brought for Alexander out of their bag, but Vanessa subtly shook her head. He gave her a puzzled look, but didn't argue.

"Thank you for your time and effort, Ms. Svetlana." Jared shook the director and the social worker's hand.

Vanessa retrieved her coat off the chair and followed Jared to the door. She could not wait to escape the stifling atmosphere in the office. Her throat was still parched. Her eyes burned with fatigue, and a dull headache throbbed at her temples.

"Watch your head," Elena warned them again as she headed down the narrow stairwell.

Vanessa wondered about her head, but not in connection to hitting it against the beam. What was she doing here, seven thousand miles from home, trying to pick out a new baby? She remembered what Ms. Kochnova had said: there were no healthy kids in orphanages. Could it be true? Judging by Alexander's size and appearance, she didn't doubt it.

The crisp air outside refreshed her foggy mind. After thirty-four hours without a wink of sleep, it was no wonder she felt tired. Stepping into the van, she dropped onto the vinyl bench. She tipped her head back and pretended to sleep during the ride back to the city. The Russian radio blared over the crackling speakers. Elena napped in the front seat next to Sergei, and Jared snored beside Vanessa, his mouth wide open.

Show us the way, Lord, because I don't see it right now. Please give me peace in this situation. I thought I knew what I was doing when I went to Russia, but now I'm full of doubt. I don't feel any attraction to this child.

Vanessa had expected to fall in love with Alexander. But she hadn't even wanted to hold him. Was there something seriously wrong with him? Or was she simply a cold-hearted person who could not love another child except her own?

When the van pulled into the parking lot by the hotel, Jared woke with a start. "Are we here already?"

"Yes. You slept the whole way," Vanessa said, collecting her belongings.

"Sergei and I will pick you up at eight thirty tomorrow morning to take you back to the orphanage," Elena told them as they stepped out of the van.

Vanessa feigned a smile. She was tired and dirty, and she didn't want to go back to the orphanage. "See you tomorrow," she managed to say before she hurried into the hotel.

Once in their room, Vanessa dropped onto the bed, her strength depleted.

"Are you OK?" Jared asked, bending over her.

Vanessa pressed her lips together. How could she explain what she felt without breaking down and crying? How could she tell him that

82

she was sorry they'd come to Russia? That all she wanted to do was pack her bags and leave?

"You've been quiet all afternoon. You didn't even seem very excited to see Alexander."

That was an understatement. Vanessa closed her eyes in an attempt to shut out the image of the drooling baby with the limp head and empty eyes. "I just need some rest. I'll be all right." She desperately wanted to believe that, but peace eluded her. Unable to fight her exhaustion any longer, she fell into a trance-like sleep.

CHAPTER NINE

After he'd dropped Karina off at the orphanage, David took the shortest route back to the shelter. He still had a lot of work to accomplish, and it was late afternoon already. With his repeated trips to the orphanages, the administration had been falling behind. He had to catch up before the next board meeting.

Jake hurried toward David in the hallway of the shelter. "There's a woman waiting for you in your office. Says she's from CNN and that you know about her visit. I tried to call you, but your cell phone must not have been working."

David frowned. He remembered the woman from CNN who'd requested an interview with him, but according to his day planner, Pamela Lowall wasn't supposed to arrive until the following Monday. He rubbed his chin.

"I didn't know you were expecting someone. She's not the type you'd usually see in street outreach. Friendly enough, though," Jake added.

David crossed the hall to his office. A lady in her late twenties sat on the worn-out chesterfield, a laptop on her knees. When he entered, she closed the computer and pushed herself up out of the sofa. Her auburn hair with blonde streaks swung loosely over one shoulder, held back by a butterfly clip. She wore a black leather jacket accentuated by a bright pink scarf. A shiny patent-leather briefcase with Armani in bold white letters sat on the floor.

"Pamela Lowall. Nice to meet you." She held out a carefully manicured hand with long fingernails, each decorated with a tiny diamond.

David shook her slender hand. "I'm sorry, but I don't recall your arrival being today. Did I make a mistake?"

Her laughter was fresh and bubbly. "I finished two days ahead of schedule in Moscow, so I caught an earlier flight to Perm. I'm sorry I didn't notify you. If this time isn't convenient for you, I could come back in a few days."

"It's not a problem. Have a seat." He pointed to the sofa.

She sat down, tucked a strand of hair behind her ear, and folded her hands on top of the closed laptop. "I would like to interview you about your work here at the shelter and then visit an orphanage, if that's possible."

David weighed the options. "The shelter's no problem. I can show you this one as well as our new day shelter, which is the educational side of our program. I can also try to arrange a visit to an orphanage. Would tomorrow work for you?"

"Absolutely. What time?"

"How about nine?" That would give him plenty of time to coordinate his day.

"I'll be here." Bending over, she slipped the computer into her briefcase and stood up.

"Would you care for supper?" David asked politely.

"Thanks, but I'm meeting a friend."

David escorted her to the door. "Do you need a ride to your hotel?"

"My friend is waiting for me." She pointed to a black Skoda parked at the curb. "I'll see you tomorrow, then."

The heels of her Armani boots clicked on the uneven pavement as she made her way to the car. Her pink scarf fluttered over her shoulder like a brilliant flamingo against the black night sky. David pondered the cost of the boots and briefcase: probably enough to feed a whole orphanage for several months.

———— ⚬⚬⚬ ————

Karina entered her small apartment. She placed two bags of groceries on the kitchen counter and then walked back to the hallway to take off her shoes. The meeting with Alexander's prospective parents had gone well but the lunch with David had been a fiasco. She should've restrained herself from commenting on his religion. She knew how important that was to him. Things had gone awry from that moment on. After walking back to the kitchen, she jammed the small loaf of bread into the bread box and tossed the apples in the refrigerator.

A firm knock on the door disturbed her reverie. Before she could answer, Tanya burst in, her face flushed. "You're a liar, Karina! You said you hated this dog of an American. But word has it you had lunch with him at Yung's today."

"Where did you hear that?"

"My friend Dima saw you there." Tanya dropped down on a chair by the small kitchen table.

Karina had no idea who Dima was but Tanya had friends everywhere. She placed the milk in the refrigerator. "It was strictly business." That wasn't a lie. They'd talked about God, and God was David's business.

"Why didn't you tell me?"

"I haven't seen you since he asked me."

"You could've called."

"If I called you for every business appointment I have, I'd constantly be on the phone." Her groceries cleaned up, Karina sat across from Tanya.

Tanya lit a cigarette and inhaled deeply. "I smell a romance."

"There's no romance, not even a shred of it. And there won't be, believe me." Karina's laughter was filled with sarcasm. "Can you imagine me dating a Christian pastor?"

Tanya blew a puff of smoke into the air. "Stranger things have happened. Last time we discussed this guy, you were furious because he refused to leave you alone, and now you're dining with him."

Karina's gaze met Tanya's and held it. "We had some business to talk about."

Tanya eyed her friend. "I've known you for ten years. Lots of guys have asked you out. You've always refused."

Karina pulled a cigarette out of the pack on the table. "It wasn't a date. We weren't even gone for an hour."

Tanya pouted her lips. "Time will tell." She smashed the cigarette butt in the ashtray and stood. "Keep me posted."

"There'll be nothing to tell." Not after that botched lunch today. That was for sure.

When Tanya was gone, Karina finished her cigarette, then prepared a slice of bread with butter and cheese, and poured herself a glass of milk. Just as she sat down at the kitchen table, her cell phone vibrated. *News must really be traveling.* She hesitated before picking it up.

"Karina speaking."

"It's me, David."

Her heart hammered in her chest at the sound of his voice.

"I wonder if you could help me tomorrow," David continued. "I've got a gal here from CNN, an American television news station. She wants to visit an orphanage for a program they're doing. Can we stop by tomorrow?"

"When do you have to know?"

"Right now. Sorry about such short notice, but I just found out myself. She arrived a couple days early. If you're not comfortable with it, I'll call Maya at Konava, but I'd prefer to take her to Kungur. Your orphanage is much better."

I don't want to have a reporter here. Instead, she heard herself say, "That'll be great. But please come after ten o'clock. The immigration doctor will be here in the morning to examine Alexander. I'll need to be with him and the Canadian couple."

"Is one o'clock OK?"

"Yes, that's fine. See you then." She flipped the cell phone closed and placed it on the table. She didn't want any American reporter doing an interview that would get aired on American television. That's where Frank was. Highly unlikely that he would see her, she scolded herself. But the nagging doubt remained.

———— ∞ ————

The darkness in the hotel room oppressed Vanessa like an evil monster that threatened to devour her. In front of her loomed a long, narrow tunnel with no end in sight and no way of escape. Jared had left to allow her a peaceful nap, but now that she was awake, the feelings were far from peaceful. What had they been thinking? They didn't need to adopt. They had a child already.

Vanessa remembered sitting in the hospital in early labor with this same dreadful feeling. But then she believed that she would make it through somehow, that good would come out of everything in the end. Now she wasn't so sure.

Jared entered the room and tiptoed around, placing some paper bags on the floor.

"I'm awake," Vanessa said wearily.

He sat on the bed and cradled her in his arms. "Are you feeling better, sweetheart?"

Vanessa shook her head. "I don't want to follow through with the adoption." She burst into long, heart-rending sobs. "I can't go through with it. I'm too afraid. I didn't feel anything when I saw that little boy except fear." Her tears flowed incessantly.

Jared took a Kleenex out of his pocket and handed it to her. "Why don't we pray about it?"

Vanessa wiped the tears from her eyes and blew her nose. She needed God to show her the way. Her own strength had failed, but God was the strength of her life.

Jared bowed his head and placed his hands over Vanessa's. "Thank You, Lord, that we can always depend on You. We can trust You even when life seems difficult and dark. Please guide us. We need wisdom. Show us whether Alexander is the one we should be adopting. And if not, close the doors. Amen."

Encouraged by Jared's prayer, Vanessa rose and washed her face. Her high expectations of this exciting trip had definitely not been met. The anticipation of meeting Alexander, the child they had prayed for all this time, had turned into a dread of going back to the orphanage.

"Let's go have some supper." Jared followed her into the bathroom and massaged her shoulders. "You must be hungry. You barely ate this morning."

"I'm still not hungry, but food may do me good."

Downstairs in the restaurant, they ordered breaded chicken fillet and mashed potatoes.

Jared looked up at Vanessa. "We'll go back to the orphanage tomorrow and see what the doctor has to say. He wouldn't send a child with serious problems to Canada. I'm sure we can trust his judgment."

"What if I still feel uncomfortable?"

Jared reached across the table and took her hand, rubbing it with his thumb. "We'll cross that bridge when we come to it. In the meantime, do you want to talk to Leah at Loving Hearts about your feelings?"

"No. I don't want to give them reason for concern. Besides, I don't think that would be helpful. Leah is wonderful, but she hasn't seen Alexander. She won't understand. I already seem like a picky Westerner."

"I feel good about adopting Alexander. But both of us need to be comfortable with it."

She squeezed his hand. "Thanks. Your support means the world to me."

"We're in this together. Remember that."

They finished their supper and returned to their room.

"We should call Steven Broxburry," Jared suggested. "He usually has a word of wisdom in difficult situations." Steven was one of the senior pastors at the church they attended. He had been a mentor to them for many years.

Vanessa considered the suggestion. "That might be a good idea."

Jared called Steve's number from his cell phone and turned the speaker on.

"Don't be scared," Steven told them. "The Israelites were afraid to enter the Promised Land, so they wandered in the wilderness for forty years. Because they looked with physical eyes rather than with eyes of faith, they died in the wilderness. Alexander may have some physical problems, but with God all things are possible. I believe the Lord has great things in store for this little guy. I encourage you not to stand in unbelief, but to go and overcome."

After they hung up, Jared wrapped his arms around Vanessa and kissed her. "How do you feel now?"

She didn't feel much better, but she produced a wan smile to set her husband at ease. "I just have to push through my fear."

But still the monster refused to let her go. She lay awake in bed long after she heard Jared's peaceful snore.

The trip to the orphanage was a tedious repetition of the previous day. Sergei listened to blaring Russian music, and Elena sat silently beside him in the front seat. Jared and Vanessa stared out the window at the dreary pre-winter landscape, old cars, and dilapidated buildings.

The orphanage was just as hot and stuffy as the day before. Vanessa and Jared were escorted to a different office, furnished with several desks and an old couch.

A middle-aged man with wire-rimmed glasses sat behind one of the desks, scribbling on a notepad. He greeted them with a slight nod.

Elena introduced Jared and Vanessa to Dr. Petrovich. "He will examine Alexander, and you can ask him any questions you like," she explained.

Ina carried the flaccid baby into the room and removed his sweater. She handed him to Vanessa, chattering nonstop in Russian, although Vanessa couldn't tell who she was speaking to. The doctor continued to write, his head bent over the paperwork.

Vanessa settled Alexander on her lap, again shocked at his thin frame and pale face. He wore the same blue outfit from the previous day. It didn't look like he'd been changed at all. Vanessa's heart ached for the infant. Would he, like so many of the other orphans, end up on the street if they didn't adopt him?

Dr. Petrovich's deep voice interrupted her thoughts.

"He wants you to undress the boy so he can examine him," Elena explained.

Vanessa stripped the layers of clothing off Alexander's frail body. Tiny ribs showed clearly in his pallid chest. He lay on the worn chesterfield, his hands limp beside him. His eyes scanned the room without making eye contact.

The doctor rose from his chair and lumbered over to the couch. He placed his stethoscope on Alexander's chest, listening intently, and tapped his knee with the blunt edge of a steel ruler. Then he took the boy's hands and pulled him up on his feet. Alexander wobbled back and forth, trying to maintain his balance.

"Everything is in order," Elena translated Doctor Petrovich's comments. "The doctor says there are no problems with this child. He is skinny due to a lack of nutrition, but there do not appear to be any serious problems. Sunlight will take care of the rickets."

Alexander's legs trembled as they bore his weight. When the doctor lowered him to the couch, his legs buckled.

"Are you sure the rickets aren't a concern?" Jared asked.

Elena translated the question and the doctor's answer. "It is early enough in the baby's development that it won't have permanent effects." She pointed to Alexander. "You can dress him again. I will call the director, who will speak with you about the adoption proposal."

Vanessa pulled Alexander's little outfit back on, her hands clammy. The doctor's visit was supposed to reassure her, but instead she felt even more agitated and unsure. Yet, she wanted to step out in faith as Steven had instructed them to do.

The director entered the room, her colorful skirt swishing around her legs, and shook Jared's hand. She smiled at Vanessa and stroked Alexander's cheek with her finger. "Good morning, Mr. and Mrs. Williams."

Vanessa swallowed. "Hello." She smoothed Alexander's hair and propped up his head with her arm. Drool dribbled onto her sleeve.

Karina spoke to Dr. Petrovich and picked up Alexander's file. She pulled out an official-looking document. "The doctor said there are no health concerns with the child. Would you like to sign the acceptance papers today?"

Jared gave Vanessa a questioning glance. She wasn't ready to sign anything. War raged in her heart between wanting to walk in God's obedience and paralyzing fright of adopting a child who, she feared, had serious problems. If he was as healthy as the doctor stated, why was he so lifeless and weak? Why did he not make eye contact? Why was he so terribly small?

"Please thank Dr. Petrovich for his help," Vanessa said, carefully choosing her words. "We'd like to think about the situation one more night. We'll let you know tomorrow."

Disappointment showed in Jared's eyes, but he didn't argue with her. "If we decide to go ahead, can we visit the orphanage again in the morning?"

Karina's face revealed no emotion. "As you wish." She slid the document back into the file folder. "I will be here tomorrow should you want to finalize the adoption. I will call Ina in to take Alexander back to the children's area."

Jared rose. "Can we take him there?"

"No. No one is allowed in the children's quarters until they sign adoption papers."

"Why not?"

The director's eyes narrowed. "Protocol, Mr. Williams. Not all the children are available for adoption. You might change your mind about Alexander if you saw a child you liked better."

Vanessa and Jared left the building, lost in their own thoughts. They could not discuss the situation in the van because of Elena, so they waited until they arrived at their hotel room.

"What do you think? Do you feel the doctor's opinion is reliable?" Vanessa asked.

"If he's unreliable, it's unlikely the Canadian government would use his services for all the immigrations."

"True. But is it possible that he missed something?"

"Of course it's possible, but I have no reason to believe that. Alexander is a little small for his age, but I'm sure he'll gain weight quickly once we get him home. The orphanage has kept good records from the time he was born. I'm sure if something was wrong, they would've found it by now."

"You're probably right." She sighed. "But I would like him to show some emotion. He seems so quiet and lethargic."

Jared poured himself a glass of water from a bottle. "I think we can trust the doctor's opinion. But we both need to be in agreement with whatever decision we make. That'll need to be soon, however. Especially if we decide to request a proposal for another child. We're only going to be here a few more days."

Vanessa didn't want to think of a proposal for another child. How could she bear going through all the emotions again?

The apprehension she felt about adopting Alexander *had* to be spiritual warfare. Satan didn't want these kids to get out of the orphanages and be placed under the light of the gospel. Vanessa determined to fight her fear and step out in faith.

⚬⚬⚬

Maria called Vanessa and Jared in their hotel room before breakfast. "Elena is sick and can't go to the orphanage with you," she informed them. "Sergei will pick you up at the usual time and take you there by himself. The director will speak with you about the proposal. Do you think you will sign the proposal during your visit today?"

"We don't know yet," Vanessa stammered. Her determination from the previous evening had disappeared and fear was alive and well. *God, I need You so badly! Please help us today. Give me a sign. I just need some emotion from Alexander to show me that he recognizes us and that he doesn't seem so unresponsive.*

"No problem," Maria answered. "Please tell me how it went when you return."

To Vanessa's relief, she didn't ask any questions.

"Have you decided?" Jared asked Vanessa once they were on their way to Kungur.

"No, I haven't." Her emotions swung from panic to faith and back to panic. She longed for faith like Jared's yet couldn't understand his calmness in light of the enormous decision they had to make. If only she had a sign . . . .

The baby was brought into the small office where they'd seen him the first time. Ina stepped through the door, Alexander in her arms.

93

Vanessa immediately rose from her chair, her eyes glued on Alexander's pale face.

The moment Alexander saw her, his face lit up. His arms flailed the air, his legs kicked, and a hint of a smile formed around his tiny mouth. He stretched his arms out toward Vanessa.

Overwhelmed, she took the baby in her arms and held him close. *Thank You, Jesus, for answering so clearly! You are amazing!*

Another helper brought in lunch for Alexander. One chipped dish was filled with a meat-and-potato mixture and peas. A second bowl held potato soup with a piece of bread. A ceramic cup was filled with some sort of red berry juice. A few berries floated on top. She motioned for Vanessa to sit in the chair by the desk.

Vanessa placed Alexander on her lap by the tray of food. He kicked harder, apparently excited by the sight of the food. It had the hearty aroma of the home-cooked meals her grandmother used to serve when she was a little girl.

"He seems rather young to eat this," Vanessa said, pointing to the food as she spooned broth from the potato soup into Alexander's gaping mouth.

"Perhaps milk is expensive," Jared suggested. "He seems to like it, though."

"Hello, Vanessa. Jared." Karina nodded at them as she entered the room. With a smile, she tickled the little boy's feet. "Hello, Alexander." She took her seat behind the desk. "Elena told me you would give me your decision about Alexander today."

Vanessa nodded. "We would like to adopt him." She glanced at Jared, who raised his eyebrows. She saw the question in his eyes, but he collected himself immediately.

"Yes, we would," he affirmed her statement.

Karina pulled a document out of a file on the desk. "All you need to do is sign here." She pointed to a blank line on the form. "This states that you will formally pursue the adoption."

Jared signed and then took Alexander from Vanessa so she could sign also. The baby protested loudly at being taken away from his food.

Jared grinned at his feisty attitude. "You'll fit well into the Williams household."

After they had signed the papers, Karina stood and shook their hands. "Congratulations. I'm glad Alexander will have a good family to take care of him."

Peace overwhelmed Vanessa. She had not shrunk back in unbelief, but had moved on to conquer the land.

"Excuse me for a moment." Karina moved toward the door. "There are a few more forms to finalize for the Russian government. I will go get them."

The minute Karina stepped out of the office, Jared turned to Vanessa. "What happened?"

She grinned. "God gave me a sign."

"How?"

"I asked for something to show me that Alexander recognized me when he was brought to me and that he wouldn't be so emotionless. So when Ina brought him in, I immediately jumped up to make sure that I was the first one he saw. He became so excited!"

"You're sure that you want to go through with this?" Jared didn't seem convinced.

"Absolutely. Without a shadow of a doubt," Vanessa beamed.

"I don't understand how you came to that decision so suddenly, but I'm happy nonetheless." He kissed Vanessa, then picked up Alexander and swung him into the air. "Welcome to our family, little one!"

"Yes, welcome to the family," Vanessa added with a broad smile.

CHAPTER TEN

T he orphanage is well run," David told Pamela as he parked the truck in the courtyard of Kungur Baby House. "The director is strict but fair and manages the orphanage to the best of her ability. The kids are healthy, well fed, and clean. It's a lot better than some of the other state orphanages in the region."

He opened the door of the truck for her. "Be careful of the potholes," he warned, looking at her stiletto shoes. Placing his hand under her elbow, he guided her over the rutted ground.

Ina opened the door for them before David had a chance to knock. "Hello, David." Seeing Pamela, she was momentarily at a loss for words but she composed herself quickly. David chuckled inside.

"Karina is waiting for you," she continued, ignoring Pamela. "Please follow me to the office."

David stepped aside to let Pamela go ahead of him into the building. She confidently followed Ina down the hall.

"Come in," Karina called when Ina knocked on the door.

She stood from her chair, her eyes full of disdain, as David and Pamela entered.

"This is Pamela Lowall," David said.

Karina extended her hand to the other woman. "Karina Svetlana," she said without a hint of a smile. "Welcome." She pointed at the two chairs by the desk. "Have a seat."

Karina sat down again and crossed her arms. "What can I do for you?" she asked Pamela.

"I'd like to interview you regarding your work at the orphanage, and then perhaps view the facility." Pamela smoothed her black suede skirt over her knees.

"I don't have much time, and I suspect Mr. Valensky doesn't either."

David cocked his eyebrow. Since when was Karina concerned about his schedule?

"A quick interview will do."

"What do you need to know?"

Pamela flipped her laptop open. "To start, tell me how you ended up working with orphan children."

Fifteen minutes and several evasive answers later, Karina led them through the building to the children's living quarters. "We have about seventy children here. Most of them have one or two parents alive."

"So why would they be here?" Pamela asked.

Karina gave Pamela a withering look. "Because the parents are not able to care for them, of course." She opened the door to the babies' room.

David had never visited this area. The room stank of dirty diapers and sour milk. A row of steel cribs, some with two babies in each bed, lined both walls. A caregiver bustled around the room, popping bottles into the babies' mouths. Some of the children rocked their bodies from side to side, while others banged their heads on the bars of the crib. An older infant, who had flung his empty bottle aside, tried to pry a bottle out of the mouth of a younger child. A fit of screams erupted.

"Take your pictures and then we'll go to the older children." Karina halted beside David and lowered her voice. "When are you coming with rations again?"

David tried to read Karina's face, but she was inscrutable. "I don't know yet. Are you out of supplies?"

"We could use potatoes," she said, walking with him to the door. Pamela followed behind.

"Maybe Saturday." David let Karina pass through the doorway.

"Thank you." She smiled briefly at him.

David didn't know if her appreciation was meant for the potatoes or for holding the door, but her smile faded as soon as Pamela caught up to them, her high heels clacking on the faded linoleum floor.

"How's your schedule, Pamela?" David stopped in the hallway. "When do you need to be back in the city?"

Pamela glanced at her diamond-studded watch. "It doesn't matter to me. Today I'm on your schedule."

Karina stepped back. "You can show her around," she told David. "I have to get back to work. Good-bye." Without another glance at Pamela, she turned on her heel and disappeared down the hallway.

Pamela raised her penciled eyebrows. "What's going on?"

"I don't know. She can be difficult sometimes." David narrowed his eyes as he watched Karina stride away, her skirt swishing around her legs. The woman was incorrigible. And gorgeous.

David turned his attention back to Pamela. "Follow me. I know the kids very well. We're going to have a good time with them." He headed in the opposite direction of Karina. Yet in his mind, he continued to see a dark-haired lady in a broomstick skirt.

"I'm sorry about her behavior," David apologized to Pamela.

"Don't worry about it. I'm not easily insulted," she assured him. "It'll still be a good article."

⊗⊗⊗

The twang of electric guitars from the amateur band on the rickety stage vibrated through the packed room. The odor of sweat and alcohol permeated the air as overheated bodies moved in rhythm to the music.

Karina leaned against the wall, watching the party, a glass of vodka in her hand. She hadn't been to a bar in years, and she watched the spectacle with a mixture of disgust and envy. She couldn't bring herself to join the party like Tanya, drinking, flirting, and pretending that life was good and the pain didn't exist.

Tipping back the glass of vodka, she guzzled the contents and slammed it down on the bar. She pulled a pack of cigarettes out of her pocket. Another rotten habit she couldn't beat, as often as she'd tried. The smoke tingled as it circled deep down into her lungs. The nicotine and vodka settled her frayed nerves. The room seemed lighter, happier, less crowded, and the botched afternoon with David and the woman from CNN further away.

The interview had been a disaster. She hadn't liked the journalist from the moment she strutted into the room with her multicolor dyed hair, flashy boots, and leather jacket. Most of all, Karina couldn't stand the way she followed David around like a love-sick puppy.

To make matters worse, David catered to her. "Are you thirsty, Pamela? Would you like to see the children, Pamela? How is your schedule, Pamela?"

Don't you care about my schedule? She'd wanted to scream. *Don't you care about me?*

No one cared about her. Not her father or her extended family, and certainly not Frank. No one had ever cared about her.

"Why is a beautiful lady like you sitting here all by yourself?" A tall gentleman slid onto the bar stool next to hers and leaned his right arm on the bar. In his left hand he held a glass of beer. His dark hair curled playfully around his ears and forehead.

"Tanya suggested I visit you for a while," he said with a smile, "She's worried that you might be lonely." A flirtatious light glimmered in his green eyes. A ragged scar ran across his cheek from the line of his beard to his eyebrow. His light blue shirt hung open, revealing a silver necklace on his muscular chest.

Karina looked away.

"My name is Ivan Silvanovich, from Ekaterinaburg. I'm visiting here for a few days."

His breath washed over her as he leaned closer. She inhaled the pungent mixture of beer and smoke. She shifted her weight back as he crowded in, his knee pressing against hers.

"I've known Tanya for some time." Ivan sipped his beer. "She said I should get to know her friend a little better." He laughed out loud.

Karina eyed the stranger suspiciously. What had Tanya told him about her?

He finished his beer in a single gulp and slid off the stool. "Come dance with me." He touched her thigh with his hand.

"No, thank you. I haven't danced in years."

"I'll teach you what you've forgotten." His physical presence stirred long-buried feelings in Karina's heart but she hung back. Ivan was not easily dissuaded. "Come on. We'll have a good time."

Karina thought back to her afternoon with David. Why did she let him depress her like this? He didn't mean a thing to her. She could live her life whatever way she pleased.

"OK." She hopped off the chair. Ivan caught her as she swayed on her feet.

They moved onto the dance floor, his right hand in the crook of her back and the left on her hip. Karina relaxed with the gentle movement of the dance, leaning into Ivan. How long had it been since she'd let a man touch her? Buried under layers of anger and hurt, she'd forgotten the pleasure of it.

Ivan danced well. He gracefully led her around the crowded floor in tune to the pounding rock music. His hand moved up until it came to rest between her shoulder blades. He caressed her back in regular up-and-down movements. Her breath quickened as he moved closer against her body.

The dance ended and Ivan led her off the dance floor to a dark corner of the room. Spotlights flickered in green, red, and blue above them. He pulled her close, encircling her with his arms. He bent his head, his face close to hers.

"Anyone ever told you that you're gorgeous?" he whispered in a throaty voice.

At that moment, David's prayer sprang into her mind. *"Lord, show her that You love her and that You have a plan for her life."* A shiver ran down her back. What would David think if he could see her right now? Suddenly what David thought of her mattered. A lot. She pulled back.

"No, I don't believe I've heard that before, and I don't need to hear it now."

Surprised by her reaction, Ivan's arms dropped. His eyes narrowed. "Tanya warned me you might consider yourself too good for a guy like me. She said you're fond of Americans."

Stunned by his words, Karina rushed out of the noisy room and headed toward the washroom. The music grew faint as she closed the door behind her. She splashed a handful of cold water on her face. It refreshed her burning cheeks but did little to soothe her emotions. How could she have let herself get carried away like that? Just to spite David, who was not even here? Ivan's touch had been pleasurable, especially after so many years of being alone. She'd forgotten what it was like to be admired, sought after. But she wasn't prepared to pay the price.

Karina inspected her makeup, wiping the smudged mascara off her cheeks. Opening her purse, she took out a lipstick but then stuffed it back into her purse. She was not going back into the bar room; she was going home. She pulled the cell phone out of her purse to call a taxi. Just as she was about to dial, her phone vibrated with an incoming call.

———

The little Italian restaurant on Lenin Street was nearly deserted. David and Pamela sat in a corner booth. Pamela sipped a glass of red cabernet while David pressed the slice of lemon against the edge of his glass of iced tea.

"So, what did you do before you arrived in Perm?" Pamela carefully set her wine down on the red-and-white-checkered tablecloth.

"I worked for a mutual funds company. Nothing exciting." David dodged the question. He'd rather talk about God or his work at the shelter.

The waitress arrived with their orders: a plate of spaghetti for Pamela and tortellini for David.

"Mind if I ask a blessing?" David put his iced tea aside and folded his hands.

"Of course not."

"Heavenly Father, thank You for the food and for Pamela's visit. May it be a blessing for her. In Jesus' name, amen." Opening his eyes, he thought back to his botched lunch with Karina the previous day. He'd not had lunch alone with a woman since he'd arrived in Russia thirteen years before, and now it had happened twice in two days. He picked up his fork and stirred the Parmesan cheese into the noodles.

"I've been praying for you since you arrived here in Perm. I'm wondering about your relationship with God."

Pamela stumbled on her words for the first time since he met her. "I was raised in the Catholic church."

He sipped his coffee. "But do you know Jesus personally?"

"My work keeps me too busy to go to church. And I'm never in one place very long." She shifted uncomfortably.

"I'm not talking about church. I'm talking about a relationship with Christ. Do you know anything about that?"

"I haven't given it much thought," she admitted. "I'm committed to my career."

"Being committed to your career doesn't mean you can't first be committed to Christ. God has a special task for everyone, but He first wants us to seek Him."

"Look, David, I appreciate your concern for my spiritual state but I came here to carry out an assignment, not to get converted to Christianity."

"I really do want you to think about it."

"I will," she promised but David wondered if she just wanted to get him off her back. Like Karina, except more polite.

"You won't regret it."

The waitress removed their plates, and placed the bill on the table. David paid for the meal and then dropped Pamela off at her hotel. As he drove home, it was not Pamela but Karina who was on his mind. Filled with uneasiness, he maneuvered the Toyota through the dense Friday night traffic back to his apartment.

Once home, he paced his living room as he prayed for Karina. For some reason, concern for her safety lay heavily on his heart.

Jesus, if this feeling of unrest is my imagination, let it pass. But if not, please watch over her and keep her safe, wherever she is.

At ten thirty he couldn't stand it anymore. He picked up the cordless phone and dialed her number. What if she was in bed already? Highly unlikely on a Friday night. What did she do in her spare time, anyway? He'd never given it much thought.

CHAPTER TEN

Every muscle in his body tensed as the phone rang. When Karina answered the call, relief flooded through him.

"Karina, are you OK?"

"I'm fine."

David heard faint music in the background. "I've been praying for you tonight. I had this feeling something was wrong. I wanted to touch base with you."

"Thank you." Her voice was somewhat shaky.

"Do you need any help?"

"No."

David changed the topic. "You weren't yourself this afternoon."

"I don't enjoy being interviewed."

"Anything else?"

"No."

"Good night, then. Stay safe. I'll call you soon."

Flipping the phone shut, he sank into the old chair. *OK, Lord, what was that all about?* Had he worried in vain? At least she'd thanked him for praying for her. But obviously there was nothing wrong and she didn't need him. Raking his hand through his hair, he headed to bed.

———❦———

Shook up and suddenly sober, Karina pushed the button on her cell phone to disconnect. Her hand trembled as she dialed the number for a taxi.

David had been praying for her. She closed her eyes and leaned her head against the tile wall. The room swirled around her. A heavy feeling settled in the pit of her stomach. Regardless of how hard she tried to forget about David and break the influence he had on her, the tighter the web spun around her.

The bathroom door swung open and Tanya dashed into the room, her face crimson. "Karina, I've been looking everywhere for you!"

"I'm going home. I called a taxi."

Anger flickered in Tanya's eyes. "Ivan is terribly upset by your snobbery. I'm never going to introduce you to my friends again. You can just sit at home like you've done all these years. I don't know why I keep bothering with you."

"Well, you don't need to bother with me anymore. I'm sorry I made life so difficult for you, but I don't like your friends and I don't like this place. I don't need guys who treat me like meat." The snub provided Karina with temporary satisfaction, but it immediately dissipated.

Tanya stepped back toward the door. "Like they do me, right?"

"I'm sorry. I appreciate that you took me along tonight. But I've been out of this kind of scene for a long time."

"Too long," Tanya huffed. "Don't expect any more favors from me."

As Karina stepped out of the stuffy, noisy bar, the cold night air refreshed her immensely. The taxi waited by the curb, the motor humming in the still of the night. A few loiterers hung around the entrance, drinking beer. They leered at her as she brushed by.

Slipping into the taxi, she questioned her sanity for coming here in the first place. Thank goodness she had come to her senses! It had been total stupidity. She dropped her head onto the back of the seat, emotionally drained.

Perhaps she hadn't learned as much from her experience with Frank as she'd thought. But that relationship had been different. It had not been a one-night stand. She'd loved him and he'd loved her; but he'd loved himself more.

———— ∞ ————

May, 1994. The two little lines in the pregnancy test turned blue under Karina's concentrated gaze. Her legs buckled and she collapsed on the linoleum in the little bathroom. Nausea washed over her like a tidal wave. Violent shivers ran over her back and into her arms until her entire frame shook with the intensity.

Someone knocked on the bathroom door. "Karina? Are you in there?"

Frank! She hadn't expected him home from his afternoon class yet. She tried to speak, but her throat closed.

"Open the door, honey!"

She melted at the concern in his voice. Maybe he would understand. Maybe they'd get married and he'd take her to the States with him next year when he finished his studies. Maybe everything would be all right.

She pulled herself to her feet and unlocked the door.

Frank pushed the door open and burst in. Seeing her face he halted. "What's wrong?"

He tried to pull her into his arms, but she put her hand on his chest and pointed to the test stick on the bathroom counter. "I'm pregnant," she said in a monotone voice, searching his face for his response.

Frank stared at the blue lines, his mouth taut. His eyes narrowed. "How could you be so stupid?"

He grabbed the stick off the counter and tossed it into the garbage. "Just get an abortion, and don't bother me with it. I can't waste my time on stuff like this. I've got a degree to finish."

"This is our baby. We love each other." Tears welled up in her eyes. She sank onto the toilet and wrapped her arms tightly around her belly.

"I don't want a baby. And what about your career? You have years of medical studies ahead of you." He roughly pulled her up off the toilet.

She jerked herself loose and pushed past him out of the bathroom. Frank followed her to the living room. Stopping in front of the window, she stared out over the drab back alley. "I don't care about my career. I just want us to be together. As a family."

He laughed sarcastically. "How romantic. I'll bring in the dough and you'll look after the kids, change the diapers, and wash my underwear. And one morning you'll wake up, find out you hate it, and walk off. I've seen enough of that."

Karina understood. He'd told her about his family. She'd lived in a similar situation herself, but she'd believed they could make their relationship work. Now that belief was rapidly dying.

Frank collapsed on the couch. "I'm sorry, Karina, but it simply won't work. Our relationship has been fantastic, but this doesn't fit into my plan for the future. We need to make a rational decision. Why don't you meet with your doctor tomorrow and make the arrangements?"

He patted the couch cushion beside him. "Come sit down."

As Karina joined him on the couch, Frank pulled her into his arms and stroked her hair. She sobbed against his shoulder, longing to believe that everything would be OK. Yet deep in her heart she knew that nothing would be the same again.

That night she noticed a change in Frank's behavior as they ate the pork stew she'd prepared the previous day. His brooding attitude, the sullen look on his face, the palpable silence. His eyes were cast down to his plate and he didn't bother with small talk, which was rare for him. He pushed the half-empty plate of stew away and walked in to the living room. Flicking on the television, he didn't speak another word.

Frank's dark mood continued throughout the evening. At nine o'clock he stood up and grabbed his coat. "Don't wait up for me. I'll be back late." The door slammed behind him.

Karina sank onto the kitchen chair and cried until her tears ran dry. At ten o'clock she went to bed, worn out from the disturbing ordeal, but sleeping proved impossible. Just after midnight, the door opened. She didn't stir when Frank crawled into bed. He immediately turned his back toward her, and within minutes she heard his peaceful snore. Apparently Frank did not lay awake over the change that had so rudely interrupted their life.

She couldn't understand his callous words toward the baby and his coldness toward her. She hadn't brought this upon them intentionally. They were in this together. Not that Frank seemed to think so. He blamed the whole mess on her. Hardly fair. But then, life wasn't fair. Yet the child should not have to suffer the consequences of their actions. Too many children in Russia faced that lot. What could she do? Without Frank's support, what were her options? She tossed and turned all night, but answers continued to elude her. Toward morning, she fell into a restless sleep.

By the time she woke up, the sun shone through the small bedroom window. The apartment was quiet. Frank had apparently left for class. Emotionally and physically tired, she pulled herself out of bed. A single plate and glass, Frank's breakfast dishes, stood on the counter in the small kitchen. Next to them, she saw a strip of paper with writing. Frank's writing. Reeling, Karina gripped the edge of the counter as she read the note.

Dear Karina,

I've had some time to think about the situation and its implications. I've come to the conclusion that I no longer wish to be in this relationship. I'm sorry. We had a good time together and I want to thank you for that. I'll always remember you as a good friend. I am moving in with Nate today. Please box up my stuff and I'll pick it up one of these days.

Sincerely,
Frank

Outraged, she crumpled the note into a tiny ball and flung it to the floor. "A good friend"? "Sincerely, Frank"? After all the promises he'd made, the life they'd shared! Gagging, she ran to the bathroom and vomited yellow bile into the porcelain bowl.

What could she do now? She had no close friends in Moscow. Her mom was dead and she considered her dad as good as dead to her. All of Frank's friends would agree with him and tell her to get an abortion.

Shivering, Karina sank onto the floor, pulling her thin nightgown over her knees. Classes started in an hour, but she had no strength to get ready. She didn't want to run into Frank at the university anyway. She never wanted to see him again as long as she lived. Her heart ached so deeply she thought it would burst. Sobbing, she covered her face with her hands.

Three days later, she returned to school, pale and shook up but ready to move on with her studies. Everyone had already heard, through the grapevine, that her relationship with Frank had ended. Karina held her head high, pretending it didn't matter, but inside pain seared through her broken heart.

Frank's friends told her that he'd transferred to the University of St. Petersburg. He'd apparently been too upset with the breakup to stay in Moscow. Karina let them believe the lie. Obviously, Frank hadn't told them the true reason for their split, and she was grateful for that. Her secret secure and without a single person to support her, she chose the only option open to her. An irreversible choice she carried to this day.

The taxi halted in front of the concrete housing complex. Karina paid the driver and headed up the dark stairs to her apartment. Her feet clanked hollowly on the steps. Another botched night. She should be used to it by now. Every situation she was involved with seemed to fail. As she made her way to the bedroom, it suddenly dawned on her that David's prayers had kept her safe tonight. She sank onto the bed. No one had ever cared enough to pray for her. It was a frightening yet fascinating thought.

With shaking fingers, she pulled out her pack of cigarettes. Only two left. That would have to do until morning. She smoked both, one after the other, changed her clothes, and crawled under the blankets. A restless sleep enveloped her.

CHAPTER ELEVEN

David picked up Pamela at her hotel early to catch the six thirty A.M. flight to Moscow. Three enormous suitcases sat on the floor in the foyer.

"Good morning." She hoisted a carry-on bag onto her shoulder and tucked her purse under her arm.

"Hello." David picked up two of the heavy suitcases.

Pamela followed him to the Toyota, pulling the third suitcase behind her. "Thank you." She smiled broadly through bright red lips as he opened the truck door for her.

"You're welcome." Starting the engine, he silenced the noisy Russian radio station.

He pointed to the sparse snowflakes that fluttered onto the windshield. "That's September in Perm for you."

"Life is so brutal here," she said. "I don't know how you manage."

David shrugged. "Only with God's grace."

"I'm jealous of you believers sometimes." Her voice held no animosity. "Your world seems so idyllic."

David grimaced. "We face plenty of reality, but we hold on to the belief that God is in control of everything."

"How well do you know the woman at the orphanage?" Pamela asked, abruptly changing topics.

"Not well."

"I've been thinking about her. I hope you don't mind if I tell you this but I think she was jealous." She fiddled with the zipper of her purse.

"Of what?" He couldn't imagine how she'd come up with that.

"My being with you."

Caught off guard, he glanced her way. She smiled. David didn't see any humor in the situation. Was she serious?

"What makes you think that?"

"Every time you looked at me or spoke to me, she became angry. I may be wrong, but I think she has a crush on you."

A crush on him! More like she tolerated him because she had no other choice. He pulled the truck into a parking space by the airport and carried her suitcases into the terminal. "Thanks for coming to visit us here in Perm. I look forward to seeing the report."

"I'll keep you posted. Good-bye." She swept her multi-colored hair over her shoulder and shook his hand.

David waved as she disappeared through the rotating doors. He descended the steps to the parking lot, hands shoved tightly in the pockets of his jeans. After stepping into his vehicle, he jammed it into reverse. The worn tires protested with a screech as he shifted into first gear and floored the accelerator.

Was Pamela right about Karina's feelings during their visit to the orphanage? No, David concluded as he made his way back to the shelter, Pamela had misread the situation. A little calmer, he parked the truck behind the building and crossed the courtyard to the back door.

On Saturday, his day off, David decided to go to the orphanage in Kungur. Karina had mentioned that they needed potatoes, and he didn't want to leave the children in a lurch.

Karina met him at the entrance, wearing a faded pair of blue jeans, a cotton T-shirt, and worn sneakers. Her hair hung down, held together at the nape of her neck with a cheap plastic clip.

David caught his breath. He had never seen her like this, so young and girlish. Her lips were full and her eyes dark and intense as she smiled at him. He scolded himself for his response. *I'm not here for romance. I want to witness for God.* Distracted by his wandering thoughts, he lifted a box of potatoes off the truck.

"Ina has today off, so I'll help you with this," Karina said, opening the cellar for him. She pulled the string that hung from the small light bulb on the ceiling. "Be careful with the stairs. A few weeks ago, one of the girls fell and sprained her ankle."

Are there no good single women in Perm? His mother's voice resonated in his mind. The box of potatoes slipped out of his hands and cascaded down the stairs. Potatoes scattered in all directions. Embarrassed, he hurried into the cellar.

Karina followed him down the stairs. "At least you didn't fall," she said, crouching on the floor beside him to pick up the potatoes.

David nodded grimly as he threw the potatoes into the box. He *had* fallen . . . for a dark-haired woman with penetrating eyes. *Why, Lord? Why her?* Thoughts twirled through his mind as they worked side by side.

After gathering the potatoes, they carried in the rest of the supplies.

"You should be set for a while," David told her, placing the last box on the shelf. "There are enough supplies here for a whole month."

"The government rations also came in, so we're in good shape."

He rubbed his neck. "I guess I won't need to come back for a few months, then." His eyes scanned her face. Did he detect a hint of disappointment, or was that his imagination?

"Care to go out for coffee?" he asked as they emerged from the cellar. How could he come all the way to Kungur without at least trying to connect with her?

Karina pulled the string on the light bulb and closed the cellar door. "I'm sorry, but Ina's off today, so I need to stay to answer the phone until the other worker arrives. We could, however, have a cup of coffee in my office."

"Sure." He followed her down the hall.

Karina offered him a chair and plugged the kettle into the outlet.

David sat down and watched her. *How can I reach her, Lord? I don't know what to say.*

Fear not.

Peace settled over his inner being. God wanted him here. Why, he still could not explain, but his steadfastness rebounded. God had a plan, and his feelings had to disappear into the background for now.

She measured two teaspoons of instant coffee into each cup and poured boiling water on top. "Cream or sugar?"

"Please."

She stirred a teaspoon of cream-colored milk powder into her cup and then sat down, placing David's cup in front of him.

"Thank you," David said. "How has your week been?" He hadn't seen her since his visit with Pamela.

"Nothing new." She sat behind the desk and stirred her coffee.

"That can be a good thing. Too much change sometimes turns into chaos."

"Drudgery is another problem, though." She sipped the hot coffee without looking at him.

"The orphanage is drudgery?"

"At times. Just like life. Work till you die. What's the use?"

"All of our lives have a purpose, whether we believe it or not."

"Some people just have a greater purpose than others. Like your friend, Pamela."

"She's no more important than anyone else. Everyone is important to God."

"How noble of you to believe that. It is, of course, the correct response."

"I really do believe that. That's why I'm in Russia."

"Those of us who'd like to get out of this country can't, but you stay here voluntarily. A rather foolish decision, I must say."

"Not foolish if God calls you. He has a specific calling for all of our lives. Yours also."

She put her half-empty cup down on the saucer and stood up. "Well, I should not hold you up any longer," she said brightly. "I'm sure you have other important people to visit."

David followed her out of the office. Why did he allow her to get under his skin?

"Good-bye." Without a backwards glance, he stepped out the door, but then hesitated. They'd parted too often in anger. He wouldn't let that happen again. Turning back, he said, "Care to go for a walk?"

Surprise showed on her face. "Well, uh, I think Svetlana just arrived, so I can go for a while if you like."

Svetlana? David thought about her last name. Svetlana was a common first name for a woman but he'd never heard it used as a last name until he'd met her. *Karina Svetlana.* Why did Karina use a first name as her last name? Or was it really her name? Had she stopped using her patronymic name and her last name for some reason?

As she shrugged into her coat, Karina pointed to the treed area behind the orphanage. "We can walk along the river."

They strolled side by side, their hands thrust deep into their pockets. Crossing the gravelly riverside, they reached the water's edge.

David picked up a rock and skipped it along the surface of the water. "I used to do this with my brother, Roger, back in Colorado," he said. "Do you have any brothers or sisters?"

"No."

He threw a stick into the river. It bobbed up and down a few times and floated downstream.

"I had a golden retriever named Treela. She loved water."

"Sounds like your childhood was perfect."

David heard the bitterness in her voice. "I used to think it was." Even when he married Sheila and worked for Imperial Mutuals, he thought he had his life under control. That was before the death of his children and Sheila's betrayal.

"When life was good, I didn't realize that I needed God. But after I lost my wife and kids I began to see that I couldn't go through life alone." David sat on an old log and patted the bark. "Join me?"

She seated herself on the far edge of the log.

He rested his chin in the palm of his hand and gazed at the water. "Do you ever wish you could float away with the current and never come back?"

"I prefer to live in the here and now." Her voice was sharp. "I don't focus on nonsense."

"When we think about good things instead of bad, we can be encouraged."

"I used to imagine things. All I received was disappointment." She stared into the distance across the river. "Does focusing on good things bring your family back?"

Her words hit a raw nerve. The pain had eased with time, but it was still there. He told himself that he'd forgiven Sheila, but had he really?

"Nothing will bring my family back, but that doesn't mean I'm going to stop focusing on God and all the good He has planned for me." He knew God's plans were bigger than his own. "God always wants the best for us. For you too."

"I'm not convinced that God exists."

"I won't be able to convince you. Only God can do that."

Karina gazed at David. She observed the strong profile of his jaw covered with day-old stubble. His straight nose. The serious look in his eyes. Lost in thought, he stared out over the river. If only she dared believe that God existed and that He cared for her, that she didn't have to continue to struggle alone. But no one had ever truly cared about her. Except her mother, perhaps, but she'd been gone for many years.

Karina had been too afraid to die, or she would've followed her mother a long time ago. But she had found it easier to run than to give up. Death scared her.

"What do you want from me?" she asked.

"To be your friend."

"Men only say that when they're interested in getting something from a woman," she said sarcastically.

"Do you speak from experience?"

"Yes." She expected to see shock on his face at her words, but he didn't flinch.

"That's not what I consider friendship." He stood up from the log.

Embarrassed, she rose to her feet. She felt the heat rise in her face, but David didn't seem to notice.

"Tell me about your parents," he asked as they walked back to the orphanage.

"My mom died when I was a teen."

"What about your dad?"

"He lives in St. Petersburg. Well, that's where he used to live."

"Where is he now?"

"He's dead," she answered too quickly. It wasn't a lie. He was dead to her.

David, thankfully, didn't respond. "Give me a call if you want to take me up on my offer of friendship," he said when they reached the orphanage. "I'll wait to hear from you."

CHAPTER TWELVE

After more than thirty hours of traveling, Vanessa and Jared collected their luggage from the plane's overhead compartment. A few more hours and they would be home.

Despite the exhaustion, Vanessa was excited. The trip had been successful. The medicals had to clear, a perfunctory procedure since the immigration doctor had already given the green light, and then they could return to Perm and pick up Alexander. Hopefully, everything would be complete within the next six weeks. Vanessa could hardly wait to see their new son again. Amazing how quickly they had bonded with Alexander in the few short days they'd spent with him after the adoption proposal had been signed.

They took an airport shuttle to their SUV, loaded the suitcases, and navigated out of the parking lot. Driving down the freeway, Jared blinked repeatedly to clear the tiredness from his eyes. He reached over and squeezed Vanessa's knee. "It's been a long haul, but it turned out well."

"Yes, it did. It's hard to believe that in six weeks we'll have another child. I want to show the photos to Annie and the family. I'm as excited as when we got Annie's ultrasound pictures."

The next few days passed in a flurry of activity. People called and dropped off meals. It was almost like coming home from the hospital with a baby, except they didn't have the baby yet.

"He's sweet and kind," she told her relatives and friends at the get-together that her mother hosted in honor of their homecoming. "A wonderful little boy. He recognizes us already. We're really blessed to be able to get him."

She proudly showed his pictures to whoever expressed interest. Annie jabbered nonstop about her little brother.

A week after their return, Gail Jamieson from the Government Adoption Services called. "We have a proposal for an adoption for you in Perm," she told Vanessa.

Vanessa frowned. "We've just returned."

A short pause ensued. "You've already been there?"

"Yes."

"You weren't supposed to go to Russia until we discussed the medical with you."

"The adoption agency said we could go."

"I'll speak with them about that. They should've informed you that you couldn't go until we approved it. So you saw the child?"

"Yes, we did."

"How was he?"

"The immigration doctor confirmed that there were no problems."

"That's good to hear." Gail paused. "However, we do have some concerns. There seems to be a problem with his growth curve and the size of his head. This can be indicative of FAS. We recommend you contact Dr. Hastings at General Hospital in Toronto. She's excellent at detecting problems from records and pictures. I assume you have pictures?"

"Yes"

"Good. I'll give you Dr. Hastings's phone number."

Vanessa scribbled the doctor's number on a scrap of paper and thanked the coordinator. *Hold it together. They're just going by standard procedures. There's probably nothing wrong.*

She rushed into the office and pulled out Alexander's records. After scanning the various numbers, she laid the file down. It didn't mean anything to her. She picked up the pictures Jared had taken in Perm and studied them. What did a child with FAS look like? She dropped into the chair by her computer and typed in a Google search: "FAS + facial features." It found 173,000 Web sites.

Nervously, she opened the first site. A picture of a little girl with Fetal Alcohol Syndrome jumped out at her. The girl's face had the same long, flat space between the lip and nose and slightly slanted eyes as Alexander had. *No, Lord, no!* Tears flowed down her cheeks. Was this what she'd noticed about Alexander but couldn't identify?

Picking up the phone, she dialed Jared's cell number.

"I got a call from the government adoption service," she said. "They believe Alexander may have FAS."

"I don't believe it," Jared replied curtly. "We even asked the director about that."

"Are you at your computer?"

"Yes."

"Look up this site." Vanessa gave him the URL. She heard Jared's fingers on the keyboard. Then thick silence.

"Do you see the pictures?"

"Yes. What are we going to do?" Jared's voice cracked.

"We need to submit the file and pictures to Dr. Hastings in Toronto. She specializes in FAS facial features. She'll tell us the diagnosis."

"Do it as soon as possible. Maybe this doesn't mean anything."

"Maybe." As soon as she hung up, she called the doctor's office. The secretary suggested that she fax the information sheets as well as pictures.

As she punched the fax number, she knew deep in her heart there was no hope for Alexander. He would never come to Canada.

Why, Lord? I don't understand! Is this what it will come to?

She didn't have to wait long for a reply. Dr. Hastings called her back a few hours later, confirming her worst fear.

"Based on the growth curve, head size in relation to chest size, as well as facial features, I cannot recommend this child as a good prospective adoptee. It is my suggestion that you turn down this proposal and request another one."

After hanging up the phone, Vanessa sank down onto the couch. A sob escaped her lips. *God, how can this be?* All their effort of securing the adoption had been in vain. She'd stepped out in faith, and now the entire process had fallen through. They'd never bring Alexander home. Annie would be devastated. Annie! She looked at her watch: almost three thirty. She had to pull herself together before her daughter came home from school.

Vanessa rose from the couch and walked down the hall to the bathroom. She splashed cold water on her face and rubbed her cheeks until they matched the redness of her eyes. A dab of cover-stick and some eyeliner and Annie might not notice that Vanessa had been crying. How would she break the news to her daughter?

The backdoor opened. Vanessa turned away from the mirror and forced a smile. "I'm in the bathroom, Annie," she called, as she hastened down the hall.

But instead of Annie, Jared met her in the kitchen.

"Oh, Jared." With a cry of anguish, she fell against his chest.

"It's all right," he hushed, wrapping her in his arms.

"How do we tell Annie? She's so looked forward to Alexander's arrival."

"I don't know. That's why I came home early from work." Jared kissed the top of Vanessa's head as she pulled out of his embrace.

"I'll get a snack ready." Vanessa opened the refrigerator and pulled out a carton of milk. "I baked fresh banana bread this morning." As if she could eat one bite of it.

She poured a glass of milk and buttered the bread. The backdoor opened again. This time it had to be Annie. Vanessa pasted a smile on her face.

"Hi, Mommy. I'm home." Her daughter bounced into the room, a sparkle in her eyes. She threw her backpack on the floor and dropped her coat on top. "Oh, hi Daddy. Why are you here?" She looked at Jared and Vanessa.

Jared cleared his throat. "Hi, darling. I came home early to see you and Mom." He pulled his daughter into a tight embrace. "Why don't you sit down, and we'll talk."

Vanessa hugged and kissed Annie and then laid the flowered place-mat on the table. She put the milk and banana bread on a plate and sat down opposite her daughter.

"How was school?" Better to wait to break the news until Annie had finished her food.

"We had so much fun! There's this new boy and he brought his puppy to school today, and then the puppy ran away . . . ." She glanced up at her mother. "Are you OK, Mommy? Your eyes are red."

Vanessa turned away to the kitchen counter, tears spilling onto her cheeks.

Jared cleared his throat as he reached across the table for Annie's little hand. "We found out today that Alexander is sick and won't come to Canada."

Annie's eyes grew wide. "But won't he get better again?"

"No, he won't get better. Alexander was born with this, Annie. It's because his mommy didn't take good care of him while he was in her tummy."

Vanessa sat down at the kitchen table across from Jared.

"Oh!" Annie's eyes brimmed with tears as she looked at Jared and Vanessa. She put her glass of milk down and rubbed her eyes. "But I want my little brother to come."

"I know. We all do." Vanessa pulled her daughter onto her lap as Annie grieved the loss of her little brother.

Vanessa's heart was in turmoil. *God, why? We trusted You. We followed You all the way to Russia to bring home a child we didn't know. I believed You gave us confirmation of this. I didn't want to follow my own feelings, so I put my fear aside to listen to what wise counselors told us. And then You gave me a sign. I was so sure of it. And now it all fell apart.*

She'd looked for God's leading and trusted that He'd work things out, but she felt let down. She should've listened to her own instincts, not followed some mystical sign. If she had, none of this heartache would have happened. Now it was too late. They'd been robbed of their son, and Annie had lost her brother. None of it made sense. Their dreams had been dashed, and she felt that she could never trust God's leading again.

David stapled the check stubs onto the paid bills and filed them in the appropriate folders. "Come in," he called at the short knock on the door of his office.

Jake peered around the door. "Is this a good time for you?"

David nodded.

After much contemplation he'd decided he should talk to Jake about his contact with Karina. He needed someone to confide in, so he'd asked his colleague to stop in when he had a chance.

"So, what's up?" Jake asked as he sat in the chair opposite the desk.

David fidgeted. "I've been reaching out to this lady at Kungur Orphanage. We've been seeing each other as friends."

"She a Christian?"

"No, but we're not romantically involved."

"Then why are you telling me about it?"

"I'd like you to pray."

Jake crossed his arms. "OK. What do you want me to pray about?"

"She's been deeply hurt in her past, and I'm trying to reach out to her."

"Yes?"

David could tell that Jake wasn't buying into the story. "She needs help," he explained, his voice quiet. "God has placed her in my path, and I feel a responsibility to her."

"So you have no feelings for her at all?"

David hesitated. "Well, I can't say that I don't."

Jake stood up, his face resolute. "There's your answer. I think you should leave the helping to someone who's not attracted to her. You know what the Bible says about being unequally yoked with an unbeliever."

"We're just friends. I'm not planning on a deeper relationship."

Jake snorted in disgust. "And how long will that last? That's how it all starts. And you know it. You shouldn't be reaching out to this woman. Let some of the female Christians do it."

"It's not that easy. I've just built up some trust with her. I feel that I should continue to reach out to her."

"Do as you wish. Just remember the consequences. You can't play with fire and not be burned. This is a very serious matter which needs to be discussed with the board." Without waiting for David's reply, Jake strode out of the room.

David remained in his chair, his eyes fixed on the door. Was Jake right? Should he never go back to Kungur? Never talk to Karina about God again? If that's what he did, all of her antagonistic feelings toward Americans would be confirmed. He'd be a fake, a phony. No, he had to see this through. He just had to make sure that he wouldn't get romantically involved with her.

CHAPTER THIRTEEN

Vanessa opened the closet door of Annie's bedroom. On the shelf in front of her lay neat stacks of summer clothes, washed and folded as they waited for another season.

Reaching up to the top shelf, she took down a large stack of brand new baby-boy clothes which she'd bought for Alexander. After they'd received the heart-breaking news, she'd taken them out of the baby room and put them in Annie's room. She hugged the little garments tightly against her chest. A tear dropped onto a tiny blue coat with delicate embroidery. One by one, she unfolded the garments and laid them on the bed: three pairs of sleepers with bunnies and giraffes, a cute brown sweater with snowmen, undershirts, and a beautiful Osh-Kosh outfit of matching shirt, pants, and vest. An expensive ensemble, but Alexander deserved special things.

What was she supposed to do with these clothes now? Perhaps she could give them to someone who had a little boy. It was too late to return them to the store. Besides, she wouldn't want to answer a store clerk's questions about her reasons for the return.

The ring of the telephone interrupted her reverie. She hurried through the hallway to pick it up.

Lisa, a lady from her Bible study group, greeted her cheerfully. "I heard you arrived back from Perm. When are you picking up your little boy?"

"We are not getting him. He has Fetal Alcohol Syndrome."

"Oh, I'm sorry." She paused for a moment. "But you can always get another child, can't you?"

Vanessa flinched. "Probably. But right now I am dealing with the loss of this one."

"I'm sorry," Lisa apologized.

"That's alright," Vanessa reassured her. "You couldn't know."

After hanging up, Vanessa pondered the phone call. At times she hardly fathomed her own emotions regarding her loss. How could she blame others for not understanding?

Depressed, she peeled the potatoes and put the pan on the stove. She sprinkled salt and pepper on the carrots and meat stew, and then set the plates on the table.

Just as she put the cutlery beside the plates, Jared and Annie entered the kitchen.

"Did you win the game?" Vanessa enquired of Annie, who had just finished a game of checkers with her dad.

"Yep!" Her eyes sparkled with excitement.

"She's hard to beat, that one," Jared winked at Vanessa as he seated himself at the table. "I'm hungry now."

During supper, Vanessa shared the details of Lisa's call with Jared. "I know people don't understand why I miss Alexander so badly. After all, I hardly knew him. Yet, I want to call Leah for another proposal."

"I don't want to go back to Russia." Jared pricked his fork into a boiled potato and smashed it flat on his plate.

Vanessa stared at him from the other side of the table. "You can't mean that."

"I don't want to go through all that again. It's too hard. Too painful."

Vanessa put down her fork. "I don't want to go through the pain again, either, but the children over there don't have anything. Surely you and I can go the extra mile to provide one of them with a home."

"I went the extra mile once already. I'm not ready to do it again."

"Please, Jared," she pleaded. "This means more to me than I can possibly explain. Can't we just ask for another proposal? We don't have to commit ourselves to going, but we can see what child is available."

"Yes, please, Daddy," Annie piped up. "I really want a baby brother."

Jared glared at Vanessa. "I don't think we should discuss this right now."

Vanessa bowed her head over her plate. Jared needed time to deal with the loss. She prayed he would change his mind: going back seemed the only way to ease the penetrating ache in her heart.

⸺⬦⬦⬦⸺

Although David had been hoping that Karina would contact him, her call still surprised him.

"I've thought about it and would like to take you up on your offer of friendship," she told him.

David gripped the phone. *Lord, now what do I do? If Jake's right, I should not be getting involved. Perhaps Hannah should take over.*

"Sure," he said instead. "I'd like that. How about I come to see you this week Saturday? Maybe we can go for supper. As long as it's not at that Chinese restaurant again."

Karina laughed. "I'll try to find a better place this time."

Her laughter was refreshing. David wasn't sure if he'd heard her laugh before.

"I'll pick you up at seven on Saturday."

Filled with conflicting feelings, he hung up the phone. *Why did I tell her I'd come? Jake is right. I can't get involved with her. But how can I say "no" when I told her that I'd be her friend?*

As the week went on, David struggled with feelings of apprehension and excitement. Part of him could hardly wait to be with her, speak with her, get to know her better. Yet the other part cautioned him strongly. He could not get involved with her under any circumstance.

Filled with misgivings, he made the trip back to Kungur to pick Karina up for their dinner date. Karina met him at the entrance of her apartment. He jumped out of the truck to open the passenger door for her. She was dressed in a soft cashmere sweater and black dress pants.

"Thank you," she smiled at him, slipping into the seat. Her lips had been touched with a hint of gloss, and her eyelashes were long and curly with a gentle layer of mascara. As she brushed by him, the fragrance of her perfume entered his nostrils. Stirred by her presence, he closed the door and walked around to the driver's seat.

"Tell me where to go," he said, starting the engine.

"The little down-town restaurant is the best choice. Just turn right here and you'll get to the main street."

David maneuvered the truck through the traffic. They didn't have far to go. He pulled into a parking spot in front of the restaurant. The building was old but recently repainted. The windows had been washed, the curtains clean and tidy. David opened the door for Karina. "It should be better than the last place."

"We can sit wherever we want," she told him as they stepped into the smoky room. She pointed to a booth in the corner. "How about over there?"

"Looks good." He followed her to the booth. A small oil lamp stood on the wooden table. The waiter placed two menus in front of them. The glow of the light cast soft shadows on Karina's hair as it fell over her shoulder. Her head was bent over the cardboard menu. He silently watched her, energized by her company.

He turned his attention to the list of options. "Anything you'd recommend?"

She looked up at him. "I don't eat out very often, but I've tried the liver before."

It was the cheapest item on the menu. "We could try the roasted chicken," David suggested. He wanted to order something special for her.

"Oh, I couldn't." She pointed to the price.

"I want you to order whatever you like. How about we both have chicken?"

She pushed the dog-eared cardboard aside. "That's fine."

Her favorite word. David folded his hands on the table.

"Have you decided?" The waiter stood by the table, poised with a notepad in hand.

"We'll have two orders of roasted chicken," David ordered. He looked at Karina. "Anything to drink?"

"A glass of red wine."

CHAPTER THIRTEEN

David ordered the wine and a coffee for himself. "So tell me about your name," he said. "Svetlana is an interesting last name. More like a first name, isn't it?"

She blinked. "It's my last name."

"Interesting." He didn't believe her, but couldn't prove that she was lying.

"Yes. How's your work at the shelter going?"

"Good."

She'd never initiated a question about him or his work before. He noticed her flushed face, the nervous twitch of her cheek.

The waiter placed two glasses on the table—a large goblet of wine for Karina, and a mug of coffee for himself.

David stirred the cream and sugar in the dark brew. Putting the spoon down, he looked at her. "I have another question for you. Why do you dislike Americans?"

Her hand shook on the glass as she raised it to her lips. After taking a sip, she put it down on the table. "I had an American boyfriend," she said, without making eye contact. "He ditched me." She swallowed hard.

David could tell that she was speaking the truth. Reaching across the table he touched her hand. "And he was one of those men who wanted your 'friendship'?"

Her nod was so imperceptible that he thought he imagined it. "Why did he ditch you?"

She took another gulp of the wine, her face filled with uncertainty. "I got pregnant." Her voice dropped to a whisper.

Oh, Lord. He'd known that she had a dark past, but he didn't feel ready to face her disclosure. "And the baby?"

"After he was born, I brought him to an orphanage. He died a few weeks later from pneumonia."

Reaching across the table, David held out his hand. "I'm so sorry," he said as she placed her hand in his. "But I'm glad you didn't have an abortion."

She laughed bleakly. "Oh, I had one of those as well. Years earlier. That's why I couldn't go through with this one when Frank insisted I abort the baby." She pulled her hand out of his and downed the rest of the wine.

"And that's why you work at the orphanage." Atonement. Just like himself working with the teens, spending time with kids as if he could make up the time he'd missed with Geoff and Danae.

"Perhaps." She put the glass back down on the table. "What I've told you is only a small part of my story. If you knew everything about me, you'd leave."

"Try me."

She shook her head. Her eyes were filled with deep sadness. "No. I've told you more than I've told anyone else. Some things are better left behind."

After dinner, David drove Karina home to her apartment. He put the truck into neutral and then pulled a small New Testament out of his pocket. "I brought this for you." He handed her the book.

Karina held it for a moment and then slipped the Bible into her purse. "Thank you." She gave him a slight smile.

He wiped his sweaty hands on his jeans. *I'm only here to reach out to her. Remember that, David.* But he knew that he was kidding himself.

"I hope you'll read your New Testament," David said. "If you'll have me back, I can come next week sometime and we can discuss it."

She reached out and briefly touched his arm. "Thank you. I'd like that very much." Opening the door, she slipped out and disappeared into the building.

———— ❧ ————

After David left, Karina walked up the stairs to her apartment. An empty sadness filled her heart. She'd told David more today than she'd ever told any of her friends. Yet he hadn't judged her. And she knew she could trust him. But she also knew that no relationship ever lasted. Dejected, she pulled a cigarette out of its package and seated herself on the old couch. She lit the cigarette, watching the puffs of smoke rise to the ceiling.

She didn't understand what David's motives for a relationship with her could be. Men wanted what they could get from her, even those in her own family. She'd found that out after her mother died. But David was different. He acted as if this relationship was more about her than him. He did not look at her as someone to fulfill his needs but as a friend whose feelings mattered.

She picked up the little New Testament David had given her. She'd never owned a Bible before and she wasn't sure that she was interested. But next Saturday he'd be back and he would ask her about it. She stubbed her cigarette into the ashtray. Somehow it seemed sacrilegious to smoke and read the Bible at the same time. She opened to the Gospel of Matthew and began to read.

***

David pulled up in front of the small church building shortly before eleven o'clock on Sunday morning. He was scheduled to lead the service that morning, but Vladimir, his co-pastor, hadn't called him the previous evening as usual.

He entered the small foyer. A small group of people had already gathered. David greeted them as he passed by, his eyes scanning the room for Vladimir. He spotted the older man against the back wall, engaged in an animated conversation with Ivan, another member of the shelter's board. When he sauntered up to the two men, they immediately halted their conversation.

"Good morning."

"Morning, David." Vladimir shuffled his feet back and forth.

"I should be going now," Ivan said, stepping back. "I need to start the service in a minute." He walked away.

David frowned. "I thought I was supposed to lead the service."

"The board received a call from Jake last night. Apparently there's an issue we need to straighten out with you."

"What issue? That I have a platonic friendship with a woman?"

"Many men have fallen for a woman under the guise of reaching out. Do you think you are exempt from temptation?"

"Of course not. But we're only friends."

Vladimir pushed his silver-rimmed spectacles on his nose. "I've known you for a long time and a woman has never been an issue before. We are to avoid every appearance of evil. How will the kids respond when they hear this?"

"It's a friendship, Vlad."

"With a woman. You are a single man. Apparently, you've admitted to Jake that you have feelings for her. The board considers this a serious matter."

"I'm beginning to see that."

"Please reconsider, David," Vladimir pleaded.

"I'll reconsider, but I make no promises." Turning away, David entered the sanctuary and sat down in the back row. He generally sat near the front, but today he wanted to be able to leave the building quickly. Other churchgoers took their seats around him.

David felt far removed from the usually comfortable environment. He'd helped found this church, together with Vladimir, back in the nineties. Today he seemed like a stranger. Amazing how a few events could so quickly alter one's life. He didn't doubt that Jake would pursue the board until they talked to him. But why? What was Jake's motivation? Was it true concern for him, or was there more to it?

Ivan rambled on and on about the lost coin and the great joy the woman had about finding it. If only the board had as much joy seeing him reach out to Karina.

As soon as the service ended he darted outside. Still, he hadn't been quick enough to escape Vladimir, who met him at the exit. "The board would like to meet with you at the shelter at nine tomorrow morning."

David nodded curtly. "I'll be there."

"And I'll teach the Bible study tonight."

"You're ostracizing me?"

Vladimir's cheek twitched. "Only until we can sort this out."

David shook his head. "You're overreacting."

"Perhaps. But we'd rather play it safe."

Play it safe? Had he played it safe when he'd moved to Perm after giving up his lucrative job in the States? Had he played it safe when he cashed in his savings bonds because donations were low? Had he played it safe when ministering to the kids on streets rife with violence?

"I didn't know Christianity was supposed to be safe." Without waiting for a reply, he marched out of the building.

⸻ ⚬⚬⚬ ⸻

David arrived at the shelter before nine the following morning. He hadn't slept much that night, analyzing the situation over and over. Yes, he had deep feelings for Karina, but he had not behaved inappropriately. And for the first time she'd begun to open up to him.

Ivan, Vladimir, and Ferdinand sat down around David's desk. Vladimir opened in prayer. He thanked God for the day, the shelter, David's work, and asked His to help to resolve the issues.

After the "amen," Ivan said, "It has come to our attention that you've been seeing a woman in Kungur. Is that correct?"

"Yes."

"It is against the organization's regulations for a ministry worker to have a romantic relationship with a non-Christian."

"My relationship with Ms. Svetlana is platonic. We've not been romantically involved." David glanced at the somber faces of the men.

"If you don't have a romantic interest in this person, breaking your relationship off should be easy."

"And if I don't?"

"Then the board will ask you to resign your position."

David couldn't believe what he was hearing. "Why?"

"You are a leader in this organization and a role model for the children. We cannot tolerate inappropriate relationships in our leadership."

"Perhaps we should take the parable of the lost coin more seriously and reach out to those around us."

"That's uncalled for," Vladimir said quietly. "We are as serious about the gospel as you are. But if your 'outreach' wasn't fueled by deep feelings for this woman, you would not be so passionate about this situation. Why don't you give it some serious thought and time in prayer?" He looked to Ivan. "Could you please pray for David right now?"

Ivan closed the meeting in prayer. The men stood up, shook David's hand, and then shuffled out of the office.

Vladimir lingered behind. "I care deeply about you," he said. "Don't let this situation destroy what we've built here over the years. You're a man of integrity, and I know you'll choose the right thing."

After Vladimir left the room, David leaned back in the old swivel chair behind his desk. *God, what would You have me do? I don't want the ministry to suffer, but I feel a deep need to reach out to Karina. Show me the way.*

He decided that he'd go see Karina. Perhaps speaking with her would clarify some of his questions.

CHAPTER FOURTEEN

Karina's doorbell rang around seven o'clock on Monday night. Strange. She wasn't expecting anyone. She hurried down the hallway. Opening the door, she saw Tanya with the guy from the bar. She'd forgotten his name, but remembered that he was from Ekaterinaburg. She also remembered that she'd deeply offended him when she'd refused his advances.

"You remember Ivan, don't you?" Tanya pulled a bottle of vodka out of a paper bag. "You got time for a drink with friends?"

Karina wasn't interested in entertaining Tanya in her drunken state, and she didn't trust the young woman's companion.

Tanya pushed the door open. "Ivan's been dying to see you again. Your last visit ended a little abruptly." She hiccuped, stumbled inside, and made her way to the kitchen. "We need glasses." She placed the bottle on the table.

Karina pulled two juice glasses out of the cupboard above the sink. "Only two?"

"I won't be having any." She had no intention of making a bad situation worse by becoming inebriated.

"What's gotten into you?" Tanya glared at her.

David and religion, Karina thought, but kept her mouth shut.

Ivan filled the glasses with vodka.

"Race you," Tanya challenged Ivan. She guzzled the vodka, sloshing the liquid onto her shirt.

"Slow down, Tanya," Karina warned. "You shouldn't drink so fast."

Tanya's eyes met hers in a defiant glare. "I'm not a spoilsport like you. Maybe you think you're too good for your old friends now that you've been hanging around with that rich American."

Karina's heart pounded. How did Tanya know that she'd been seeing David? Ivan leered at her. If he still harbored anger toward her for spurning him that night in the bar, she needed to be careful.

Tanya guzzled the last of her glass of vodka. "More." She tried to unscrew the bottle but her fingers slipped off the cap.

Karina grabbed the bottle. "You could kill yourself if you continue drinking like this."

In a flash, Ivan's fingers closed around Karina's wrist. "Leave her alone. She can make her own decision."

Frightened by Ivan's response, Karina released the bottle. She watched as he filled Tanya's glass again.

"Thanks," Tanya slurred. "You're a good friend, Ivan." Her hand shook as she raised the glass to her lips. A trickle of clear fluid ran down the corner of her mouth.

The scene repulsed Karina. Tanya should know better. But what if she didn't? What if she killed herself in the process?

God, if You are real like David says, please help me!
Call David.

She rose from her chair and headed for the bathroom. She locked the door behind her and dialed David's number. The phone rang, but no one answered. Where could he be? She dialed again. She flushed the toilet and turned on the tap to cover the sound of her voice when she heard him pick up the phone.

"David, this is Karina. I need help. Can you come?"

"I am almost in Kungur. I'll be there in a few minutes."

Relief flooded through her. She flipped the phone shut, suddenly calm. David's God had answered. How else could it be that David was almost in Kungur when she needed him?

She found Tanya in a kitchen chair, slumped onto the table, her face in a pool of spilled vodka.

Ivan stood by, laughing. "She's out cold, stupid woman. I guess that means we've got the place to ourselves. How about a little fun?" He moved around the table toward her.

Heart pounding, she maintained her composure. She smiled at him and pointed to the couch. "Why don't we have a seat?"

Looking surprised, Ivan followed her to the couch.

Please hurry, David! She sat down beside Ivan and folded her shaking hands in her lap.

"Why so sweet all of a sudden?" Ivan eyed her suspiciously.

"I am sorry about that incident in the bar. I wasn't quite myself that night."

Tanya made a gagging sound that turned into a choke. Karina tried to jump up off the couch to go to her, but Ivan grabbed her arm. He squinted his eyes, his face inches away from hers. "She's OK. Let's have our fun. Or did you forget?"

She hadn't forgotten. Karina kicked him in the shin.

Fury reddened his face. "Not so nice anymore, huh?" He jerked her down onto the couch. Fierce pain seared through Karina's shoulder as he twisted her arm. She screamed out in pain. He clamped his hand over her mouth. "Shut up or I'll—"

Karina heard footsteps on the stairs outside. With all her might she brought her knee up into Ivan's gut. Groaning with pain, he slipped his fingers around Karina's throat and squeezed.

David dashed up the steps two at a time. He'd never heard Karina's voice so panic-stricken. *Lord, please let her be OK!*

As he approached the door to her apartment, he heard Karina cry out. He turned the knob and threw his weight against the door in case it was locked. It flew open, banging into the wall. Bounding into the living room, he scanned the scene. The smell of vomit entered his nose. A woman lay slumped on the kitchen table, face down.

Then he noticed the man on top of Karina on the living room couch, his hands around her neck. David threw himself on the man clutching

Karina. Tossing him against the wall, he knocked a lamp off the table. With a loud bang, it shattered on the floor. As the man dashed into the hallway, David didn't attempt to go after him. Instead, he knelt by the couch and touched Karina's cheek. Red stripes marred her neck. "Are you OK?"

She nodded, and pointed to the kitchen. "Check Tanya," she stammered, pushing herself up off the sofa.

Striding to the kitchen, David looked at the girl by the table. Repulsed by the putrid odor, David lifted her head out of the puddle of vomit. Her breathing was shallow, her skin pale. He turned to Karina. "She needs help. Call an ambulance."

As Karina called the emergency service, David laid the girl on the carpeted floor in the living room.

Karina joined him. "They'll be here shortly. Is she OK?"

"She's alive," David stated grimly. "If you get me a washcloth, we can clean up her mouth."

Karina hurried to the bathroom and returned with a wet cloth. She washed Tanya's face and smoothed back her vomit-covered hair.

"How much did she drink?"

"She nearly emptied the bottle."

"That's enough liquor to kill herself. Thankfully, she's breathing. Why didn't you stop her?"

"I tried, but Ivan wouldn't let me."

"Ivan. He's your friend?"

"Hardly."

The doorbell rang and Karina led the medical personnel into the room. Within minutes they strapped Tanya onto a gurney.

"Do you want us to come along to the hospital?" Karina asked.

"Are you related?"

"No, an acquaintance."

The man shook his head. "Just give me her name, and we'll call the family."

After they were gone, Karina collapsed on the couch and buried her head in her hands.

David balled his fists and turned to the window. *How can she do this?* Two days before they'd had dinner together and he'd given her a

Bible, and today she hosted a drunken orgy. *What am I doing here? I'm an idiot to consider giving up my ministry for this!* By the looks of things, the men who were after her for sex still hadn't left her life.

He threw an angry glare over his shoulder at the woman on the couch. Her hair spilled down over her knees and her shoulders shook.

"Why don't you have another glass of vodka? Might settle your nerves."

Karina's head snapped up. "I didn't drink any of that!"

David laughed mirthlessly. "People are dying from alcohol poisoning in your apartment, but you didn't have any of it? You're lying to me, just like you lied about your last name and your father's death." His hands gripped the windowsill.

Karina leapt from the couch and strode across the room. A tangle of jet-black hair framed her ashen face. She stopped in front of him, hands on her hips, her eyes ablaze. "OK, so I've changed my last name, and perhaps my dad is still alive, but I did *not* touch a drop of booze today. Don't you accuse me!"

David smelled her clean breath.

Karina pointed to the door. "Get out." Her voice cut like a razor.

David remained by the window. "I'm sorry. I assumed . . . ."

"I'll call the police if you don't leave this instant."

David stepped toward her and grabbed her wrists. "First you ask me to come bail you out of your trouble and now you're going to call the cops?"

"I don't care. Just get out!"

"OK. I'll leave, but not unless you come with me." He eyed the puddle of Tanya's vomit on the table. "This place isn't worth being in."

"I am not going anywhere with you." She squirmed to free herself from his grip.

David released her. "Please come with me. That guy may be keeping an eye on the apartment, waiting for me to leave so he can attack you again."

Karina shivered.

"We can go to a coffee shop or something," David suggested.

She threw him another dark look, but grabbed her coat off the hook and followed him down the stairs.

He watched her out of the corner of his eye as she sat in the bucket seat of the truck, her back stiff. She was more gorgeous than ever with her hair loose around her shoulders, all tousled up. Her eyes sparked with anger, and their heated debate had deepened the rosy color in her cheeks.

David parked the truck by the restaurant and turned to face her. He'd never been so keenly aware of her femininity and her tenacious strength. He ran his fingers through her disheveled hair. Her eyes met his and lingered on his face. He slid his hand up her neck, cupping her face, while his thumb stroked the smooth skin of her cheek.

"Karina," he whispered as he encircled her with his other arm and his lips found hers. He savored the sweetness of her kiss as she melted against him.

Be not unequally yoked together with unbelievers.

David drew back. His hands dropped down. "I'm sorry," he said tautly. He raked his hand through his hair. "I shouldn't have done that. Please forgive me."

Karina sat motionless and silent, her face inscrutable. "It's OK," she said nonchalantly. "Don't worry about it."

He wasn't worried; he was appalled with his lack of self-control. So much for his reassurance to Jake and the board that his relationship with Karina was purely platonic.

"Let's go inside," he said. He needed a strong shot of caffeine to bring him back to reality.

They entered the cafe and found a table in the corner.

"Two coffees," David told the waiter, "with an extra shot of espresso." When the waiter disappeared, he planted his elbows on the table. "So, tell me what happened tonight."

Karina decided to tell David the truth. "My friend Tanya showed up uninvited tonight with this guy, Ivan."

"Why?"

CHAPTER FOURTEEN

Karina shifted uncomfortably. Then she told him about the night at the bar with Tanya. "I snubbed him that night when he made a pass at me. Today must have been payday."

The waiter returned with two steaming cups of coffee. David poured three packages of sugar into the hot brew. Did he always take that much sugar? Karina couldn't remember.

"When I called you tonight, you said you were almost in Kungur already. Did you come to see me?" she asked.

"Yes." David put his cup down. "The board asked me to resign from my position at the shelter or break off my relationship with you."

A gasp escaped her lips. "Why?"

"No one employed by the organization can have an intimate relationship with someone who's not a Christian. It's the rule." She heard bitterness in his voice.

Her hand trembled on her cup. "What did you say?"

"I told them that I had to think about it. They gave me a week to decide."

Karina sat in silence, stunned that he would even consider losing his ministry and his job on her account. "I know what the ministry means to you. You can't consider giving it up."

"There's one thing that matters more to me than this ministry, and that is giving you a picture of who Christ is. I want to be like the shepherd who leaves the ninety-nine to find the one lost sheep."

Karina remembered reading that story in her little Bible that David had given her.

"If I can show Jesus to you, the sacrifice will be worth it. Even if you and I never get together."

Her eyes grew misty. "Thanks, but you can't leave the shelter for this. The teens depend on you."

"I know. But I believe God works out all things for the good and that He'll take care of the details." He held out his hand across the table.

Karina placed her hand in his. His eyes locked with hers in an embrace that took her breath away. Yet deep melancholy penetrated her heart. Their time together had come to an end. It could not be any other way. "You've been very kind." She pulled her clammy hand out of his. "But we can't go on like this. I refuse to be the cause for your dismissal."

A tired sadness filled David's eyes. The grooves around his mouth deepened. He curled his fingers around his coffee cup. "I know, you're right, but I just wanted you to hear about God. To help you start a personal relationship with Jesus. But then my feelings for you got involved."

Her chest constricted. "I'm sorry."

She hadn't apologized to anyone for years. But she was truly sorry. Sorry that they could not go on. Sorry that her feelings had gotten involved as well.

David pushed back the chair and stood. "I'll get you home. It's late."

He drove her back to her apartment in silence.

David stepped out of the truck, opened the passenger door for her, and accompanied her to the main door of the apartment building. Turning to face her, he grasped both of her hands in his. His eyes, filled with hurt, held hers for a long moment. "I'll miss you. But God is here for you. Don't forget that."

"I'll miss you too," she said lamely.

Soft as a whisper, he brushed his cheek against hers. "Good-bye, Karina."

"Good-bye, David."

He released his hold and stepped back. Her throat tight, she watched the Toyota disappear into the blackness of the night.

"You're back awfully late."

David spun around at the sound of Jake's voice behind him. He'd dropped in at the office to pick up his cell phone charger before going home to his apartment. He hadn't realized anyone was still up.

"And what's that to you?" David asked.

"I suppose you've been to Kungur again." Jake had stepped into the hallway.

Only now David noticed that the light in Jake's office was still on. "Still working?"

"I've been here all night answering e-mails."

"Well, you'll be glad to hear that my friendship with Karina has ended. I won't be leaving the shelter. So pack it in for the night and go to bed. The work can wait until tomorrow."

"Someone had to be responsible should you've had to leave."

Had Jake been vying for the leadership of the shelter? Was that why he'd created such a ruckus about his relationship with Karina?

"Was that all your concern was about? An ego trip to the top of the organization? This ministry is not about power. It's about helping kids. If that's not the case, I don't want to continue my work here after all."

"I'm not trying to take over your job." Jake dropped his head. "I've just seen too many guys rise to the top of a church organization and then fall for a woman." He swallowed hard. "The pastor of my home church had an affair and ran out on his wife. It destroyed his family and his ministry."

"I am not having an affair." David fought to control his seething emotions. "I don't even have a wife."

"What am I supposed to think when you get back at one o'clock in the morning? That you're having tea and crumpets with her?"

"After all these years of working together, is that all the trust I've gained?" David grabbed the charger off his desk and turned away. He didn't trust himself not to clobber Jake. He couldn't believe Jake's audacity to accuse him like that.

"We'll keep this visit to Kungur between us," Jake soothed.

"Do what you want. I already told you that my relationship with Karina is over. And our friendship perhaps also." Without another word, David strode out of the building.

CHAPTER FIFTEEN

Karina squatted on the floor of the nursery and stroked the crying toddler's head. "It's nap time, Yuri."

The boy's screaming halted for a moment as he looked up at her with tear-filled eyes.

"After your nap you can play in your group again."

The three-year-old wailed louder. "I want my mom!"

Karina sighed. The new boy had been very unsettled since his arrival a few weeks ago. He'd lived with his mother since birth and now she'd passed away. There were no other relatives capable of looking after him. Karina had a soft spot for the boy. Somehow her presence had a calming effect on him.

"There's nothing wrong with thinking about your mom. But you need have a nap. If you're good, we'll play with the toys later."

"Pwomise?" He rubbed the tears away with his little fist.

"I promise. Now, go with Ina."

Yuri followed Ina to the communal bedroom filled with rows of beds.

"Spasiba." Ina threw a relieved glance over her shoulder at Karina. "Couldn't do it without you."

"Any time." Karina had been baffled by Yuri's attachment to her from the day he arrived. Children were not usually as drawn to her as they were to Ina. Yet Yuri's cry for help affected her deeply.

I want my mom! How often had that been the cry of her own heart after her mother passed away and she'd endured her father's abuse? Like Yuri, no one had cared for her. Perhaps that was why the boy had connected with her.

Karina walked from the children's area to her office. She cringed as she remembered the intense pain in David's eyes when she told him they were through. But she'd held her ground, difficult as it was. She didn't want to be blamed for the fiasco with his ministry.

But now, two weeks later, she missed him intensely. Missed his phone calls. The intimacy they'd shared.

Focus on your job. That had always worked before. But the knowledge that someone cared about her had been her lifeline.

She used to think that Tanya cared about her, but when Tanya brought Ivan to the apartment, Karina's mind had changed. That had been nothing but a devious plot to get even for the snubbing in the bar.

Tanya had survived the alcohol poisoning, though barely. The doctors had warned her that next time she would probably not be so lucky. Her liver already showed serious damage.

Karina had sworn off vodka weeks ago. Now her smoking habit had to go. She was tired of being a slave to her addictions. She had tried to quit so often that depression set in whenever she even thought about quitting.

The day Tanya and Ivan were at her apartment, she'd prayed and God had answered. Maybe she should pray about her smoking habit, too. That's what David would tell her to do. She closed the office door behind her. She'd pray later. Right now she had to focus on Alexander's case. The Canadian couple had refused to continue with the adoption once their doctor had alleged that the boy had Fetal Alcohol Syndrome.

She jerked the file out of the drawer. He did not have FAS. Sure, he was behind in his development, but that was to be expected considering the long orphanage stay. But the couple's decision could not be changed. The Canadian government would deny the child access to the country, all based on a doctor's opinion from a photograph.

Karina had to reenter Alexander into the system and try to find other prospective parents for him. The Russian authorities would present him as a healthy toddler, regardless of what had happened.

Half an hour later Ina knocked on her office door. "Yuri's awake already. He wants you to come."

"I'll be there in a minute." Karina finished her work on Alexander's file and then made her way to the play area. As soon as Yuri spotted her from across the room, he darted over.

"Come play with me," he insisted, grabbing her hand.

Together they sat on the big rug and built Lego cars.

"*Machinka*," he squealed as he pushed a newly constructed vehicle around the room. Karina could not understand why the boy liked playing with her. Did she remind him of his mother?

"I want you to be my new mommy. I want to go home with you." He hugged her tightly.

"I can't take you home," Karina explained. "But I will try to find you a new mommy and daddy."

"Will they take me home with them?"

"Yes."

Was it possible to find adoptive parents for Yuri? He was at a difficult placement age for the international adoption program. People wanted babies; a clean slate with no baggage. As if there was such a thing.

She'd contact Maria in Perm and see if she knew of a prospective couple. Perhaps they could find a home for Yuri after all.

―――∞∞∞―――

David hadn't talked to Karina for two weeks. He wondered how she was doing. Did she miss him? Or was she happy that he was out of her life?

The board had asked him to spend more time in the office to catch up on the administrative work that had fallen behind. Jake now traveled to the orphanages. David stayed at the shelter, but didn't feel that he belonged there. His trust in the board had been eroded, and his relationship with Jake was in shambles. The kids were the only reason he hadn't left yet.

He continually prayed about whether he should stay in Perm and hope that his relationship with Jake and the board could be repaired in time. God had led him throughout his life and ministry, and He would not forsake him now.

Losing Karina, his friendship with Jake, and his joy in the ministry had created a huge hole in his heart. That hole ached so much, it threatened to swallow him.

He *had* to talk to Karina. A plan had been percolating in his brain for some time. It was a long shot, but it might just pan out.

———

Exhausted after a long day, Karina crashed on the couch to watch a late-night rerun of *Dallas* translated into Russian. Her phone rang in the middle of the show. She turned down the volume on the TV and answered the call.

"Hey, Karina." David's voice sounded strained.

"Hi, David. It's good to hear from you." She pressed the phone closer to her ear.

With a minimum of small talk, they were friends again. She told him about Yuri having grown so attached to her, and how she was trying to find adoptive parents for him. And she told him about Alexander's failed adoption and the accusation of FAS.

David listened intently, asking questions from time to time. When she finished speaking, he asked, "Would you come to church with me Sunday? I could pick you up on Saturday evening. Hannah, a girl who looks after the east-side shelter, has offered to share her apartment with you for the night. A young couple from Kungur who attend church here in Perm can drive you back on Sunday night."

She hesitated. He'd never invited her to his church before. And she hadn't spent the night with anyone since Frank walked out on her. Staying with the woman David mentioned did not appeal to her. "What would the board say?"

"I've already discussed it with Vladimir. It's all been OKed."

Her grandma had taken her to a Russian Orthodox cathedral when she was a little girl. She remembered the awful smell of incense, and men with flowing beards dressed in long, dark robes. Would David's church be like that?

"I don't want to cause any trouble for you," she said.

"I explained to the board that we're not seeing each other anymore, so they didn't make any fuss about it. I'll pick you up Saturday at six."

Dazed, she hung up the phone.

She looked forward to seeing David again. And not only for a few hours, but an entire Sunday! Humming a soft tune, she turned off the television and entered her bedroom.

What did one wear to church? Opening her closet, she scrutinized its contents. She flipped through her straight skirts, drab suit jackets, and blouses. Perhaps this event called for a little shopping trip. After pulling her pink chiffon nightgown over her head, she climbed into bed.

Just before she drifted off to sleep, she realized she'd forgotten about her habitual bed-time smoke.

Karina opened the door for David as he arrived promptly at six on Saturday night. His hair tumbled over his forehead from the drizzling late-September rain. He shook the water off his hair and coat like a wet greyhound and smiled at her. "How've you been?"

Karina's heart skipped a beat. "Great." She'd had a fantastic week once he'd asked her to come to Perm. She'd anticipated being with him from the moment he'd called.

"I'll grab my bag," she said and walked back into her apartment. Her hand trembled as she lifted the small overnight bag off the bed. She'd packed only the bare necessities, and no cigarettes for this weekend. God would certainly frown on that. But she had no idea how she would survive without them.

CHAPTER FIFTEEN

The shopping trip for a new outfit had not materialized, so she had chosen a long black skirt, candy-pink blouse, and black suede high-heeled pumps from her wardrobe. She hoped it would do for the service.

"God deserves our best," her grandma had said as she hoisted five-year-old Karina into an ill-fitting leotard with the crotch at her knees. Perhaps that's what she had learned to hate about church. Stinky incense, morose looking men in long, flowing gowns, and ill-fitting leotards.

Grandma had passed on in the early eighties, so it had to be at least twenty years ago since she'd gone to church.

"I'm ready." As ready as she could be.

David took the bag out of her hand and carried it to the truck.

Karina slipped into the passenger seat and cranked open the window, breathing deeply as the cool fall breeze touched her face. Would David pursue the questions he had for her when they met last time? Why she'd changed her identity and why she'd lied about her dad? Her dad's red face appeared before her eyes, his liquored breath in her nostrils. *"If you ever tell anyone, I'll kill you,"* he had said. So she'd been silent and never told a soul. Good girls didn't do that kind of thing. Shivering, she wrapped her arms around her body.

"Are you OK?" David touched her arm.

Embarrassed, she closed the window, color rising in her cheeks.

David popped a peppermint in his mouth. "Want one?" He held the roll out to her.

"No, thanks." She folded her shaking hands on her lap.

"You'll like Hannah," David said, obviously attempting to make small talk. "She's a great gal. She looks after the day shelter on the east side."

Sure she'd like Hannah, a total stranger. As if. And now she had to spend the night at her place. People could not be trusted. Not even one's friends or relatives. Especially not one's friends or relatives. Her mom had been right. Karina had found out the hard way.

David's gut dropped as he watched the woman beside him. Their separation had not cooled his feelings for her, but flamed them into a fire that burned brightly in his heart.

He gripped the steering wheel. *Lord, why am I so weak? I wanted to be her friend, lead her to Christ, but that's not how things are turning out.* He shouldn't have asked her to come to Perm. He had no business pursuing an unbeliever, regardless of how close she might be to the kingdom. And if he was honest with himself, being with Karina had been the real reason for his invitation.

"Tell me about the service. I'm not sure what to expect."

He saw uncertainty on her face. "It's really informal. The pastor, Vladimir, is a great guy and the people are kind. We simply worship God, help one another, and take care of those around us."

"Sounds like a great system. Sort of like communism. Except it didn't work."

David glanced at her profile. Her mouth formed a tight line and her eyes focused straight ahead.

"Christianity has stood the test of time. But you'll have to find that out for yourself." He didn't intend to get into a debate with her. Only God could convince her otherwise.

Hannah opened the door for them before David had a chance to knock. "Come in," she said, hugging David. "And you must be Karina. Welcome." She greeted Karina with the same affection as David. "Let me take your coat and bag."

She bustled around the hallway, hanging up Karina's coat. "There's no one here at night except myself," she explained to Karina. "We'll have the place to ourselves. I'll show you your room."

"I'll be going then," David said, but Hannah stopped him.

"Oh, do stay for coffee! I'll show Karina her room, and then we'll be back down. Why don't you go to the living area? We'll be right there."

Karina followed Hannah up the stairs.

"I haven't had a female companion overnight since my arrival here last year," Hannah explained. "I'm so excited about your visit."

Karina frowned. How did one get excited about a visit with a total stranger?

"Here's your room." Hannah opened the door to a cubicle-sized room on the left side of the hallway. "My room is right across from yours. We'll share the bathroom at the end of the hall."

The room was sparingly furnished but clean and tidy. A little heater purred softly, spreading its welcoming warmth. A few fashion magazines lay on the bed, topped with a bar of chocolate. The small lamp on the nightstand beside the bed was turned on. An old rocker chair stood in the corner, half covered with an American quilt. On the wall above the bed hung an English plaque. "Trust in the Lord with all your heart," Karina read silently.

She smiled at Hannah. "Thank you," she said sincerely. "It's a lovely room."

Hannah beamed. "Small but comfortable, I hope. You can let me know if you need anything else." She stepped back. "Now, let's join David for coffee."

When they arrived in the living area, David had already set three cups on the table, each with a scoop of instant coffee. He was just in the process of retrieving the kettle from the kitchen.

"Thanks, David." Hannah waited until David poured the hot water into the mug and then handed it to Karina.

Soon, all three of them sat around the table, each with a mug of coffee in front of them.

Surprisingly at ease, Karina listened to the friendly banter between David and Hannah. Their relationship was one of camaraderie, without the physical tension that Karina was familiar with between men and women.

"David's like an older brother," Hannah said after David left. "I miss my family in the States sometimes, but he always encourages me. He's a very special person." She looked at Karina from her vantage point. "He's very special to you as well, I see?"

"Yeah, he is." There was no sense denying it. Her heart leaped every time David looked at her.

"Do you have other friends?"

"No." At one point she'd considered Tanya her friend, but that was over. She couldn't think of anyone else.

Hannah nodded. "I see many women who long for connection with other women," she said, "but they have no close friends, especially in this post-communism generation when people's lives are falling apart. So a lot of women end up lonely and hurt."

Karina knew all about that.

"God has created so much beauty and potential within people, but they don't see it. When they begin to walk in what God has for them, transformation takes place. It's like a light radiating from the inside out," Hannah said with a smile. "I love connecting with other women."

Fascinated, Karina watched her. She hadn't experienced what Hannah spoke about, but she could see the light Hannah spoke about shining on the face of the young woman. She exuded peace and joy.

"Well, I should let you get to bed," Hannah concluded, standing up. Karina followed her example. Hannah hugged her again. "I'm praying for you," she said. "And for David. That God will make all things well for both of you."

<hr />

Filled with misgivings, Karina entered the church building on Sunday morning, Hannah at her side. To her surprise, she quite liked the young American girl and had enjoyed their visit the previous night.

"Hello, Fayina," Hannah called out to an elderly lady in the foyer. "I would like to introduce you to Karina. She's a friend from Kungur, and is here for the service."

Karina was glad that she'd not mentioned David's name. She hung back as she shook the old woman's hand. News travelled like lightning in a small community like this. Everyone was probably already aware of her connection to David.

A few more women introduced themselves to Karina. She was happy when Hannah entered the building and sat down in one of the pews.

Karina took a seat next to Hannah and watched the building fill up with all sorts of people. There were ill-dressed street kids and business-men in three-piece suits, older ladies in skirts or dresses with scarves draped over their heads, and younger ones in jeans. Most were lower-class women with rough, work-worn hands.

The open atmosphere of the church surprised her. At her grandma's church, the people sat silently, with somber faces. These people were sociable, visiting with one another across the pews, apparently happy to be in church.

A girl at the piano played a soft tune while a few other young people strummed guitars.

Karina had not seen David since he'd dropped her off at Hannah's house the previous night. She kept an eye on the aisle.

"David is leading the service this morning and will come in later," Hannah told her. Whatever "leading the service" meant.

The piano picked up the tempo, and the congregation rose to their feet, joining the Russian chorus. Karina stood as well. She didn't remember music being part of the service with her grandma certainly not such joyful, spontaneous music. The entire building reverberated with the sound of voices.

Accompanied by an older man, David entered. Her heart lurched at the sight of him. He wore black dress pants and a dark-brown blazer which accentuated his light hair. He stepped up to the podium and took the microphone.

"On this first day of the week we remember that Jesus rose from the dead. Death did not have the last word, and we rejoice in that. We have a hope that never fades away. Let's praise God for what He has done for us."

"Praise the Lord!" an older man in front of her proclaimed loudly.

Karina had never encountered such an exuberant group of people. She listened to the singing, all the while watching the joy on people's faces. Something was different here. Something she had also observed in David and Hannah.

The singing ended and the people took their seats. David opened his Bible. "Today I'm reading from Philippians chapter four, written by the apostle Paul to encourage this group of believers."

He read from the text. "Rejoice in the Lord always. I will say it again: Rejoice! Let your gentleness be evident to all. The Lord is near. Do not be anxious about anything, but in everything by prayer and petition, with thanksgiving, present your requests to God. And the peace of God, which transcends all understanding, will guard your hearts and your minds in Christ Jesus."

David paused. "Is this where you are this morning? Anxious for nothing, resting in the Lord, and giving all your requests to Him? Does the peace of God surround your heart? Or are you anxious and restless?" His eyes drifted across the crowd until they spotted Karina in the back row. A faint smile curved his lips. "Allow God to work in your life and you'll have the peace you're looking for. Find someone who can help you and pray with you. Someone you can trust."

Karina didn't dare move lest she attract attention to herself. She hoped others would not see David's eyes fixed on her. She cast a sideways glance at Hannah, but the young woman was leaning forward, her arms propped up on her knees and her chin resting in the cup of her hand.

David's eyes moved to the front row of pews. "Vladimir, could you come up and share your thoughts with us?"

The older, bearded man who'd accompanied David into church rose from the straight-backed wooden bench. With a slight limp, he made his way to the platform. David shook his hand, and then walked to the back of the church.

Karina's breath stopped in her throat as he approached. Surely he wouldn't sit beside her! She stared at the ring on her pinkie finger, nervously twisting it. Everyone would be watching them.

Be anxious for nothing, but in all things let your requests be known to God. Taking a deep breath, she straightened her back and dropped her hands in her lap. David and she were friends. Nothing more. She should not worry about what people thought of them. David sat beside her, stretched his legs, and folded his arms across his chest. His presence settled Karina, but even so, she could not concentrate on the message.

The enigma of church intrigued her. Why did people gather together every week without fail? Was it really possible to trust God the way David had explained? To give up all her worries? Perhaps. But share them with someone? Highly unlikely!

One of the men picked up a gold-colored plate and handed it to the people. David brushed his shoulder against her as he reached in his pocket and pulled out a small envelope. Karina blanched. She remembered that in her grandma's church people used to put money in the plate. She dug in her purse and extracted a few coins.

"You don't need to give anything," David whispered in her ear. Embarrassed, she lowered her purse. She felt socially inept. The inevitable story. She touched her forehead in a weary gesture.

———— ∞∞∞ ————

After the service, David quickly led Karina out of the church. He didn't feel like being subjected to a myriad of curious eyes and questions.

"We're going to Hannah's for lunch," he explained as he opened the truck door. "But I want to show you the shelter before we go there." Hannah would not arrive home from church for a while, as she usually lingered after the service, chatting with her friends.

Within minutes, they reached the day shelter. "This is our educational center," he explained as he unlocked the door. "We teach the kids a variety of skills, including computers and accounting." He pointed to the long hallway. "My apartment is upstairs. I lived in the main shelter for twelve years until we got this building. Now Jake supervises that shelter."

He climbed the stairs ahead of her and opened the door to his apartment. "It's plain, but it's serviceable." He'd never looked at his apartment through a woman's eyes, but he suddenly noticed the bare walls and old furniture.

"It's spacious." Karina stepped into the living room. "Big enough for a family." David swallowed hard. He knew her comment didn't have a double meaning, but he found it disturbing nevertheless. She ambled to the bookshelf and fingered the English titles.

"You're a reader." She glanced over her shoulder.

Of course he was. What else was there to do in the long winter months without anyone to share his apartment? He turned to the door. "I think Hannah should be home by now. She'll be waiting with lunch." He wasn't hungry, but Karina's presence in the apartment aroused feelings he'd rather not face and certainly could not share.

The rest of the afternoon passed quickly. Hannah had invited a few others from the church also. After lunch, the men gathered in the living room while the women washed the dishes. Despite David's insistence that he do part of the work, Hannah had smiled and waved him away. "Next time you'll get a turn."

When they finished, it was time to bring Karina to Vladimir's apartment, where her ride back to Kungur would depart from.

David waited in the hallway as Karina said good-bye to Hannah. "I've enjoyed my stay," he heard her say. "Thanks for having me." Voluntarily, she reached out and embraced Hannah.

"Come again any time. You're always welcome. We need to get to know each other better." Hannah stood at the door and waved them good-bye.

David opened the truck door for Karina.

"Thanks, David."

Karina had changed out of the formal black skirt and now wore a pair of faded blue jeans and a baggy sweater. It didn't make a difference to David what she wore; she was as gorgeous as ever.

"You're welcome." He'd gone through this routine a dozen or more times, yet he knew that today was different. He'd have to call it quits once again.

Lord, how do I explain to her? I so badly didn't want to hurt her. I wanted to show her Your love and that people could be trusted. I feel like I've failed on all accounts. He started the engine and maneuvered the truck out of the parking lot. "I shouldn't have asked you to come."

"Did I do something wrong?"

"No, of course not. It's me. I can't go on like this." How could he explain to her how much he cared for her? "Every time I see you I want to be more than just your friend. I wanted you to come to church, but it mainly was an excuse to see you. I'm sure you realized that. But I can't pursue a relationship unless we both agree to put God first in our lives."

David turned the street corner that led to Vladimir's apartment. "I have to say good-bye to you. If we see each other again someday, that'll be great, but I won't be pursuing you." The decision tore at his heart. He parked alongside the curb by the concrete apartment building where Vladimir and his family lived, and held out his hand.

Karina gripped his hand in return. "I care about you, too, David. I'm sorry." Tears welled up in her eyes.

Reaching up, David wiped them away. "Don't be sorry. If God wills it, things will come together." He kissed her cheek. "God be with you. Until we meet again."

He took Karina's bags out of the back of the truck and turned toward the entrance of the building.

CHAPTER SIXTEEN

Large raindrops dripped off the edge of the orphanage roof onto Karina's head and shoulder. She entered the low hallway and shook the water off her coat. It had rained the entire weekend.

The gray sky matched her Monday morning mood. The peace David had talked about in church eluded her. She clenched her teeth and booted up the old computer. Another day to add to the endless chain of worthless baubles that summed up the grand total of her life.

She'd had a nightmare the previous night. David had been in her apartment, arms outstretched. "I am leaving, Karina. I've come to say good-bye." He advanced toward her, but the apartment rose and fell like the giant waves of an earthquake. A huge crack split the floor under her feet. She tried to run toward him, but the crack grew wider. With excruciating effort, she jumped, falling short. Her fingers clawed at the periphery. David reached out to grab her hand, but she let go of the edge. With a terrifying scream, she fell into the black abyss.

Her scream had jolted her back to reality. Sweating profusely, she'd sat up in bed, her heart pounding. The dream had left her unsteady and shaken.

Karina shook her head. Dreams had no meaning. They were just the idle imaginations of an overactive mind. She hung her coat on the rack and strode to the kitchen for a steaming mug of strong coffee.

CHAPTER SIXTEEN

David knew he was in trouble when Vladimir called and insisted on another urgent board meeting, right on the heels of Karina's visit. A sick feeling washed over him. He covered his eyes with his hand.

Lord, now what do I do? Will they listen if I explain that it's over? Will they believe me? Lifting his head, he looked up. "Jesus, I need You. Give me grace to answer wisely."

At the knock on the door, he stood. The time of reckoning had come.

Jake, Vladimir, and the two other men on the board of directors greeted him curtly as they entered. Vladimir's face was mottled red. He blew his nose loudly.

"Let's open this meeting in prayer," Ivan said, folding his hands.

What happened to Vladimir being the spokesman of the board? David glanced at the old pastor. His mouth was a tight line and his eyes were open during the prayer. Ivan rattled on about repentance for David and putting away all idols. David had no idea what he was referring to.

After the prayer, Ivan stared at David. "It has come to our attention that you have breached the board's decision through unauthorized contact with Ms. Svetlana. Although we agreed to your arrangement to bring Ms. Svetlana to church, you assured us that you were not involved in a serious relationship. Yet, Jake, who was visiting Vladimir, saw you kiss her when you dropped her off."

So that was it! Jake, of all people, had watched him as he kissed Karina good-bye. David sat in silence and looked around the circle. Every face was grim except Jake's. David saw a smug look in his eyes as if he savored the moment.

"Yes, I kissed Karina good-bye," he admitted. "But I told her that I would not be calling her again. I broke off all contact."

"You told us that once before. How will we know that this is indeed true? If you're physically involved with this woman, will you stay away from her? After in depth discussion with the board, we are asking you to resign from the organization."

David rubbed his hands across his knees. "I tender my resignation. I'll evacuate my office tomorrow and the apartment as soon as I make alternate plans."

He looked at Jake's triumphant face. "I give you my blessing in leading the organization. God has done mighty works here in Perm, and I pray that will continue." He stood up. There was nothing left to say. His throat constricted with sheer emotion.

Vladimir rose to his feet and shook David's hand. "May God be with you." His voice cracked.

Ivan and Ferdinand shook David's hand and exited the room without another word.

When they were gone, Jake approached David. "I pray God will forgive you for what you've done to the board and this organization. I believe that you carry a spirit of rebellion against higher authority that will not go unpunished."

David moved toward the door. "My conscience is clear. But something's wrong with you. I pray God will reveal it."

"Please don't hang around the shelter," Jake said, ignoring David's statement. "It's going to be hard enough for the kids when they hear that you're leaving. A quick, clean break will be best."

David bit his tongue. "I'll do what I think is right for the kids. This isn't about you or me. It's about them."

Heat stained Jake's cheeks. "Seems to me you've been the one putting your own interests first. Had that not been the case, we might not be having this conversation."

"Good bye, Jake." David wasn't about to pick an argument with him. The situation didn't need more fuel on the fire.

Vladimir stood in the hallway, his shoulders drooped. "I tried to stop this, but Jake convinced the board. It was three against one."

David put a reassuring hand on his shoulder. "It's all right. God has a plan. We need to trust that He'll work out all things for the good. As far as Jake is concerned, I don't understand why he would stir the others up like this."

"Perhaps he's truly concerned about your spiritual state. Or perhaps he's jealous."

CHAPTER SIXTEEN

David walked with his friend to the back door. "He's changed so much. I can't believe that we used to be close friends."

"God will restore what is rightfully yours. You've done so much over the last thirteen years. I don't believe it's been in vain."

David rubbed the back of his neck. "Thanks for being a faithful friend. I'm going to miss you."

He was going to miss everyone. All the kids who'd come to the shelter, some when they were very young and now were maturing into teenagers.

How am I going to live without the kids? They are the reason for my existence. The very essence of my call here.

At a snail's pace, he drove through the dark streets to his residence. Where would he go? Should he stay in Perm or head back to the States? What would he do there?

He killed the motor as he parked behind the shelter, then dropped his head onto the steering wheel and wept.

Vanessa bolted upright in bed as Jared and Annie bounded into the master bedroom, carrying a large box.

"Happy Birthday!" Annie dumped the box on the duvet and scrambled onto the bed, throwing her arms around her mother's neck. "Here, Mommy," she said as she thrust the home-made card into Vanessa's hands.

Vanessa opened the card and read the inscription, made out of awkward, squiggly letters. "I love my MOM! Happy Birthday. Annie."

"Thanks, sweetheart. It's lovely." She kissed her daughter's cheek.

"Open my present, Mommy!" Annie bounced up and down on her hands and knees.

"Wait a minute." Jared sat on the edge of the bed and kissed his wife. "Happy thirtieth, honey." He wrapped Vanessa in his arms and kissed her on the lips. "God bless you always."

"Now open the present," Annie insisted, handing her mother the large box.

Vanessa ripped the flowery paper off the cardboard box and lifted the lid. Removing the crepe paper wrapped around the contents, she saw a satiny black winter parka with silver fur trim on the hood and sleeves.

"It's gorgeous. Thank you." Vanessa took the elegant winter coat out of the box and held it up. She stroked the fur trim.

"It's fake fox," Annie explained. "The lady in the store said so. I don't know what a fake fox is."

Vanessa bit her lip to stifle a chuckle. "It's beautiful."

"You're going to need it very soon." Jared's eyes twinkled.

Holding the coat, she looked up at him. "What do you mean?"

"Leah from Loving Hearts called with another proposal. She said they have a three-year-old boy waiting to be adopted."

Vanessa's hand flew up to cover her mouth. "Oh, Jared!"

"There's no trace of FAS or any other medical problems. Leah said she'd send pictures as soon as we tell her yes."

Vanessa threw off the covers and swung her legs over the edge of the bed. "Let's call her now!"

"They're an hour behind our time, so we need to wait. In the meantime, Annie and I will serve you breakfast in here." He winked at his daughter.

After they left the room, Vanessa lay back down in bed.

Another proposal! She could hardly comprehend it.

She thought of the last trip they'd made to Russia and the frightening experience she'd had there. She still could not reconcile the events of Alexander's loss. How could she be certain that God would lead her this time?

Soft as a whisper, truth dawned in her soul.

God did not let you down, Vanessa. In Russia, He warned you through your feelings but you wouldn't listen.

She'd known something wasn't right with Alexander, but she'd wanted to squelch her fear and step out in faith. God, in His mercy, stopped them from adopting Alexander by alerting the government officials in Canada to his health problems.

Feelings are a gift from God; don't set them aside. She suddenly realized that God had been with her all along, but she hadn't wanted to listen. She'd looked for a sign when she'd already received an answer.

Tears flowed down her cheeks as she released her emotions. She'd wanted so much to have faith that she'd never thought of her fear as a warning voice. She'd looked for outward revelation while God had given her inward knowledge of what to do. Her feelings had been God's way of telling her no. She'd missed the obvious and mistrusted God's leading.

Rolling over, she buried her head in the pillow. "I'm sorry, Lord," she whispered. "You were there all along, and I missed it. Thank You for Your grace. Please forgive me for mistrusting You."

She sat up as Jared entered the room, carrying a tray of coffee, fresh muffins, toast, and a ham, green pepper, and cheese omelet, Vanessa's favorite.

"Are you OK?" he asked, concerned, seeing her tears. "I was sure you'd be OK with another proposal."

Vanessa smiled through her tears. "Yes. I've just had an unexpected revelation, but it's good. God is good."

He placed the tray on the night stand. "When I spoke to Leah, she mentioned that I can go alone on the first trip and simply take a power of attorney to represent you in Russia. So you won't have to come along this time. Then after I come back, we can go together to meet the child to finalize the adoption."

Vanessa picked up the cup of coffee. "Either way, I don't mind. I know that all things will work out for the good."

Jared kissed her cheek. "You're a real trooper, Mrs. Williams."

CHAPTER SEVENTEEN

David methodically removed his personal possessions from his office. He lifted the picture of Geoff and Danae off the desk. He held it close to his chest and then carefully placed it in his briefcase with a few other items. Amazing how little he had accumulated in thirteen years. But God did not want His people to lay up treasures on earth.

David didn't have the heart to call Karina and tell her the news. She'd think that she was to blame for his dismissal, and wish she'd never come to church with him.

Thirteen years of work, and not even a thank-you from the board. *That's not what you did it for, remember? You did it for the kids. Don't lose sight of that.*

David appreciated his faithful friend, Vladimir, more than ever. *A seasoned veteran for the Lord. A true man of God.*

A knock on his door stirred him out of his reveries. Without waiting for a response, Georgi, one of the older shelter teens, stepped inside, followed by Alik, Sasha, and several others.

"We heard you were leaving, Pastor David," Georgi said, his eyes hard and angry. "Is it true?"

David flinched. "Yes, I've resigned. Not that I wanted to, but I didn't have a choice." He'd planned to tell the kids in the next few days after he'd finalized his plans, but the gossip mill had beat him to it.

"All of us want you to stay," Georgi said.

The other teens nodded their agreement.

"Your enthusiasm is a blessing to me, but things can't be changed. Jake will handle the shelter, no problem."

Alik stomped his foot on the floor. "We don't want him. He's a snake."

"I'm sure everything will work out," David soothed.

Georgi shook his head. "If you're outta here, we're outta here."

All the teens responded unanimously.

David knew it was no idle threat. Georgi had connections outside the orphanage; he could find the teens a place to stay. But he hated to think of what would happen to them.

"Please don't make any hasty decisions. I'll discuss this with Vladimir."

"Do what you want, but our mind is made up." Georgi moved toward the door.

David watched the teens leave with a heavy heart. Everyone at the shelter had worked hard to keep them off the streets, off drugs, away from the mafia and prostitution. Now what would happen to them?

He dialed Vladimir's number and explained the situation to him.

"The teens are in good hands," Vladimir responded. "I think they're just trying to put pressure on the board to rescind the decision about your dismissal. But I'll discuss it with them."

"Thanks." David hung up the phone.

Vladimir called back within minutes. "The board believes the teens are trying to manipulate the situation. We are not too concerned. They have it good here. Free food, education, a place to live. They're not stupid."

"But they're angry, and that's all it might take for them to leave."

"The board will take it from here, David. Don't worry about it."

Bone-weary, David hung up the phone. Would his work here in Perm be completely laid to waste? He dropped to his knees and poured his heart out to God.

David's phone rang just after seven o'clock the following morning. Seeing his brother's number on the call display, he frowned. Roger never called except on his birthday, and even then he occasionally forgot. They'd not been very close the last few years. His brother, a driven executive with his own trading corporation, was financially successful without God in his life, while David was an unsuccessful missionary who, in Roger's eyes, had thrown his career away.

"David. Mom's not doing well. You need to come home."

David gripped the phone. "What's going on?"

"She's had a stroke and is in a coma. The doctors don't think she'll come out of it. They said she could have another stroke at any time, which would be the end. If you want to see her alive, you need to come right away."

"OK. I'll book a flight immediately. Tell her to hang on till I get there."

Roger laughed flatly. "Mom's not hearing anything right now. She's too far gone."

"I'll be there as soon as possible."

After hanging up, David entered the Aeroflot web site on his computer. The next flight from Perm to Moscow left at one P.M. He still had enough time to catch that one. He booked the Moscow-London flight, too, and checked out British Airlines for a flight to Denver. There were no direct flights available, so he booked his route via Chicago.

Lord, what's going on? I'm rolling from one crisis into the next. Give me strength to cope.

He rubbed his eyes and smoothed his unkempt hair. He whispered a prayer for his precious mother, who'd been such an encouragement to him all these years. Glancing at the clock on the computer screen, he calculated that he'd have to leave for the airport in two hours. Not a lot of time to prepare for an extended trip. Depending on his mother's condition, he could be there for several weeks or even longer. And there was nothing to come back to in Perm.

Except Karina. He'd wanted to wait for a while before breaking the news to her about the termination of his position at the shelter. Should he tell her now, or merely inform her of his unexpected trip to America? No, he needed to tell her. With Jake doing the food drive, the news would leak quickly. She might feel betrayed if she heard it from someone else. He'd call her after he'd packed.

He informed Vladimir of the sudden change of plans and called Hannah.

"Keep an eye on the kids, Hannah, especially Georgi and his friends." He explained what had transpired the previous day. "Vladimir doesn't take the situation seriously, but I don't think their threats are idle. Also, could you stay in touch with Karina? I'll call her, but I won't be able to see her before I leave."

"Of course. I'll try to make it out to Kungur sometime soon."

Feeling more at ease, David hung up the phone and focused on preparing for the extended journey.

At ten, he went to the full-time shelter. En route, he dialed the orphanage from his cell phone. No one picked up. He'd have to try again later.

David parked and entered the building. A strange feeling settled upon him. He no longer had any involvement in this ministry that he, by God's grace, had pioneered.

Jake met him in the hallway, animosity in his eyes.

"I've come to say good-bye," David announced. "My mother is very ill so I'm flying out this morning."

"Sorry to hear that," Jake replied, his face inscrutable.

David walked to the kitchen, where the kids had gathered for their morning break.

"My brother called this morning," he told them. "I need to go to the States right away." He glanced at Jake, who had entered the room behind him.

Georgi stood. "I guess we're leaving, then, hey guys?"

"Please don't," David pleaded. "I'll be back when I can."

The young teen shook his head. "We told you that if Jake was in charge, we were leaving." He stood, followed by half a dozen other teens.

Jake blocked the doorway, his face stern. "You can't just leave."

Georgi shoved his chest. "You pushed David out. We don't want nothin' to do with you."

"Georgi, hold on," David called. The boy turned around at the sound of his voice. "How about you move to the other shelter? There's lots of room there, and Hannah does a great job."

Georgi cocked his head. "That might work. We'll do anything to get away from Jake." He looked around the group.

The others nodded their consent. "But if we don't like it, we're outta here."

Jake threw a furious glare at David, wheeled around, and disappeared down the hallway.

The kids thronged around David in a tight cluster. He hugged them one by one, then made his way to the door as the kids continued to cling to him.

"I'll try to come back soon. Make me proud of you. I don't want to hear that any of you are back on the streets by the time I come back."

The kids crowded in the courtyard as the Toyota pulled out. David waved, the smile on his face a far cry from the feelings in his heart. He'd miss them terribly.

He called Karina again. Still no answer. Where could she be? He tried her home number. No answer there either. Hannah would have to tell her the news. Dejected, he threw his phone down on the passenger seat.

<hr />

"We are now approaching Denver International Airport. Please turn off all electronic devices. Flight attendants prepare for landing," the captain spoke over the intercom system.

David closed his small laptop and slipped it into his briefcase. He was happy to have arrived. The trip back home had never seemed so long.

His brother Roger met him at the Denver airport dressed in an immaculate suit with matching shirt and silk Armani tie. A diamond ring glistened on his finger where his wedding ring had once been.

"Hey, bro, how have you been?" His gold canine tooth sparkled as he flashed David a broad grin.

"I've been better. How's Mom?"

"Hanging in there but barely. She's on IV. They're talking about tube feeding her if the coma lasts much longer."

David felt sick and exhausted.

Roger led him out of the terminal to his shiny, canary-yellow Corvette. Business must be good. It always was good for his older brother.

David lifted his suitcase into the car and slipped into the creamy leather seat. Roger might have the toys, but he lacked substance and stability. He had a new mistress every few months while his ex-wife and kids were somewhere across the nation with another man.

David wondered how he could be genetically linked to his brother. But then again, his own ex-wife was somewhere else with another man as well. . . . He sighed and leaned back against the seat as Roger pulled away from the curb.

<hr />

The aged hospice smelled musty, like stale water and old mold. The tiled, brown floor camouflaged most of the dirt, but the walls were smeared with fingerprints and grime.

David lifted his eyebrows. "I thought Mom was in the hospital."

"I didn't think Mom would notice the difference. No use wasting her pension plan on expensive care."

Anger exploded in David's chest, but he didn't respond, afraid of the tirade that would burst loose should he open his lips. There was no sense arguing right before they saw Mom. Struggling to regain control of his emotions, David quickened his pace.

Roger followed close on David's heels. "Hey, you don't have to get mad. You may not need the money out there in Russia, but my business is a going concern, and I need to clear some debt. Besides, you haven't been around to help look after Mom."

As if Roger had looked after her. Stopping in mid-stride, David turned to his brother. "I'm here now, and I *will* look after her."

Roger opened the door to the room. "Be prepared. She doesn't look good."

David's heart leapt into his throat as he approached the bed. "Mom!"

He bent over the pale form on the bed and took the bony, limp hand in his. Tears streaming down his face, he kissed her. Her pale-blue skin was cold beneath his touch, and her wrinkled skin hung flaccid on her thin cheeks.

His fingers slipped around her wrist. Roger, standing at the foot of the bed, shook his head. "She's not dead. She's been like this for days."

David detected a faint pulse. He cradled her hand as he sat by the bed. "Mom, it's me, David. How are you feeling?"

Roger chortled. "Don't bother, man. She's not going to hear you."

"I'm sure she does. And if not, it can't hurt."

Roger glanced at his watch. "I should be going. Call me when you need a ride. Where are you staying?"

"Mom's house."

"Mom's house is dirty. And it stinks pretty bad."

"I'll get it cleaned up and make it presentable."

Roger's face lit up. "Excellent idea. I'll list it as soon as possible. With some work, it's a good piece of real estate."

David scowled at him. "We'll talk about it later. Thanks for picking me up."

With Roger out of the room, he turned his attention back to his mother. "Hey, Mom," he whispered as he touched her hand. "I'm so glad to see you." He talked to her while stroking her hands and arms. He smoothed her hair back from her face and sponged her mouth with cold water.

"Are you hungry, Mom? Just squeeze my hand if you need something."

Paralyzed, the doctor had said, but David held out for more. With God all things were possible. He took his little Bible out of his pocket. "I'll read Psalm 23 to you, Mom. The Lord is still your Shepherd, even now."

He opened the book and began to read. "Even though I walk through the valley of the shadow of death, I will fear no evil, for you are with me; your rod and your staff, they comfort me."

Nurses came and went, looking after his mother's basic needs. "She might be able to perceive sound," one of them said. "But at this stage it's doubtful. Too far gone, I think."

"But it can't hurt for me to assume that she can hear."

The nurse smiled as she adjusted the sheets. "No, it can't. Where there's life, there's hope, right?" For a brief moment their eyes met. Her dark brown eyes reminded him of Karina's. He turned back to the bed.

"I found this lady, Mom," he told his mother when the nurse had left. "Her name is Karina. She's beautiful, with chocolate-colored eyes and long, black hair. She's the director of an orphanage, and she loves kids. She went to church for the first time last week. I'm praying she'll come to know Jesus. I'm sorry you couldn't meet her. I think you'd like her. Maybe you can pray for her." *And for me too. I need it every bit as much as Karina right now.*

He sat by the bed for a few hours while confused thoughts circulated through his mind. Finally he stood up. "I'm going to your house, Mom. I'll take care of the plants and the garden. I know that's important to you. I'll trim the roses just like Dad used to. And I'll deadhead the perennials. I'll even paint the trim and clean the garage. You won't recognize the place after I'm done. I'll take you home when you're feeling better."

Slim chance.

Dejected, he kissed her good-bye. His mother was going home, but not with him. He wondered how much time he had left with her.

Karina's nightmares came with recurring frequency. Grotesque monsters with glowing red eyes, huge outstretched claws, and slobbering fangs chased her around her apartment and out into the darkness. Usually they had her father's face.

Shook up and sweating, Karina woke up and lay silently in the dark room, waiting for morning to come. The memories rolled over her in waves even as she lay awake. She recalled the smells, the sounds, and the belt her father used on her when she would hide from him. She remembered the other men he'd bring home, and the horrible things they'd done to her so her father could have vodka.

Nauseated and exhausted, she crawled out of bed and splashed cold water on her face. A generous layer of cover stick lightened the dark rings under her eyes. The thought of breakfast filled her with disgust, so she brewed herself a cup of dark coffee and then set out for the orphanage.

Maria, the adoption coordinator from Perm, called her on the phone as soon as Karina stepped in her office. "I've found a prospective couple to adopt Yuri. They're the same people who were unable to take Alexander. They're very excited about this. It should be a good home for Yuri, as they already have an older child. The gentleman will be here in about two weeks."

The good news encouraged her. A bright ray in her gloomy day. She poured a cup of hot water from the kettle and threw a tea bag into it. Letting the beverage cool, she stepped outside for a smoke. Her nicotine intake had doubled the last few days. The fix soothed her emotions. If only it would last.

She still had not heard anything from David, although she could hardly expect it after last Sunday. He'd said good-bye, and she knew that he meant it. Yet her feelings for him were unmistakable.

In love with him, Karina? Frustrated, she shook her head. No, she would not go down that path. David needed his work, the shelter, the kids . . . and she did not fit in that plan. Still, she'd hoped that despite his definite good-bye he would ask her to come to church again. After all, he'd changed his mind before. But several days had gone by, and she had not heard from him or Hannah.

She decided to call Hannah herself. Picking up the phone, she dialed the number.

Hannah sounded delighted. "Karina! I was going to call you today. David tried to get in touch with you yesterday, but couldn't get through. He received a call from his brother to come home. His mother is in critical condition. He left yesterday for the States."

David went to the States? Karina swallowed hard. "I am sorry I missed his call. How long will he be gone?"

"Well . . ." Hannah hesitated. "At least as long as his mother is alive, but she may not have much time left. But there's also another issue. David resigned from the shelter."

Karina nearly dropped the phone. "When did that happen?"

"Monday. Jake took over as director."

Karina gripped the receiver. "Does it have anything to do with my visit on Sunday?"

"Well, that does seem to have sped up the process. But it would've happened sooner or later."

"Not if I hadn't been in the picture." Guilt washed over her.

"Don't worry. It's all part of God's plan, and I know good will come out of it," Hannah tried to encourage her.

"Yes, I am sure," Karina replied sarcastically.

"Don't condemn yourself; it's not your fault. Let's keep in touch. Maybe I can come out to Kungur sometime to visit with you."

"Maybe," Karina responded, flat and uninterested.

She hung up the phone and sank down into her chair. David was gone. He might never come back. Why should he? There was nothing left to come back to. He'd resigned from the shelter, and it was all her fault. Again.

CHAPTER EIGHTEEN

David pounded another nail into the rickety wooden gate of the backyard fence. Perspiration dripped off his forehead and ran in rivulets down his stubble-covered cheeks. He paused, wiping the sweat away with the sleeve of his faded T-shirt.

He lifted the hammer again. He wasn't used to this climate anymore. Perm didn't offer mid-eighties Fahrenheit weather in September.

He drove a few more nails into the chipped post until the gate swung open without dropping in the middle of the turn.

Looking around the yard, he felt pleased with the work he'd accomplished. The trim on the house had a fresh coat of paint. The lawn had been watered and mowed, and the perennials were trimmed and ready for winter.

Even Roger had been impressed with the results. "It should be easy to sell like this," he'd commented when he stopped by.

David realized that the day was coming when they would list the property, yet he dreaded the moment. He knew every inch of the house and the backyard, having lived here during his teenage years. Countless memories were attached to the place, and he wanted to savor the moment.

His dad had passed on in the early eighties, leaving his mother a widow long before retirement. Dad's employment had provided his mom with a reasonable pension plan thanks to his faithful work for the same company for over thirty years.

David walked to the apple tree. Tiny branches crowded one another. A thorough trim would be beneficial next spring. Opening the tree would prevent disease and help it produce more fruit. Some fertilizer to jump-start the growth might be helpful as well.

David hoped that whoever bought the place would care for it just as his parents had. Mom had always babied the trees and the garden until old age prevented her from working outside. Yet she'd lived here until the day of her stroke. David was proud of her tenacity. She had a strong spirit and deep faith in God.

Every time David visited her, sadness penetrated his heart. He remembered his mother as capable and strong; cooking, cleaning, and canning, always caring for her family. Not that he and Roger had appreciated it much as teenagers. They took the clean laundry and wonderful meals for granted. But he'd expressed his appreciation later on as a grown man. The last few years, he and his mother had been close, albeit via a long-distance telephone relationship.

Although Roger was still too busy to take note, David knew he loved his mother in his own way. Too bad he'd chosen such a shabby place for her care. But his brother was right; Mom didn't notice.

David had sat at her bedside for the last week, usually several hours a day. He'd read to her from his Bible, recalled stories from his childhood, and shared articles from a magazine. He still held on to the faint hope that she could hear him and that someday she would open her eyes and speak.

With a sigh, he left the garden and entered the house, placing his shoes on the mat by the back door. He poured a glass of water from a pitcher in the fridge and settled in the leather recliner by the living room window.

His thoughts traveled back to Russia; to the kids and to Karina. He'd spoken with Hannah several times over the past week. Apparently, the teens had taken his advice and moved to the other shelter. He didn't know what Jake's response had been; Hannah avoided all contact with him. She'd spoken with Karina, though. Hannah told David that Karina blamed herself for his forced resignation.

After speaking with Hannah, David had called Karina at the orphanage. The assistant director told him Karina had not been in for a few days. He tried to call Karina at home, but without success.

David carried the glass back to the kitchen sink, and then climbed the stairs to the shower.

He kept a steady visiting schedule with his mother to provide her with a sense of time and routine. Roger hadn't been around for several days. Important business trip to Texas, he explained. David didn't blame him; Mom could be in the same state for weeks.

The staff at the convalescent home had inserted a nasal-gastric tube to prevent starvation. Thankfully, Roger and he were on the same page on that issue.

"Mom's not going to starve to death," he had said, to David's surprise, especially considering his reluctance to spend money on his mother's care.

How long would she hold on to life? Mom had never wanted to be in a palliative state. "Just let me go on to be with the Lord, David," she had said the last time he was in the States. "No artificial machines for me." As if she had known something was about to happen.

It was hard to see her lie there, helpless, a fading shadow of the feisty woman she'd been all her life. The cycle of life and death continued, but David struggled with that reality now that it touched his own life so deeply once again.

He pulled on his boots and walked over to the gray Dodge Aries that had been his dad's vehicle until his passing. With a groan, the old motor chugged to life. The gear creaked into reverse and David backed the car out of the narrow driveway.

I need direction, Lord. I don't mind spending time with Mom, but after she's gone, what then? What do You have for me?

He parked the car adjacent to the palliative-care building and entered the main foyer. The smell of mold beleaguered his nose. *Why are You keeping her here, Lord? This place is not worthy of a woman like my mother.*

He trudged down the hallway to her room. She was still in the same position on the bed, her color the same ghastly bluish gray. David bent over the pale form and kissed the parchment-like skin, crisscrossed with tiny blue veins. Her cheek was cold to his touch. He felt the indomitable hand of death upon her. Filled with gloom, he sat down on the orange plastic chair.

He would've liked to hear what she had to say about the situation at the shelter, and about his senseless, destructive love for a woman who didn't know the Lord. She'd tell him the same thing as the board. Walk away. Don't get involved.

Dr. Hudson entered the room, a beige file in his hand. David had spoken with him on several occasions during the last week. He was a good man with a heart for his patients. Probably the only good thing about the care center.

"Your mother's condition has been deteriorating rapidly today. Her heart rate has been erratic and her blood pressure has dropped considerably, despite the increased IV fluids. Her chest has been getting congested. I can't give you a time frame, but it won't be long. I'll be here most of the day. Feel free to call me if you need to."

David swallowed the lump in his throat as a sick feeling oozed into his body. He clenched his fists. Every fiber in his being fought against the impending reality of her passing, but he'd known this was coming. Death crept stealthily forward and he was unable to stop it.

David called Roger on his cell phone. "If you want to see her alive one more time, you need to come."

Roger promised he'd return as soon as his business was finished, but it might be a day or so. David flipped the phone closed. He hoped Mom would hold on until Roger returned.

David made his way to the cafeteria, ordered the daily special, and sat in the corner by the window. Chewing on dry spaghetti and garlic bread, he watched the sun set behind a willow tree. A picture-perfect September day . . . . if one didn't need to spend it in a palliative-care unit. He sipped coffee out of the plastic mug and pushed back the half-empty plate of spaghetti. His mind wandered across the parking lot, down the road to the airport, and across the ocean to the orphanage in Kungur.

Karina moved her chair away from the desk and reached for the bottle of aspirin. Another pounding headache had settled across her forehead. She hadn't suffered from migraines for at least ten years. Nauseated, she washed the pill down with a cup of lukewarm tea. She couldn't stomach the coffee at the orphanage anymore. She couldn't stomach much, for that matter. Her clothes hung on her thin frame. The mere thought of food brought on a wave of bile.

Cold sweat formed on her forehead. She had not been sleeping well, the nightmares vivid and intense. For hours, she lay awake, waiting for the morning light. Her hand trembled as she picked up the pen again. She had to finish the papers for Yuri's court case. The father had arrived and would be at the orphanage tomorrow.

Hannah had called her every couple of days until she shut off her phone in the apartment. She couldn't talk to anyone. David had left, and it had been her fault. Just like her little boy who'd died. If only she'd brought him into the orphanage rather than put him on the steps . . . .

Hannah told her on the phone there was no condemnation in Christ. But her life was full of condemnation. She didn't deserve a man like David. He was better off without her. She missed him so much she thought her heart would explode. Dared she hope that he missed her as much as she missed him?

Taking a deep, shaky breath, she picked up the phone and dialed his number.

<hr>

David sat by his mother's bed until late in the evening. He read the *National Post*, his Bible, *Time* magazine, and *Gardening Today*. His options of reading material depleted, he dropped his head back on the chair and prayed.

The nurse woke him during the final evening rounds. "It's twelve o'clock, Mr. Valensky," she whispered. "Perhaps you should go home."

"Do I need to stay with her tonight?"

The nurse shook her head. "She's stable enough. Why don't you come back tomorrow morning?"

David agreed. He really didn't look forward to a long night on a lumpy cot in a suffocating hospice room.

By the door, he cast one more glance at his mother's silent frame. "Good night, Mom. I'll be back tomorrow."

He walked down the corridor to the after-hours exit and stepped out into the crisp, clear night. Breathing deeply, he looked up at the millions of twinkling stars.

"God, I know You're at my side and I have nothing to fear. I'd rather go with You in the dark than go alone in the light. But please guide me."

A quiet peace settled over him. A peace which had its foundation on the knowledge that God was in control of every detail of his life.

Vanessa glanced at her watch for the twentieth time in half an hour. Jared had left for Russia early the previous morning for the first visit with Yuri. Rather than going together on this trip, they'd decided that Jared would go by himself to sign the proposal and Vanessa would join him for their court appearance.

He should have been there by now. Why hadn't he called? Had he missed a flight? A bad accident? A plane crash?

Stop it. You'll drive yourself crazy!

Pacing in her kitchen, she prepared a simple evening meal. She wasn't hungry, and Annie didn't like vegetables, so macaroni and cheese would be enough.

"Why don't you pray, Annie?" she asked her daughter.

"Bless this food and drink," Annie prayed loudly after Vanessa placed the pan on the coaster in the middle of the table. "And be with my daddy in Russia. And my little brother. In Jesus' name, amen."

"Amen," Vanessa echoed.

After supper, Vanessa cleaned up the dishes and tucked Annie into bed.

"I'm sure Daddy will call soon," she assured her daughter. "As soon as he visits your new brother."

Annie nodded. "I'll share my toys and my room with him and teach him English!"

Vanessa kissed her daughter on the top of her crown of blonde hair. "Good night, sweets."

For the rest of the evening Vanessa busied herself with different projects around the house to stay occupied. Just as she'd convinced herself that he was dead, Jared called.

"Why didn't you call sooner?" Vanessa blurted out. "It's eleven o'clock. I've been waiting all night. What happened?"

"Lots of things happened," Jared replied. "I had a delay in London, and then again in Moscow. I missed the evening flight to Perm and had to book a different ticket. I got stuck in that small airport without cell phone reception and couldn't figure out how to use the land line."

"Did you get in touch with Maria?"

"I am going to see Yuri this afternoon."

Vanessa sighed with relief. "Call as soon as you return from the orphanage."

"I will. In three days, the mandatory visits will be completed, and I'll be on my way home. Then we just need to wait a few weeks until the court date is established and we'll come back together."

Vanessa pressed the phone closer to her ear. "I love you, Jared."

"I love you too, baby. Take good care of yourself and Annie. I'll see you soon."

Vanessa placed the telephone in the cradle on the desk. Relieved, she hugged her arms around herself. The end of the journey was in sight.

CHAPTER NINETEEN

David watched Roger park the yellow sports car in their mother's driveway and hop out of the car. He surmised from the buoyancy in his brother's step that his business trip had been successful. As always. David laid the paintbrush on the tray.

"Good work, David!" Roger admired the fresh coat of olive-green paint on the trim of the house and the white siding. "The real-estate market will gobble this place up in a snap, especially with the amount of outsiders moving into Denver. I think we should list it soon."

David glared at him. "Not until after Mom passes on."

"Of course, of course." Roger smoothed his shirt. "Have you been to see her today?"

"I went this morning. She's hanging by a thread." He had spent the entire morning with her and planned to go back that night, but he needed a few hours of physical work to soothe his weary emotions. "Did you stop by to see her on your way here from the airport?"

"No, I came straight to you. You know I've always hated hospitals. If I go, I probably won't stay long."

The hospice was closer to the airport than his mother's house. Roger obviously had driven by. David lifted the paintbrush to the window frame. "I suggest that you come tonight. She's not going to last long."

The dark, dingy room smelled of death and decay. The dim hallway light shed a small beam into the room. David sat by the bed and held his mother's cold hand.

Roger had fled the scene an hour ago. "Mom doesn't know I'm here anyway," he'd said.

The attending nurse stopped by occasionally to check up, but there was nothing she could do. David swabbed his mom's mouth with a small sponge on a stick and read the Scriptures to her.

"The Lord is my shepherd, I shall not want." He knew the psalm by heart, and it comforted him every time. God was always by his side, leading him beside still waters, restoring his soul.

"Her heart rate and blood pressure have dropped very low," the matronly nurse told him on her next round. "It won't be long now." She placed her plump hand on David's shoulder. "Be strong. A better place is waiting for her."

David nodded. He wiped his eyes and continued to pray. The minutes slipped into hours. He kept his finger on her pulse, watching the shallow rise and fall of her chest under the thin, white sheet.

Roger showed up again at midnight, pale-faced and shaken. "I can't take this, David," he whispered. "It's too tough."

"Go on home, Rog," David answered gently. "I'll call you when she's with the Lord." He preferred the peace and quiet over Roger's nervous presence.

The hands of the large clock moved slowly, ticking away each minute. He prayed and meditated on the Word. "Any time now, Mom, and you'll see Jesus face to face."

At two o'clock, her chest ceased its gentle rise and fall. Checking her pulse, David confirmed that she was gone. Tears descended down his face as he folded her hands on top of each other.

"Good-bye, my dearest mother," David whispered, his voice thick with tears. "Until we meet again." He kissed her wrinkled cheek and dropped his head on the edge of the bed.

Images of Danae and Geoff rolled through his mind like a film. Pictures of the black limo with two little coffins, two tiny open graves accepting the two caskets into the fresh earth. His friends and family milled around him with empty words of comfort. He saw Sheila in her black velvet dress, a heavy string of expensive pearls around her creamy neck, her hair done up in an elaborate coiffeur. She'd thrown a red rose in each grave, her face pale and drawn. Her mascara had smudged along her ashen cheeks.

David remembered the pain in her eyes that evening after the funeral, and how he'd stabbed her with his words. "If only you had picked them up . . ." He couldn't touch her, be close to her. No wonder she'd left with Andrew. If only he could change the past.

He remembered Karina, her eyes fearful, saying, "If you knew everything about me, you would leave." He'd been so sure that he wouldn't, that he'd love her forever, even after she'd told him about her abortion and her fling with an American guy. Why hadn't he loved Sheila like that?

Fear not, for I am with you. Be not afraid, for I am your God. I will strengthen you. The Scripture reached him like a soft hush in the night.

Yes, Lord. I will trust You. Just let me make things right.

He straightened his back and sat up in the chair. He needed to let the nurses and Roger know about his mother. One last time he touched her hand. Then he reverently stood and left the room.

The funeral took place in a small Baptist church on the edge of Denver, the one his mother had faithfully attended for many years. Old friends and a few remaining family members showed up to honor Martha Valensky and to support David and Roger. Roger's children had flown in from the East Coast. They stood silently by their father at the head of the wooden casket. David stood alone on the other side.

People filed by in slow procession and greeted him with a hearty hug, kiss, or simple handshake. The warmth of the crowd should have comforted him, but he'd been in this setting before, and the cloying smell of the sanctuary swarmed into his nostrils. Woozy, he rested his left hand on the casket. *Lord, help me get through this.*

After the people finished paying their final respects to his mother, the funeral director motioned for the pallbearers to proceed. They lifted the casket off the gurney and carried it to the black limousine. The funeral procession inched through town, lights blinking, until they reached Grace-Mount Memorial.

"Ashes to ashes, dust to dust," the pastor read in a monotone voice. "Martha Valensky has finished her earthly journey and is now praising her Savior in heaven. May God bless the family and friends who will miss her presence."

David didn't know the pastor. He hadn't seen him in the hospital. He didn't blame the man. After all, what was there to do or say?

The black-clad funeral director handed each of the relatives and friends a white carnation to throw into the grave. David stood at the edge of the precipice and threw the delicate flower on the oak casket. *Good-bye, Mom. I miss you so much.*

Roger touched his shoulder, his eyes filled with tears. "I'm so sorry she's gone." His voice cracked. "I should've spent more time with her."

I tried to tell you that, but you wouldn't listen. "Your kids are still alive, Roger. Invest in them. You'll never regret it."

Roger squeezed David's shoulders in a tight bear hug. "Are you coming to the luncheon at my house?" he asked, turning away from the grave as the crowd dispersed.

David shook his head. "Not yet. I want to spend some time here by myself. I'll come in a while."

The two little graves on the other side of Grace-Mount beckoned him. When the people had left, he trudged across the graveyard to the children's section. His shoes seemed to be filled with lead; every step weighed him down.

He knelt on the marble stone, touching the picture of his kids. "My precious Geoff," he whispered. "I miss you so much." He touched Danae's grave with his other hand as he wept, his forehead on the cool marble.

CHAPTER NINETEEN

"Why, Lord? I don't understand." Sobs wracked his body. A nippy wind blew across the graveyard, rustling the leaves of the tall oak above him.

When he finally stood, he noticed a woman on the other side of the path. Sheila! She was dressed in an immaculate turquoise business suit topped with a short suede jacket. Her hair tumbled down her shoulders in long blonde curls. She looked exactly like he remembered: beautiful and striking, the picture of perfection, outwardly at least. Hesitating, she approached him.

Roger had told him he'd seen her at the back of the church. He appreciated her coming to pay her respects to his mother, her mother-in-law at one time, but resentment rose in him at the thought that she'd been watching him here. His pulse quickened as she came close. He hadn't seen her in twelve years.

She stopped in front of him and held out her slender, manicured hand. David looked in her eyes, the eyes that had mesmerized him as a young man. He noticed the pain on her face.

"I'm sorry about your mother," she said, her voice low and melodious.

"Thanks for coming to the funeral. And thanks for looking after these." He pointed to the two ornate Roman vases filled with silk flowers on each side of the double grave. Little purple violets grew around the border of the marble slab. Only Sheila had been close enough to Geoff and Danae to do something so thoughtful.

Tears filled her eyes. She forced a wan smile. "I think of them every day," she said, "as I'm sure you do too. I'm sorry. For everything." Her eyes were downcast, her shoulders stooped.

"I'm sorry I acted as if you were an accomplice to their deaths. It wasn't your fault." He'd carried years of guilt over that accusation.

"No, I mean with Andrew." She dabbed her eyes with a white tissue.

His head jerked up. "I treated you like dirt. I only got what I deserved."

She shook her head. "No. I had no right to cheat on you. I'm sorry."

He turned from the grave and started down the path. Why did she have to bring that up? Why had she even come here?

"I know what you went through," she said, following him.

He stopped and faced her. "How can you know anything about the betrayal, pain, or loneliness?" He spoke sharper than intended and immediately regretted it.

She looked at him with troubled eyes. "Andrew left me for his secretary." Her voice was a mere whisper. Shame filled her beautiful face.

"When?"

"I found out a few weeks ago, but no one else knows yet. We're still the perfect married couple. Respectable citizens." Bitterness laced her voice. She walked to a park bench and sat down, her hands folded in her lap. "I hope you can forgive me for the pain I caused you."

David sat beside her. "I rejected you when you needed me. I took out my grief and anger on you, but it wasn't your fault. Please forgive me."

Sheila nodded solemnly. "We've both made big mistakes. There's no turning back the hands of time, but I want to be able to go on without the guilt. When I saw you come over here, I followed you. I'm sorry if I intruded."

"I forgive you for all you've done. Please forgive me as well. We've both been through a lot." He looked at the broken woman beside him.

She lifted her chin and waved her hand as if to dismiss the pain. "When are you going back to Russia?"

"I don't know." David stood and raked his hand through his hair. He didn't want to talk about the situation in Russia with an ex-wife he hadn't seen in years.

She got the hint. She rose on her high-heeled pumps. "I should be going. Take care, David." She dropped her head and started down the path.

David caught her sleeve. "Wait." He wrapped his arms around her slender frame.

For a brief moment, she returned his embrace. "God bless you, David." A curtain of tears shimmered in her eyes.

"God bless you too."

As she made her way down the cobblestone path, David felt a weight slide off his shoulders. Despite his mother's passing, he felt freer than he had in years.

CHAPTER NINETEEN

—◦◦◦—

"We have to put that place up for sale," Roger told David in the granite-floored foyer of his elaborate home as David got ready to leave the gathering. "May as well do it now before you head back to Russia."

David still hadn't told his brother about the turn of events at the shelter, and he was in no mood to discuss a home sale on the day of the funeral. "Let's get together later this week and talk about it."

"Of course. I understand." Roger had lightened up considerably after his last two martinis. He draped his arm over the shoulder of his latest girlfriend, a twenty-something-year-old with dyed red hair and pale skin. Resisting a frown, David bade them good night.

Stepping out into the fresh night air, he walked to the car. He picked up his cell phone from the faded seat of the Aries. The "low battery" light flashed orange. He checked his list of received calls. Three from an unknown caller. Some distant relative trying to express condolences, no doubt. They should have left a message. After powering the phone down, he threw it back on the seat.

—◦◦◦—

Bathed in sweat, Karina jolted upright in bed. Her hand trembled as she reached for the light switch on the lamp beside the bed. Had she heard a noise in the apartment? Or on the street below?

It's just another spooky dream. No one is here.

She listened for another minute and then trudged to the bathroom. Two dark eyes, lined by blue circles in an ashen face, stared back at her in the mirror. Shaking, she opened a vial and popped a Valium into her mouth. She washed it down with a tumbler of tepid tap water.

The baby's cry in her dream had been intense and piercing. Karina had searched around, groping to find the little one, but when the crying died down Karina saw the baby, dead, on the steps of a stark gray building. His eyes gaped in a blank stare. Karina tried to reach him,

185

but he evaporated into thin air beneath her touch. He didn't look like the baby who had been placed on the steps of the Kungur orphanage. He had dark hair, framing a cream-skinned face. Her baby.

"I am so sorry, Dmitry," she whispered into the mirror. "You'll never know how sorry."

She splashed cold water on her face. Heading back to the bedroom, she pulled on her jeans and sweater. There was no sense going back to bed. She would lie in bed, wide awake, too afraid to go back to sleep.

She trundled into the dark kitchen and flicked on the light switch above the small stove, then grabbed the kettle. After filling it with water, she put it on the small stove. Hopefully a cup of tea would settle her emotions. She glanced at the clock: three thirty. This past week she had not been able to sleep any later. No wonder she felt tired and sick. She plopped down on the couch and picked up the television remote. Not that there would be any good programs on at this hour. She dropped the remote.

She'd dialed David twice the previous day, but he hadn't answered. Should she try again? It would be mid-afternoon in the States right now. She picked up the phone and called. Still no answer. Karina threw the cordless phone on the couch by the remote. Obviously, he didn't want to talk to her anymore.

No one cared for her. If she killed herself, the police might find her rotting corpse a week later when the neighbors complained about the stench. Unless the orphanage decided to see why she wasn't coming to work.

If you die, no one will miss you. You are worthless, good-for-nothing trash, like your dad always said. You killed your baby, remember? If you'd taken care of him, he wouldn't have died. Finish off that bottle of Valium and your pain will be gone for good.

Karina shook her head. She didn't want to die; she wanted to live, but not in this pain.

God, I don't know what to do. Help me! I'm an awful person and I am all alone.

Karina walked to the living-room window. Thousands of stars lit the sky. *Jesus, help me. I don't want to die, but I feel this force and I'm afraid.*

CHAPTER NINETEEN

She stood at the window until the night sky gave way to a glorious crimson dawn. Low-lying fog covered the ground like smoke. In need of fresh air, Karina shrugged into her cardigan and pulled on her shoes. Exiting the apartment building, she walked down the street. Yellow and crimson-colored leaves crunched beneath her feet. More floated down in the breeze and joined the myriad of others on the ground.

Karina came to the river, following the path that she and David had taken together. She strode to the riverbank. The calming flow of the water buoyed her spirits. The sinister dreams ebbed out of her soul. She wandered along the river to the edge of town. Sitting on the gravelly ground, she skipped a few pebbles across the water.

David was gone and she missed him intolerably. If only she could have a second chance. . . . She would search the Bible to see if his faith held any truth for her. She couldn't deny that she'd had some interesting answers to prayer, but that could simply have been coincidence . . . .

Why not still do that now? Even if David never comes back, don't you want to know the truth? She'd have to prove the Bible factually.

She threw another pebble into the water. Apparently, Jesus walked *on* water. Rather tough to prove *that* factually.

Following the river, she walked back to the main thoroughfare. Enormous billboards lined the poorly paved road. The first one featured a huge, empty cross with a large throng of people in the background. "Power to Change," the caption read. "Wait no longer for freedom!" IRR/TV, Channel 14, 10:00 A.M., Saturday and Sunday.

Karina's heartbeat quickened. She glanced at her watch; eight thirty. She had plenty of time to get home to watch the broadcast.

CHAPTER TWENTY

A realtor listed the house the day after the funeral. David didn't try to stop Roger. After all, their mother was dead. She didn't need the old abode anymore now that she had a mansion of gold and diamonds. Yet David thought the whole deal was disrespectful. Could they not wait a week, or even a few days?

"I may not be going back to Russia," David told Roger as he stopped by his office to sign the real estate contract. He related the story of his resignation.

Roger laughed. "All that trouble over a woman? And knowing you, I'll bet you didn't even kiss her."

David smirked humorlessly. He didn't feel like divulging the details of his relationship with Karina to his brother. "I'll move out of the house as soon as the place sells. Why don't you stop by sometime and see what you'd like to have from Mom's belongings."

Roger dismissed the offer with a wave of his hand. "I have enough stuff. I don't need her retro junk from the sixties. Just get the lawyer going on those stocks of hers."

"I'll call him soon," David promised.

After returning to his mother's place, David busied himself in the house. Roger insisted the furniture stay until the place sold. "It doesn't look good empty," he'd said, which David knew to be true.

But he could empty the cupboards, closets, and dressers and box up the clothing and other items as donations to the Salvation Army. He ended up with a few dozen boxes to be sent to the thrift store.

Lord, where am I going from here? What is there for me to do?

As he took the bedding from the hallway closet and placed it in a cardboard box, he realized that he, like the kids at the shelter, had become an orphan.

David loaded the boxes into the Aries. The passenger seat, backseat, and trunk were crammed to the brim. Slipping into the driver's seat, he drove to the south side of town.

The lady at the thrift store welcomed him with open arms when he told her he had an entire household to dispose of. He left the store, steering the car south onto the I-25.

A soft breeze whispered through the trees and the sun shone vibrantly. Despite the exhaust fumes on the freeway, he detected a hint of mountain air. He inhaled deeply. Something stirred in his soul.

Why not take off for one of Colorado's beautiful scenic areas? He had no obligations, no one waiting for him, no one to question his whereabouts. The melancholy of the previous days lifted as the car chugged down the busy four-lane highway. An hour later he parked by the Garden of the Gods in Colorado Springs. The mystical sandstone formations towered before him while the mighty Rockies stood guard in the distance. David slipped out of the car and headed down the winding red shale path. He slung his small backpack over his shoulder. A Bible and a water bottle were all he needed.

The sun had risen to its zenith and pushed the temperature into the eighties as he climbed the trail straight up between the peaks. At the top of a hill he found a comfortable spot against a stubby pine tree and sank onto the needled ground. He leaned back against the tree and pulled out his Bible.

Lord, I commit my way to You. I don't know what to do or where to go, but I rest in the assurance that You do all things perfectly. You make no mistakes. I am at peace with my situation and I will wait upon You.

He tugged on the snap of the leather Bible cover. The worn Bible flipped open on his lap. David's gaze fell on Genesis 28:15, the account of Jacob fleeing Esau because he had deceived him.

"I am with you and will watch over you wherever you go, and I will bring you back to this land. I will not leave you until I have done what I have promised you," God told Jacob.

David stared in wonder at the turquoise-and-crimson sky as the sun painted a brilliant pallet of colors behind the peaks. *Lord, are You speaking to me? Do You want me to go back to Russia someday?* He knew this promise in the Bible was for Jacob, but God spoke through His Word to His children today.

He read the text again. The words leaped up off the page as if they were magnified. God *was* speaking to him. Clouds drifted across the horizon, casting a dark shadow over the top of the mountain. David watched the heavenly spectacle unfold. Dark had battled light even from the brink of creation.

The clouds parted, and once again the sun shone down on the garden and its rocky formations, warming David's skin. He pondered the story of Jacob, who had fled Canaan because of his brother Esau. His own doing, but God promised to bring him back. Jacob was heir to the promise that God had given to Abraham.

He, David, had been wronged, but would God restore him to his rightful position? He didn't know, but one thing was clear: God vindicated His people in Bible times, and He would vindicate His people now. It was only a matter of time.

After seeing the billboard with the TV advertisement, Karina rushed home to watch the ten A.M. broadcast, "The Power to Change."

She threw her shoes in the hall and hurried into the living room to turn on the television. Spellbound, she watched as dozens of young men in a Russian prison listened as the pastor gave the message of God's love and forgiveness.

"God wants to forgive your sins," he said. "You don't need to live in the mire of your bad thoughts, your addictive habits, and all those things you struggle with. Jesus came to set you free! He came to earth to die for your sins. Not only will you go to heaven with Him, but

He'll also enable you to overcome addictions like alcohol, pornography, lying, and stealing." He paused to look at the prisoners. "He'll also deliver you from your suicidal thoughts and fears. *You* can be free. Put aside your doubts about God's existence: repent and believe on Jesus. He will show you the truth."

Tears streamed down Karina's face. As the prisoners knelt on the floor of their concrete prison, she knelt on the carpet. Without a shadow of a doubt, God had sent this program for her.

"Confess all you have done to Him," the preacher continued, "and He'll forgive your sins. He'll wash you clean, and you'll know His peace in your heart."

Karina wept as she told God all the sinister secrets of her life. Time stood still as Jesus entered her heart and commanded the darkness to leave.

For several minutes, she lay on the floor as a quiet peace enveloped her. The program ended, and a text message flashed on the blank screen, giving a Web address for the program and the message "Get in touch with other believers in your town." She filed the site away in her brain and turned off the television.

"Thank You, Jesus. Thank You for forgiving me. For not giving up on me when I was about to give up on life. Thank You for Your love." She basked in the overpowering presence of God, who had given her such an amazing gift.

Karina slept more peacefully that night than she had in years. She woke up at nine o'clock on Sunday morning as the sun cast its bright rays through the creamy sheers in front of the bedroom window. She spent the day reading the Bible, particularly the Gospels. She loved the Sermon on the Mount and the parables, remembering many of them from David's visits with the children at the orphanage.

Mary Magdalene reduced her to tears. Mary, whom Jesus had delivered from many demons. Mary, the prostitute who washed Jesus' feet with her hair, totally against the tradition of the Pharisees. "A loose woman," they said to one another. "If this man is a prophet, He would know who is touching Him." But Jesus didn't care; He loved her just the way she was. Just as he had her, Karina Svetlana Ilyanova Gorsky.

The following day at the orphanage, she looked up the IRR/TV site and punched in "Kungur" under the search button of "church fellowship." The name Leonid Molotov appeared with a phone number. Hesitating, she dialed the number.

Leonid's deep voice boomed through the phone line. "We'd be delighted to meet you," he told her as she shared her story. "We are just a little group," Leonid told her, "but we love the Lord and we would love to meet you too."

She obtained the address where the meeting would be held and promised to come.

Karina shifted uneasily on the wooden chair in the hazy living room at Leonid's home. Good to her word, she'd come to meet the other Christians. A dozen people had gathered around on this cold October evening. As the only newcomer in the group, she felt out of place. She sat in a corner by the door, having snuck in at the last moment. She hoped with all her heart that she could leave unnoticed at the end of the service.

Leonid clapped his hands to silence the noisy group. "Welcome, everyone," he thundered. His intense eyes surveyed the group and came to rest on Karina. His penetrating gaze sent nervous shivers up her back.

"Tonight is a special night. We have a new guest with us: Karina Gorsky. Our sister is new to the faith, so please make her feel welcome."

Karina had read Leonid's biography on the Internet site of IRR/TV. He had spent ten years in Siberia on account of his faith. After his release he became involved with outreach to needy families in the Kungur area. His wife, Anja, sat next to him, wearing a traditional scarf on her head. Her hands were folded in her lap over her straight black dress. Every time her husband spoke about God, her face lit up with a joyous smile.

The group was divided equally between men and women, most of them elderly. Their attire told Karina that they were working-class people, most likely employed on farms or in factories around the town.

A young man played a hymn on a guitar, and the group joined the song. Karina listened to the words. "Christ the Lord is risen today." At the hallelujah chorus, the voices rose like a mighty wave crashing on the shore. Karina had never heard such volume from so few people. *These people sing with their hearts.* She closed her eyes, allowing the lyrics to sink into her soul.

She heard deep conviction in their voices as they sang of their Savior. Their eyes were filled with joy and hope, a hope that Karina finally understood. The past had not changed, nor had the present, but she now saw beyond it all to One far greater than anything she faced. God was for her, and everything else paled in comparison. For the first time, she grasped the significance of David's ministry in Perm among the street kids whose lives reflected the hopelessness so evident in atheistic Russian society.

"There is no God," they'd been taught in the schools and universities, even after the fall of communism. They'd been duped and lied to by the authorities. Thank God she'd found out the truth before she came to the point of no return!

She had not told Ina about her newfound faith. If she told her she'd become a Christian, Ina would suspect Karina had done so for David's sake.

Nor had she told Hannah; David didn't need to hear about the change in her life. He had not answered her calls. She refused to stir up something that was not meant to be. Her heart ached. He would've been so excited to hear what had happened to her.

The music died down, and Leonid opened his Bible. Karina took the small New Testament David had given her out of her purse.

"Isaiah chapter nine verse six," Leonid said. "For to us a child is born. To us a son is given. And the government will be on his shoulders."

She couldn't find the book of Isaiah. The rest of the group didn't seem to have a problem. They eagerly followed along in their Bibles.

The young man who had played the guitar during the singing caught her eye. He was dressed in simple clothes: a navy blue sweater, faded jeans, and black shoes. His sandy brown hair lay flat against his high forehead. He smiled, creasing the tiny lines around his lively brown eyes.

Heat crept up into Karina's neck and face. He probably knew she couldn't find the passage! *And so what, Karina? Is that such a big deal? Don't worry about it.* Lifting her chin, she met his gaze and smiled back.

CHAPTER TWENTY-ONE

David boxed the last few of his mother's belongings. Contemplative, he folded the flaps of the box closed. An era of his life had come to an end. Both his parents had passed on to be with the Lord. He no longer had a home in Colorado. In fact, he no longer had a home anywhere. The house had sold two days after it went on the listing, with possession scheduled for the middle of November, giving him only a few weeks to find new accommodations.

Where do I go from here, Lord?

That night, during a CNN update on the "war against terrorism," Vladimir called. "We need to talk."

"What's going on?"

"We're having problems at the shelter. The board would like to know if you could return as soon as possible."

Just like that? No apologies, no explanations?

"I don't understand."

"The board realizes they made a mistake by dismissing you. I'm sorry for all that happened."

David chewed on his cheek. "So what's the problem?"

"Almost all of the kids are gone. Both shelters are empty except for a few younger children. The older kids left the east-side shelter and have disappeared. If the older ones don't come back, we may

CHAPTER TWENTY-ONE

have to close the place down. You warned us, but we didn't take it seriously."

"Where did they go?"

"Back on the street."

David's heart sank. All their work in Perm seemed to have been spoiled in a few short weeks.

"We'd like you to work as shelter coordinator and oversee the orphanage program again. Jake will take care of the administration."

So he wasn't getting his position as CEO again. Apparently, they only wanted him there to get the teens back. And he might have to answer to Jake.

"I need to pray about it. I'll call you tomorrow."

David struggled all night. He tossed and turned, thought and prayed. Perhaps his wounded pride wanted too much. Why did he care about being in charge of the leadership of the organization? But why did their request leave such a bitter taste in his mouth?

Trust in the Lord with all your heart, and lean not on your own understanding. Remember Jesus, who made Himself of no esteem but took on the appearance of a servant.

The first glimpse of daylight filtered through his window when he finally reached a conclusion. He slipped out of bed and picked up the phone.

"I'm coming," he told Vladimir. "I'll call you when I get to the airport."

Karina's life had settled into a peaceful routine. She went to the weekly meetings at Leonid and Anja's house on Sundays and attended the mid-week prayer service, which was held in the home of one of the church members. The people regularly invited her over for dinner before the service. Contrary to her previously solitary disposition, she enjoyed the evenings away from her apartment.

She looked forward to the weekends, eager to learn more about her newfound faith in the God of the Bible. Her fears had disappeared and her restlessness had settled down.

Leonid had invited her to share her testimony at one of the gatherings, but she had tactfully refused. The transformation in her life was too fragile to put into words and her past was still too painful to speak about. To her dismay, her feelings toward her father had not changed. Anger still bubbled in her heart like molten lava looking for a place to vent.

She straightened a few papers on her desk and glanced at her watch. It was almost time to head home from the orphanage.

Ina peeked around the corner of her office. "A young man is waiting for you at the door."

Karina frowned. She wasn't expecting anyone. Standing up, she followed Ina to the front door.

Boris, the guitarist from the home group, leaned against the doorjamb. His navy blue sweater hung loosely on his thin frame. His chocolate-colored eyes lit up when he saw her. "Hello."

Karina returned his greeting. Boris, Leonid's youngest son, attended the Technical University in Perm during the week, while spending his weekends in Kungur. She guessed him to be in his mid-twenties, several years younger than herself.

"I wondered if I could walk you home," he said cheerfully. "Seeing it's almost five o'clock, I thought you might be ready to go."

Karina found herself at a loss for words. "That would be fine," she mumbled. "Let me turn off my computer and grab my coat."

He waved his hand. "No hurry. Take your time."

A slow drizzle dripped from the lead-gray sky, carrying yellow and red leaves off the trees to the ground, creating a slippery surface on the asphalt. Karina and Boris carefully navigated their way around the puddles.

"My favorite time of year," Boris announced. "Cool, crisp fall weather." He kicked leaves into the air. A healthy red glow colored his cheeks and his eyes danced with hidden pleasure. His wet hair lay plastered against his forehead. "It's a marvelous time to be alive."

Karina laughed. Yes, it was good to be alive, fully alive for the first time in her life.

"Care to come in for coffee?" she asked as they arrived at her apartment.

He shook his head. "Mom's waiting with supper. How about I pick you up tomorrow afternoon? We'll have to walk because I don't have a car, but we can go to the coffee shop on main street."

Karina nodded. "That would be great. I look forward to it." To her surprise, she meant it.

She hummed a little tune as she walked into the apartment and took off her jacket. The fresh coat of buttercup yellow paint on the walls greeted her warmly. She looked at the new picture on the wall. Cost her a fair penny, but she'd been unable to resist the sweet scene of ladybugs and butterflies on purple and yellow irises.

In the dining room, she had hung a wallpaper border sporting the same flowers. The sunny environment lifted her spirits. She had not bought anything new for her house since she moved in a year and a half ago. The second-hand, dilapidated furniture that furnished her suite had been included in the rental.

Entering into the living room, she stopped by the phone. During her depression, she'd left the answering machine off for weeks. Anyone who needed to get in touch with her could call her at work, she'd reasoned. But since attending the church and their various get-togethers, she'd turned on her answering machine again. The little light blinked steadily. She pushed the button to retrieve the message.

"Hey, Karina, this is Hannah. I tried calling you several times but couldn't get through. I wanted to let you know that David is coming back to Perm."

Karina dropped onto her couch. Had he asked Hannah to call her? Probably not. He could have called her himself if he had wanted to let her know. Of course, he might have tried to call when her answering machine was unplugged. But he hadn't answered her phone calls either. She hadn't left a message, but he should've recognized the number. *And what if he didn't?*

Beads of sweat formed on her forehead and upper lip. His mother had died a few weeks ago, Hannah had mentioned in a previous phone call. What must he be going through right now? Would he start working at the shelter again? Why was he returning to Perm? Perhaps Jake had left? Should she call David? Quickly, she rejected the idea. No, he could easily contact her now that her phone was working again. She would leave the first contact up to him. If he sought to renew their relationship. But why would he?

She dialed Hannah's number. Hearing Hannah's exuberant greeting sent a wave of guilt through Karina. She should've called Hannah sooner.

"I got your message," Karina said as nonchalantly as possible. "David's coming back to Perm?"

"We've had some difficulties at the shelter. The board asked David to return. They're hoping he can remedy the situation. He should be here by the end of this week."

"Did he . . . say anything about me?"

"I didn't speak to him: Vladimir did. But I tried to call you several times. Have you had phone trouble?"

"No." Psychological trouble was more like it.

"I'll tell him you called."

"Please don't. I'd rather wait for him to contact me when he's ready."

"As you wish. But do visit us sometime. I had such a good time last month when you were here."

Karina promised she would, then she sat on the bed, her legs crossed, and stared at the drab October cityscape.

She picked up the phone and called Leonid's residence. Boris answered.

"I won't be able to go out for coffee with you after all," she told him. "I've changed my mind."

―――❧❧❧―――

Moscow greeted David in dismal gloom. The city lay shrouded in a haze of gray fog. Cab drivers huddled deep into their black wool coats, their breath forming puffy clouds that hung in the frigid air.

He crossed the double-lane road to the bus stop and glanced at his watch. Eight-twenty P.M. The shuttle to Sheremetyevo Terminal 2 came every half hour. He jerked the two heavy suitcases onto the curb and put his computer bag on the ground.

Another ten hours and he would be in Perm. What would he find? Would the kids confide in him, or would they distrust him now?

And how about Karina? He hadn't spoken to her since he left over a month ago. He'd given up trying to call her after the first week, and following his mother's death he lacked the mental energy. He tucked his gloveless hands in his pockets and stomped his cold feet. He should've been more prepared, but who could have guessed this after the balmy weather in Colorado?

The bus pulled up to the curb. David hoisted his suitcases up the steps and placed them in the cargo bin. Dropping onto a seat, he contemplated his reunion with Jake. How would he react to his return? Would they be able to have a civil relationship at all?

In the waiting room at the airport, David settled onto a steel-gray chair. A well-dressed young couple sat down next to him. Surprised to hear them speaking English, David glanced up from his *Daily Times*.

"English?" he queried.

The man focused on David's face. "Canadian. You?"

"American. Where are you going?"

"My wife and I are going to Perm. We're picking up a little boy we've adopted."

"I lived in Perm for thirteen years." David folded his newspaper. "My name is David Valensky." He extended his hand.

"Jared." They shook hands. "This is Vanessa." The man pointed to his wife.

"What did you do in Perm?" the lady asked.

"I was in charge of shelters for street kids, as well as an orphanage ministry."

"Not there anymore?"

David grimaced. "I took a break. A death in the family. I'm heading back now. Which orphanage are you going to?"

"Kungur," the woman answered. "Djetskii Dom Number Two. Do you know it?"

David hid his surprise. "Yes. A friend of mine is the director there."

"Ms. Svetlana?" Jared asked. "Small world. We'll have to mention you when we see her tomorrow."

David swallowed his chagrin.

"Such a nice lady," Vanessa said, "and so good to the kids. We met her last spring when we came to see another little boy, but he couldn't come to Canada due to FAS."

That was you? David wanted to exclaim, but he refrained himself. "I know the boy you tried to adopt. Alexander's mom was in our shelter while she was pregnant. I picked the baby up at her residence right after birth and transferred him to the hospital."

The woman stared at him, her eyes wide. "Could you please tell us more?" She slid to the edge of her seat. "Any information would be welcome."

David related Alexander's story, starting with Sofia's arrival at the shelter in the middle of the winter, inebriated and half frozen, and then her sudden disappearance, only to appear again through the call of an acquaintance in Kutchino, asking him to transport the baby. After that he had lost track of the child until Karina told him about the failed adoption. Not until then had he known the baby was in Kungur.

He also remembered Karina's anger when the adoption fell through, but he didn't tell Jared and Vanessa about that.

"Don't talk about this to anyone in Russia," he cautioned. "I probably shouldn't have told you all this."

Vanessa's eyes misted over. "You are an answer to prayer. We were told that Alexander had FAS but we didn't have proof. Now we know for sure that this was God's will. I have closure."

David smiled at her. Closure was important. He'd come to understand that even deeper after seeing Sheila. His mother's death still grieved him deeply, but God had renewed his call once again, and he was ready to go back.

The city of Perm greeted David with dismal sobriety. But David didn't care about the gloomy gray buildings. He was home!

Vladimir met him at the airport. "I brought the old Toyota," he grinned, slapping David on the back. "I thought you might like that."

"Thanks, man." David lifted his suitcases on the back and hopped in the driver's seat. "Tell me about the shelter," he said as they drove away from the airport.

"I don't know much other than what I told you on the phone. There seems to be an issue with Jake and the kids."

David frowned. "I never noticed that when I was there, but I could've missed it."

"There are only a few kids left at the main shelter," Vladimir said. "One of the older teens looks after them."

Half an hour later, David parked in the courtyard behind the building. He followed Vladimir into the familiar building. The door squeaked as if reluctant to let them enter. Oppressive silence hung in the air. Their footsteps echoed on the wood floor.

Except for four people at the table, the living room was empty. Katya, Anton, and Inna, the three youngest children at the time of his departure, leaped off their chairs at the sight of him.

"Papa David!" Screaming wildly, they rushed for his outstretched arms.

"Hey, you rascals!" He swung Inna into the air and caught her again.

"We missed you so much!" Katya clung to his neck, and Anton hung on his leg.

"I missed you too." Flopping down onto a chair, he placed them on his knee. "Tell me all that's happened while I've been gone."

Katya's face grew somber. "All the older kids have left and we're the only ones here now."

David eyed the little ones intently. "That's not nice for you, is it?"

They shook their heads. "We want the others to come back."

"I don't know if I can bring them back, but I can take you to Hannah and the other younger kids."

Rachael, one of the older teens who'd been at the shelter for several years, rose from her chair and sauntered to Vladimir and David.

"Jake hired Rachael to look after the children," Vladimir explained.

"Welcome back," she said, looking at David without a hint of pleasure.

"I'll take the younger kids to Hannah's. You may as well go there also," David told her. "Please pack up the children's stuff so that we can go."

Resentment crossed her face, but she didn't resist. "I'll be ready," she said as she turned to leave the room.

⁂

Hannah greeted David exuberantly as he stepped inside.

"Thank God you're back." She threw her arms around him in a tight embrace.

David returned her greeting. "I have three more kids and a teenager who want to come here from the main shelter."

Hannah frowned. "We're very full, even though the older teens have left. We have all the younger kids here. Several of them are sleeping on the floor."

"I think the main shelter will be up and running in a very short time." He threw a tote bag of clothing on the floor. "The little ones really missed the others." He walked to the outside door. "Can I bring the kids in?"

The three children hid behind David's back, but Hannah's warm greeting drew them out of their shell. She ushered the children into the living room to play with the others.

David entered the room behind them. His arrival was met with loud enthusiasm. The children thronged around him, smothering him with hugs and kisses.

"OK, OK," he laughed, loosening himself from their grip. "It's great to be here with you, but I need to go now. I'll come to visit tomorrow."

He wanted to get out on the streets to search for the teens as soon as possible. The weather had taken a turn for the worse, and although he believed that Georgi would find a good hide-out, he wasn't sure all the kids were together.

From Hannah's, he drove back to the main shelter; the weather was cold and he needed extra clothes before heading out.

Jake met David at the door of the shelter as he pulled his heavy suitcase up the crumbly concrete steps. Tension filled the air. "Where do you think you're going?" Jake asked, pointing at the suitcase.

CHAPTER TWENTY-ONE

"I'm staying here with you."

"Any particular reason?"

"I want to be here should the kids return."

"I see you've emptied the place."

"If you call taking the last four kids to the other shelter 'emptying the place,' then yes, I did. There used to be thirty kids in this building." He didn't wait for Jake's reply. "I'll take one of the upstairs rooms."

"Rachael lives up there. Second room to the right."

"I'll pick a different room."

"Oh, no problem. I just thought you might like to be close to her, seeing you lost your little girlfriend in Kungur."

Anger coursed through David's body. He gritted his teeth. "Rachel is staying at Hannah's with the other kids."

"Too bad."

Ignoring Jake, David climbed the stairs, a suitcase in each hand. He opened the door to one of the rooms and dropped onto the cot in the corner. He felt the claws of evil lash out at him. He balled his fist. He'd fight for the young people, and he'd get them back. How and when he didn't know, but like a shepherd, he was ready to lay down his life for the sheep.

CHAPTER TWENTY-TWO

David pulled the collar of his turtleneck sweater over his nose and descended into the dark, dank sewer system. His flashlight chased away the empty darkness. A few rats scurried into the corner. Other than the rodents, the culvert revealed no sign of life. David pulled himself up out of the opening.

He'd been searching for the teens for hours, but without success. The old hang-outs were empty and deserted. He rested against the lamppost on the edge of the dim street. His watch showed nine o'clock. Still early in the evening, but considering his exhaustion from the long flight that morning, he decided to head back to the shelter. The idea of being in the same building as Jake did not appeal to him in the least, but his body begged for rest.

This does not feel like restoration, Lord. It feels like starting all over again, like I did when I first arrived. Where are the teens? What's been happening to them?

He trudged down the empty road in the direction of Lenin Street. How glamorous the mission field looked on the overhead projector in the Colorado Springs People's Church where he had held his fundraiser presentation last spring. Bravely, the entire audience sang "Onward Christian Soldiers, Marching as to War." They probably still sang that song whenever a missionary came to visit. The little old ladies cried in their white hankies and the teens triumphantly raised their hands heavenward.

But where were they now? The battlefield lay empty and deserted before him, the enemy hidden in the bushes like snipers in a phantom war as the soldiers watched the Superbowl back in Colorado, eating popcorn.

OK, cut the cynicism. Deliverance will come. Somehow, sometime. In God's time. Not mine.

What had he expected? Walk back into the shelter and everything would be OK? Hadn't he fought this battle thirteen years ago when he started the shelter? The need of the teens had driven him on then, relentlessly, day after day.

Lord, will it always hurt this much? I asked that question thirteen years ago, and I am asking it again. I am sorry if I am complaining. . . . Forgive me . . . .

He turned a corner into the back alley behind the shelter. Faint light shone through the office window. Jake was probably on the Internet or checking e-mails. David's key creaked in the lock. He promised himself to grease it soon. Careful not to disturb Jake, he plodded up the stairs to his room.

Vanessa hugged Maria as she greeted the couple at the airport. Vanessa was glad to have arrived in Perm once again. Their journey would soon be finished.

"Welcome back," Maria said. "It's good to see you again. Unfortunately, we have no driver available to take you to Kungur today—Sergei is ill—and the other driver is occupied with a couple from the States. I will contact you tonight with arrangements for tomorrow."

Vanessa was relieved: at least they'd get some time to sleep and rest.

That evening, Maria called to announce that Sergei was feeling no better. "I can drive you myself, but I have two court hearings tomorrow for other adoptions. I will call you in the morning."

After hanging up the phone, Jared gave Vanessa the news.

"I really don't want to wait for two days." Vanessa threw her cardigan over the brown, imitation-leather chair. "Are there no other options?"

"I wonder if that man we met on the plane today might be willing to drive us out there. He did say he had an orphanage ministry here in Perm and travels out to Kungur. I'll call Maria and see if she knows him."

Moments after calling Maria, he hung up the phone. "She knows him and will call him. We should know as soon as she can get in touch with him."

David got up early the following morning. The board had requested a meeting with him and Jake. The meeting might provide insight into the dynamics at work, as well as the solution that might be needed to regain momentum. He brewed himself a potent cup of coffee and went to his office.

Vladimir, Ferdinand, and Ivan filed into the room and shook his hand. David greeted the men in return, but remained aloof. Their attitude was not overly welcoming, and he'd been deeply hurt through their actions.

Jake entered and sat down on the faded couch, folding his arms across his chest. He greeted the men around the table with a curt nod, refusing to make eye contact with David.

Ferdinand opened with prayer. "God, please give us a heart to work together in unison so the teens can continue to have a home rather than living on the streets. Please give us all wisdom. Amen."

Vladimir looked at Jake over the top of his metal-rimmed reading glasses. "Let's begin with the financial statements. Jake, you have those?"

"I didn't quite finish." Jake shifted uncomfortably. "Sorry." He licked his lips. "I'll have them ready for the December meeting for sure."

David raised his eyebrows. Two months behind on financials? What *was* Jake doing during those long nights he spent in the office?

Ferdinand cleared his throat. "I suggest that David help you prepare the financials. With the end of the year coming up, we need to have them done in the next few weeks."

Jake looked chagrinned. "Yes, sir. We'll look after it."

Vladimir leaned toward him, elbows on the table. "Why didn't you get those records done in time?"

"Carrying the entire load of the administration for both shelters is a lot of work."

"What a relief it must be for you to have David here then," Vladimir said, leaning back.

Jake responded by casting a dark glance in David's direction.

"For our next item," Vladimir continued, "how are we going to get the teenagers back to the shelter?" He looked around the circle, his eyes coming to rest on David.

"I have some ideas about programs that we could create to draw them in," Jake said.

"I don't think programs are going to make the kids want to come back," Vladimir said gently but firmly.

Ivan nodded. "We just need to find a way to let them know David is back."

"I've looked around the city for several days," David remarked. "I haven't been able to find a trace of them."

"The word will spread as new teens come," Ferdinand spoke up. "I think we need to get the financial records in order immediately so we know where we're at. David can work on those. Once we know, we can decide on what route to take."

Jake stood up out of his chair. "I may as well go then. Sounds like David will have things perfectly under control."

"We do expect you to assist David in whatever he may need."

"Of course." Jake smoothed his shirt. "I'd be happy to."

But the anger that filled his eyes as he looked at David belied his words.

The Canadian couple met David in the hotel lobby at three o'clock that afternoon.

Vanessa greeted him with a huge smile. "Thanks so much for taking us to Kungur, Mr. Valensky. We were afraid that we'd have to miss going today. We missed yesterday too. I haven't met Yuri yet, so this will be very exciting!"

They squeezed into the tiny Toyota; Jared sat next to David in the front, and Vanessa scrunched herself into the narrow space behind the seats.

"A little tight," she laughed, "but we'll get there!"

David listened half-heartedly to her chatter as he maneuvered the Toyota out of the city. He pondered the prospective meeting with Karina. He hadn't spoken with her since her visit to Perm in September. So much had happened since then.

Did she know he was coming? After all, she was expecting Sergei, not him. And if so, did it mean anything to her? Occasionally, he'd been able to break through the thick shield she carried, but did he know the true Karina? Did he even know her real name?

"God's ways are amazing, aren't they, Mr. Valensky?" Vanessa mused as she surveyed the Ural landscape.

"Indeed." He agreed, but had no idea what she was referring to.

"After our last trip here, we were devastated by the loss of Alexander, and now it looks like we'll have another child instead. It's been an incredible journey of learning to trust God in everything."

She slipped her hand into Jared's. "I didn't realize it at first, but God has used this experience to increase our trust in Him. I haven't met Yuri yet, but I know this is the child God has for us. God is at work even when we don't see it."

David glanced at Vanessa. "Thank you for sharing that. I believe that was what God wanted me to hear."

They continued on in silence, all three of them lost in their own thoughts.

"Nervous?" Jared asked Vanessa as David pulled into a parking spot behind the orphanage.

"Not at all. I have complete peace, regardless of what happens."

David chewed on his lip. If only he could say the same thing!

He followed Jared and Vanessa into the building, where Ina welcomed them exuberantly. David translated her rapid Russian for Jared and Vanessa. "She's glad to see you. Yuri has been waiting for you."

Was Karina waiting for him as well?

Ina waddled ahead of them down the long corridor with its peeling plaster walls and faded linoleum.

"I'll wait here," David told Jared as Ina led them around the corner to Karina's office. "Take as much time as you need. I'm not in a hurry."

He walked through the hall and out the back door. Cool winter air flooded his nostrils. Absorbed in thought, he followed the pot-holed road to the edge of the fast-flowing river. The water had frozen solid. He picked up a rock and sailed it far onto the icy surface.

He couldn't shake his bitterness at Jake for destroying the ministry he'd built with his own money, blood, and tears. Thirteen years of work destroyed in six weeks. And now he had to clean up the remains and start from scratch. He had a right to be angry, didn't he?

It's not your ministry, but God's. Release it to Him.

The old log still lay in the same spot as the previous summer. At least some things remained predictable. He sank down on the moist wood and dropped his head into his hands.

If it's God's ministry, don't you think He can take care of it?

"Yes, Lord," David spoke into the stillness. "You are able to care for it, even without me."

So why do you act as if you don't believe that? Has God not been with you all these years?

"You've always been with me. You built the ministry. Gave me what I needed."

How about Karina? Did you not trust God's plan for your life in that situation? Why did you run ahead of God's timing and try to force His hand?

David closed his eyes. Had he not trusted God's timing? Had he desired a woman more than the leading of God? Had he marched ahead in his own strength when he'd invited her to church?

Lord, I'm sorry. I've not followed You as I should have. Forgive me for my bitterness against Jake. I'll take up my cross again, and I will follow You regardless of what happens at the shelter or with Karina. You are in command of my life. I surrender to You. I will not take one step in any direction unless you clearly show me. And that includes Karina.

The heaviness in his spirit lifted, and a song of jubilee rose in his heart. The peace of God rested upon him like a tender blanket. Tears of repentance were replaced by tears of joy.

Karina nodded politely at her visitors. "Good to see you, Mr. and Mrs. Williams. Welcome to Kungur again." She gestured to the chairs on the other side of the bureau. "Can I make you some tea or coffee?"

"Yes, tea please," Jared responded as they sat down.

Karina took the kettle off the shelf. She'd noticed the Toyota as soon as it pulled into the courtyard. Thankfully, she'd had a few minutes to recover from the shock before Ina escorted the guests into her office. Even better yet, David had not come into the office with them.

Plugging in the kettle, she wondered where he was. "Mr. Valensky gave you a ride here?" she asked nonchalantly, spreading a cotton napkin on the desk.

Jared nodded. "I hear you know him."

Karina placed three china cups and saucers on the napkin. "Yes, through his orphanage ministry." She poured the boiling water into the teapot.

Ina tapped on the door and entered with Yuri. Vanessa bent down, holding out the small present she'd brought.

Eyes wide, Yuri sucked on his clenched fist and clung to Ina's leg.

"This is your new mama," Karina told the boy in Russian. "She brought you a gift."

Refusing to look at Jared and Vanessa, he inched toward Karina.

She picked him up. "I'm not sure why he's so shy. He was OK with Jared a few weeks ago." She took the present from Vanessa. "This is for you. You can open it."

Yuri clutched the gift to his chest but refused to take the paper off the box.

Karina sat down and put him on her knees.

CHAPTER TWENTY-TWO

He peeled the tape back carefully so as not to damage the paper. Then, with a wide grin, he pulled a shiny police car from the box. "Spasiba," he whispered, clasping the package against his frayed sweater.

"He said thank you," Karina translated. She cut the plastic off the car with the scissors from her desk and gave it to Yuri, putting him and the toy on the ground. "He is a good boy. You will like him a lot. He is very sweet."

She poured tea into the cups on the desk. "I will leave you for a while to get comfortable with Yuri. There is some tea for him as well." She pointed to one of the cups. "Help yourself to the cookies also. Ina will show you the playroom once you have had your tea."

She translated the information for Ina and then stepped toward the office door. "I'm just stepping out for a few minutes. I'll be back," she said to Ina in Russian.

The matronly lady nodded. "I saw David disappear in the direction of the river."

Color rose in Karina's cheeks. Without another word, she grabbed her coat off the hook and hastened to the door.

Karina spotted David by the river before he saw her. She slowed her step. What if he had found a different woman during his time in the United States? What if he didn't care for her anymore? What if. . . . Unanswered questions crowded her mind. Well, she would soon find out. Lifting her chin, she picked up her pace.

David turned around at the sound of footsteps behind him. He stood in silent surprise as Karina approached. She wore a three-quarter-length cream-colored coat and black trousers. Her face was fuller than he remembered, softening the sharpness of her features. Mesmerized, he watched the woman of his dreams. The woman who had cost him so much. The woman he still loved with all his heart.

"David!" She smiled broadly, her cheeks and lips crimson from the nippy weather.

He didn't know how to respond. *It's in Your hands, Lord. I'm not moving in any direction until You tell me. It's simply too costly.*

Stepping toward her, he held out his hand. "How have you been?"

"I'm doing well." She shook his hand.

"You look like you are." *Gorgeous, ravishing, smashing.* He released her hand and mentally steadied himself. She had a different air about her, a gentler spirit. He scrutinized her face. The long hair was gone, replaced by a shoulder length bob. "You cut your hair."

She smiled. "You like it?"

Her smile was breathtaking. He felt the heat rise to his face.

"Yes. It makes you look kinder and younger."

She laughed out loud. "Kinder, perhaps, but not younger." Her face became serious again. "I've been praying for you. Losing your mother is a difficult thing."

"Yes, it was." Did she say she'd been praying?

She pushed her hands into her pockets. "Hannah told me you are back at the shelter. How are things there?"

"Not good. I'm dealing with some difficult situations."

"I'm sorry to hear that. What brings you here today?"

"I drove the Williams' out as they couldn't get a ride today."

"Yes, I should get back to them. They might have questions."

"I'll come with you," David said.

In amiable silence, they strolled back to the orphanage.

"Thanks for coming out to see me," David turned to her when they reached the building. "God bless you."

She nodded, her eyes dark and mysterious. "God bless you too."

As she disappeared through the door, David slowed his breath. Sweating, he pulled on the collar of his turtleneck sweater. Had she mentioned that she'd been praying for him? Had he really heard her correctly?

The door opened as Vanessa and Jared came toward the truck, broad smiles on their faces. "Yuri's everything we could've hoped for," Vanessa exclaimed, as they climbed into the truck. "Playful, happy, and so cute. First he was shy, but then he warmed right up to us."

David listened as they shared the details of their visit.

"We'll be going to court in a few days to finalize the adoption," Jared said. "We're hoping they'll waive the ten-day waiting period so we can go home early. If not, I'll stay here while Vanessa goes back to Canada to take care of our daughter."

"God has brought us so far," Vanessa said. "I know He'll see us all the way through."

David smiled. "I'm glad the visit went well for you. If you need a driver tomorrow, let me know."

But upon returning to the hotel, Maria told them Sergei had returned to good health. David's service would not be needed the following day.

Disappointed, David said good-bye to Vanessa and Jared, climbed into his truck, and drove back to the shelter.

CHAPTER TWENTY-THREE

David's alarm rang at 5:45 A.M. the following morning. He pulled himself out of bed, determined to get an early start on the financials. Jake would almost certainly not be around at this hour.

Entering the office, he booted the old computer, opened the desk drawer, and fished the bank records out of a manila file folder. He organized the statements month by month, putting the canceled checks on top of each statement. August had been done prior to his departure for the States, so at least he had a starting point. He worked through the records until only the petty cash had to be accounted for.

With a yawn, he stood and stretched. The cash box was kept in the closet. After retrieving it off the shelf, he placed it on the table and reached under the desk for the key. The hook was empty. Jake probably had it. No problem; David carried a spare on his keychain.

He inserted the small key in the lock, which squeaked open. The money tray in the top had been removed. A row of little plastic bags filled with a brownish powder lay in the bottom of the box. Several hypodermic needles and syringes, held together with an elastic band, were neatly arranged next to the bags.

David gripped the edge of the desk. Steadying himself, he locked the box and put it back on the shelf. Devastated, he sank down in the chair behind the computer.

Now he understood why the teens had left the shelter. They must have known the truth all along.

His jaw clamped tight, David powered the computer down. He grabbed his coat off the hook in the hall and stepped out the door. Icy wind and sleet swirled around him. He forged on with no particular destination.

Stefan's tragic death flashed through his mind. He remembered standing in his room, looking down on the rumpled sheets and the empty bed with the blood stain, wondering how Stefan had acquired the drugs. At the time, David had thought the drug lord from Moscow had driven the boy to suicide, causing him to go out and buy the drugs. But more than likely, he'd been supplied internally.

Lord, I thought Jake had the same goals I did, telling kids about Jesus. But he fooled me. Why did I not know this sooner? How can I be such a bad judge of people?

Trudging on through the blinding snow, David reached the river. He gasped for air through the thick storm. Panting, he halted and dropped against a thick, leafless poplar tree. Tears slid down his cold cheeks. Dropping to his knees, a strangled cry escaped through his clenched lips.

Now what, Lord? Do I turn him in to the police? Is this the death knell for the ministry?

The bleak light of dawn mingled with the dusk of the night, blending the snowy sky into a drab shade of gray. He left the path along the river to cut back across the open field toward town. On his right, he noticed the barbed-wired fence edging the sprawling graveyard. After climbing across the fence, he stumbled between the rows of snow-covered wooden crosses. The wind whipped around him with howling fury, as if the forces of hell battled the earthly elements. He wandered around in search of Stefan's grave, overwhelming sadness in his heart which turned into seething anger.

No, Lord. I will not walk in anger. Vengeance is Yours, not mine. I need to do what is right. Please guide me. I can't do this in my own strength.

Unable to find the grave marker, David turned back to the city, his feet numb with cold. The industrial area of Perm rose starkly before him. Soot-covered chimneys belched their hideous fumes into the morning air. Unfamiliar with the area, he meandered through a maze of almost deserted streets.

A few shadowy forms lurked in a large stairwell of a decrepit building.

Fear tingled up and down David's spine. He'd never been in this area of town on foot. Ruthless gangs were well established in diverse parts of the city, and crossing their territory could prove lethal. He slipped his hand into his pocket to cover his wallet.

A gangly youth stepped out of the shadow onto the street, bringing David to a halt. "Hey, man. What are you doing here?"

David planted his feet, ready for an assault from behind. He knew the game. He also knew the inevitable end, unless he could meet their demands. Squaring his shoulders, he held his ground. "I've come from the graveyard."

The teen laughed mirthlessly. "Foolish to pick this route back, man. This is our territory."

David nodded. "I understand. I'm sorry. Perhaps I can buy some food for you?" It was a long shot, and he didn't think it would work. They'd undoubtedly prefer his wallet.

The mottled face of the boy-man came close to David, his alcohol-soaked breath washing over him. "Food, uh? How about just giving me the money?" He shoved David in the chest.

Praying hard, David regained his balance. "I'd prefer the food," he answered calmly. "I don't have a lot of money on me. Just enough to buy us all a meal. And I could use a good cup of coffee."

Stepping back, the teen considered for a moment, then flipped his head to the side. "So you wanna feed us, uh? OK, but it'd better be good, man."

"Wherever you want to go." David looked at the teens. Their ragged clothes hung haphazardly on their thin bodies, their faces pimpled. Pity welled up in him. "I don't know the area, so you'll have to take us to a café."

"Alright, follow me." The teen marched off down the street, the other teens in tow, with David sandwiched in between.

"I'm David," he introduced himself as they sat down in the small, grimy restaurant.

The skinny leader of the gang pointed to himself. "Pasha," he said, slurping the hot coffee with eager gulps. "And those guys are Grisha, Denya, and Valik."

"I work with young people," David said. "We have a building on Lenin Street. If you ever need a place to stay or some food, look us up."

"Thanks, but no thanks, man. Life's good here," the leader of the group bragged, devouring the sour rye bread and hard boiled eggs that the waitress had brought.

"Hey, I'm looking for a bunch of guys. Georgi, Sasha, Alik. You ever heard of them?" David carefully watched the leader's expression.

Pasha's jaws suddenly came to a halt. He wiped his mouth on his grimy sleeve while giving the others a hard look. "No, never heard of them."

"Well, if you see them, please let them know that Pastor David is looking for them."

Pasha nodded. "Will do, man."

Breakfast done, David excused himself from the group and called Vladimir. "I'm in the industrial area. I need a ride back to the shelter."

"How'd you get there?"

"On foot. It's a long story. I'll wait at the café on Tolstoy Street just off the corner from the old rubber plant. You can't miss it."

Vladimir arrived within half an hour. "Don't you understand how dangerous this area is?" he scolded, carefully navigating the car over the icy roads. "You could have been killed by those gangs that roam here."

"Actually, I had breakfast with a bunch of them. They're just like other teens. Hungry for attention."

David stared out the passenger window, his thoughts on his discovery in the office. "Listen, Vlad. I've got some very bad news to tell you."

Vladimir's head jerked up. "What's going on?"

"I got up early this morning to work on the financials. When I went to balance the petty cash, I found a stash of heroin in the cash box. Needles and syringes too. It has to be Jake's."

Vladimir gripped the steering wheel. "Are you sure?"

"No one else has a key to the box."

"Oh, Lord," Vladimir whispered. "How is it possible?"

"I don't know. But what do we do now?"

"You need to call the police,"

"Yes, we'll need to call the police."

"*You* need to call the police."

"I'm afraid you're right."

David placed the call to the authorities, and Vladimir informed Ferdinand and Ivan.

War raged in David's heart. How could Jake do such a thing? How did one fall into such cold-blooded deception? And then he'd pretended to be concerned about David's relationship with Karina. It had all been a cover-up to remove David from his position in the shelter.

Vladimir parked alongside the shelter building.

"The police are on their way," David told him. "They should be here any time now."

A police cruiser pulled up a few minutes later. Two uniformed officers, guns on their hips, stepped out and greeted David and Vladimir.

"Don't go in," the officer told them. "The suspect may be armed. We'll let you know once he's apprehended."

David and Vladimir waited in the car as the officers walked over to the door. One of them pulled his gun out of the holster. Without knocking, they entered the building.

"I hope Jake is here," David said. "If he noticed the box has been moved, he may have left the premises."

About ten minutes later, one of the officers approached the car. "We've made an arrest. You can go in now."

Vladimir and David followed the officer into the building. Jake stood beside the desk in David's office, his hands cuffed behind his back, his eyes fixed on the linoleum floor. The cash box stood open on the table.

The gloved officer transferred the little plastic bags into a metal case. "Nice cache. Probably smuggled in from Afghanistan."

Jake's head snapped up. For a split second his gaze met David's, filled with smoldering hatred.

Oh, Jake, why did you do it? How did Satan get into your heart?

The officer closed the box and tucked it under his arm. The other officer grabbed Jake's arm. "We'll have to lock the building until we've done a more thorough investigation." He nodded at David. "You'll be expected to testify."

They shoved Jake into the backseat of the police vehicle and slammed the door. Side by side, Vladimir and David watched the car disappear around the corner. Overcome with emotion, David sank onto his haunches, tears streaming down his face.

"I don't get it, Vlad." Dismayed, he looked up at the elderly man.

Vladimir rested his aged, shaking hand on David's shoulder.

"Be strong, my son. Be strong. Although we grieve, we also rejoice. Satan did not have the last word in this situation. God is good."

CHAPTER TWENTY-FOUR

T he judge sat tall and stiff in the straight-backed wooden chair, dressed in austere black garb. He flipped through the pages of Jared and Vanessa's dossier, halting here and there to read for a few minutes. The prosecutor, a grumpy woman in her mid-thirties, sat on the other side of the room. The clerk manned an archaic manual typewriter.

Vanessa folded her hands on her lap. *Just formality. Don't worry about it. Surely they wouldn't turn down an adoptive couple at this point.* Beside her, Jared looked relaxed, as did Maria, seated on the other side of Vanessa. She translated the prosecutor's speech into English for Jared and Vanessa. The prosecutor fired a rapid succession of questions at Vanessa, Jared, and the social worker from Kungur.

"Is there no family to look after this boy?"

"No, Madame. His mother passed away and there are no other known relatives," the social worker informed the prosecutor. Vanessa detected a hint of nervousness in the petite woman. Could something still go wrong? She wiped her palms on her black, A-line skirt.

Apparently satisfied with the answer from the social worker, the prosecutor transferred the question period to the judge.

"He's a kind man," Maria whispered, "He should not present any problems."

CHAPTER TWENTY-FOUR

"Unless a Russian relative comes forward in the next ten days," the judge stated, "Yuri will go to Canada with the Williams." He closed the binder.

Excited with the verdict, yet also disappointed that they'd have to wait ten days, Vanessa was filled with conflicting emotions. What if a family member showed up and claimed Yuri?

"Highly unlikely, but possible," Maria told them outside the courtroom. "It's happened only once in all the years that I have been facilitating adoptions. And Yuri has no family to look after him. I would not be concerned."

Jared and Vanessa walked into the hotel after Maria dropped them off. Jared wrapped his arm around Vanessa's waist. "It'll all work out. No other family has come forward up to now, so they probably won't in the next ten days either."

"You're right." Vanessa's spirits lifted.

"And now you get to go back to Canada!"

Vanessa reached for Jared's hand. "Yes, I get to go back to Annie. And very, very soon, Yuri and you will be there too."

⧉

Karina paced back and forth in her apartment. She hadn't been able to rest since she met David at the river. Her intention had been to walk up to him and say, "Guess what? I have become a Christian!" But when she saw him the words had stuck in her throat. Why should he believe her?

She'd thought of discussing the situation with Leonid, but his son, Boris, still had a crush on her. Finally, she overcame her trepidation and called the old pastor.

Her hands shook as she explained the situation with David. Leonid listened intently without interrupting her. "Have you read the story of Ruth in the Old Testament?" he asked when she finished.

"I don't remember." She hadn't read much of the Old Testament yet.

"Read it carefully, and then pray and see what God leads you to do."

221

Dissatisfied with Leonid's answer, she flipped through the index in the Bible which Leonid had given her in addition to David's New Testament, to find the reference to Ruth. She read the short book without pausing. Ruth, the foreign woman, embraced the God of Israel. She went back to Canaan with her mother-in-law, Naomi, where she met Boaz, the rich landowner. Although she didn't understand the references to Boaz as a "redeemer," one thing became clear: when Ruth wanted to marry Boaz, she didn't wait for him to come to her. She went to him.

"I would like to see Jake," David told the police officer at the station.

"No visitors allowed," the officer said, crossing his arms. "And rubles won't work." David recognized him as the same officer who'd assisted him after Stefan's death.

"Just a few minutes," David insisted, resisting the urge to pull out his wallet to see if the officer's words held truth.

"No."

"Is there anyone else in authority that I can talk to?"

"I'm the only one here." The officer leaned forward on the counter. "Your seedy friend doesn't need company."

Jake wasn't his friend. Not anymore. David turned around and left the station.

The shelter greeted him with dark silence. David closed the door behind him, sliding the deadbolt in place.

Vladimir had invited him to stay at his place, but David refused. The investigation had been completed so he'd moved back in. The shelter had to assume a sense of function again. *He* had to assume a sense of function again. He hung his coat on a hook and made his way to the dining room. His footsteps echoed in the empty hallway.

The room was cold and dark. David flicked on the light, placed a few logs in the wood stove, threw some old newspapers on top, and lit the paper. With crackling greed, the flames attacked the wood.

Lifting the coffee pot off the wood stove, he poured the day-old brew into a mug. He lowered himself onto the wooden bench by the table, his stare fixed on the blank paper on the table. The pad had been lying there since he'd returned to the shelter. He hadn't been able to bring himself to write the letter . . . until now.

Dear Jake,

I forgive you for supplying drugs to the teens while they came to us to try to come clean. I forgive you for destroying the ministry here at the shelter and for driving the kids away.

I've been so angry with you, but I choose to forgive you. God tells me that vengeance is His, and He will repay. I pray that you'll return to God and that He'll forgive you too.

The loud ring of the doorbell shattered the silence. David laid down his pen and trudged out of the dining room to the door. Moving the deadbolt, he opened the door.

"David," Karina nodded at him, hands thrust deep in her pockets. Her breath formed a frosty cloud in the cold air.

"Karina! How'd you get here? Is something wrong?"

"Oh, no! I caught a ride to Perm with some friends." She gestured to the small car waiting in the alley. "Is it all right if I come in or are you busy?"

No, he wasn't busy. David opened the door wider.

"Hannah told me what happened with Jake. I'm sorry," she said, stepping inside.

"Thanks. It's been tough." He took her coat, hung it up, and led the way to the dining room. "Are you in Perm for the night?"

"Yes, I'm staying at Hannah's."

"I'm glad to hear you've stayed in contact with her." He motioned to the wooden bench by the table. "Have a seat. Care for coffee?"

"Please." Karina sat at the table.

David busied himself by the wood stove with the coffee pot. "Do you need supper?"

"No thanks. I'm fine."

Like always. David poured the hot coffee into a mug. "I'm out of milk," he stated apologetically as he placed the steaming cup of coffee in front of her.

"Black's good. Thank you." Karina smiled at him as she cradled the cup between her hands.

Her presence disturbed him. He poured himself another cup of coffee, ladled some lukewarm stew into a bowl, and sat across from her. She wore a knit rust-brown sweater and a necklace made from bulky wooden beads. His eyes fell on the cross suspended on the necklace.

"I've done a lot of thinking this week," David said quietly, toying with his spoon. "The events that have transpired here have done terrible damage to Living Hope, and once again I've been fooled by people close to me. I don't know why you've come tonight, but first I have a question." He surveyed her face. "Karina Svetlana, who are you?"

Her eyes were clear as she looked at him, her face calm as if she'd expected the question. "My name is Karina Svetlana Gorsky."

"And your patronymic? Your father's name?"

"Ilyanova."

"So you've lied about your name?" His voice was sharper than he'd intended.

"No, my full name is on my official documents. I just chose not to use it." She set her half-empty cup down on the table and folded her hands.

"Because?"

She stood up from the table and moved close to the wood stove. For a moment she stood in silence, apparently soaking in the warmth of the fire. She turned and walked back to the table.

"I was abused by my father for years," she whispered, unable to make eye contact. "When I was old enough, I ran away. I wanted to forget."

Her openness surprised David. When she raised her eyes to his, the depth of pain shocked him.

"When I decided to come here, I knew I had to tell you everything," she said, her voice trembling. "What my father did isn't all."

David lifted his hand. "You don't need to tell me."

"Yes, I do." A determined look crossed her face. "My father brought other men home as well. To supply him with vodka. That's when I had my abortion."

David closed his eyes. "I'm so sorry." He'd had no idea. But why was she telling him all this? Why had she come? "Why do you tell me this?"

She pointed to the cross suspended on the necklace. "I've become a Christian."

He didn't doubt her words—her sincerity was evident—but he didn't know how to respond.

"Leonid, the pastor from the fellowship I've been attending, suggested that I go to you," Karina went on. "I knew that after you dropped me off at Vladimir's that one Sunday that you wouldn't pursue a relationship again. I needed to get my life straightened out first." She laughed softly. "It didn't happen that way, though. God straightened my life out for me instead."

"What happened?"

"After you left I became very despondent. Suicidal, actually. One day I watched this broadcast 'Power to Change.' I then gave my life to the Lord. Whether you ever returned or not, I couldn't go on without God anymore."

David rose to his feet. He moved around the table toward her, a lump in his throat. "Karina," he whispered, spreading his arms wide.

In one fluid motion, she rose and entered the circle of his arms. The words from the prophet Jeremiah sprang into David's mind. "I know the plans I have for you," declares the Lord, "plans to prosper you and not to harm you, plans to give you a hope and a future."

He slipped his hands through her hair, then cupped her face and kissed her tenderly. "I've waited for this," he said, his voice hoarse. "But I never dared believe." He drew back, his hands still around her face. "But God's timing is always better than we can imagine. Tonight when I came home I would never have guessed . . . ." He let go of her face, put his arms around her, and held her against his chest. With his cheek on top of her hair, he savored her nearness. Peace pervaded his being.

Thank you, Lord. God had answered above all he could've asked or imagined.

CHAPTER TWENTY-FIVE

K arina sat at her dining room table, pen and paper in front of her. David had suggested she name the babies she'd lost and write a letter of repentance. She also had to write a letter of forgiveness to Frank and her dad. "It'll bring healing for you," David had said.

Tears burned behind her eyes. *Help me, Lord! I don't feel up to this.* She didn't even know if the child she'd aborted had been a boy or a girl. Somehow she imagined her as a daughter.

She began to write.

My dearest Julia,

I'm so sorry you died just because I wanted to cover my sins. I didn't think of you as a baby. But after losing you, I wanted to die. I was so empty and the pain was so deep, I cried every night. I thought of killing myself, but I guess I was a coward. So I ran away. I'm sorry. If you were here, I know that you'd forgive me.

She dropped the pen and wept, her tears creating dark blotches on the paper. With great effort, she picked up the pen again.

My dearest Dmitry,

I gave you up because I didn't think I had a choice. I tried to keep you, but I couldn't. There was no one to help me. I wanted you to live, so I gave you away. Much later I heard you died. I loved you, and I still do.

She clasped her hands to her heart and steadied her breath. She envisioned his tiny, purplish face, his first cry when he emerged from her womb. No one had been with her during the delivery. She could've died right then and there. She'd tried to nurse the baby, but she had no milk. Her apartment stone-cold without heat, she'd bundled him up and brought him to the nearest orphanage.

I now work at an orphanage. I think of you every time I see a little baby boy, and my heart aches for what could have been. I miss you, and I love you still. I wronged you so much. You paid with your life, and I am so very sorry.

Love,

Your mom

She wept until her tears dried up and a quiet peace pervaded her spirit.

Fear not, Daughter, she heard a quiet voice say to her spirit. *Your sins have been forgiven. If no man condemns you, neither do I. Go and sin no more.*

Lord, I want to walk in Your commandments, she breathed. *Thank You for everything. Especially for David.*

Next she wrote the letter to Frank. Compared to the tears she'd shed about her babies, she felt surprisingly calm.

You hurt me, Frank, and I have hated you because of it. You walked out on me, dumped me during a difficult time. Dmitry died because you forsook us, and for years I held his death against

you. But God has found me and I don't hate you anymore. I forgive
you for all you've done to me and Dmitry. The memory of you will
no longer have power in my life. I am free in Christ.

"Good-bye, Frank," she said, folding the letter and shoved it into the
envelope with the others. "I have an amazing man in my life, better
than I could've imagined."

She pushed her chair back from the table and walked to the balcony
window, gathering the courage to write the letter to her dad.

She balled her fists at her sides. Her lips formed a thin, tight line. *If*
you do not forgive, neither will your heavenly Father forgive you.

God required that she forgive her dad. She picked up her pen.

> *Dear Dad,*

With a harsh stroke, she crossed out the "dear." *I hate him. I can't*
forgive him. Picking up the paper she scrunched it into a ball and threw
it to the floor.

"The kids have moved back to the main shelter from Hannah's,"
David told Karina as they drove through Perm. He'd picked Karina up
in Kungur to spend the weekend in Perm.

"You can stay with us rather than at Hannah's. We've prepared a
room for you." Relaxed, he held her hand as he pulled up in front of
a red light.

She squeezed his hand. "Thanks. I look forward to meeting everyone."

"I wish you could meet the teens, but we've never heard from them
again." That had been his deepest regret since returning to Perm. David
accelerated as the light turned green. "Rachael and the younger kids are
preparing dinner for us tonight. They're very excited about it."

Pulling up behind the shelter, he parked and opened the door for
Karina. "Welcome," he said, lifting her bag out of the truck box.

"It's a wonderful building," she told him, looking up. "We visited only the day shelter last time I was here. You aren't living in that apartment anymore?"

"No, but I'll probably move back there once I find someone to replace Jake."

David opened the door. "Noisy here tonight," he commented as he hung up Karina's coat. "I'd forgotten the amount of racket a few kids can make." He crossed the hallway to the living area.

"Hey, Pastor David!" A few gangly youths jumped up off their chairs and charged toward him as he entered.

"Georgi! Alik, Sasha!" Astonished, he halted in his tracks as he looked around the room. About ten exuberant teenagers crowded around him, cheering and laughing.

"Good to see you, Pastor David!" Georgi slapped him on the back.

"What a surprise! Did you know I was back?" David asked, grinning broadly.

Georgi pointed to a few teens who hung back. In the excitement, David had not noticed them until now.

"Pasha here told us."

David recognized the him and the other boys: he'd fed them the morning he'd found out about Jake's betrayal. Stepping forward, he shook their hands. "Welcome to Living Hope. Good to see you again." Turning around, he motioned to Karina. "I'd like to introduce you all to my lovely girlfriend, Karina Gorsky."

With a smile, Karina stepped forward and greeted the teens. "David has told me about you," she said. "How nice that you're back."

With a grin, Georgi elbowed David in the ribs. "I didn't think that you had it in you, Pastor," he whispered.

David elbowed him back. "The ol' man has some surprises left yet!"

"Good choice," Sasha winked. "She's a real looker, that one."

David observed Karina as she mingled with the teens, introducing herself individually. She seemed completely at ease among them, not in the least put off by their dirty clothes and disheveled appearance. *Thank You, Father.*

After supper, David picked up his worn Bible. "It's our habit to read God's Word after supper," he explained to the newcomers as they sat around the large table.

"I sought the Lord, and He answered me," David read, "He delivered me from all my fears. This poor man called, and the Lord heard him: he saved him out of all his troubles."

"I don't have enough words to tell you how happy I am that you're back." David looked around the group. "This is an answer to my prayers. God is very good to us."

After cleaning up the dishes, they played ping-pong, foosball, Chinese checkers, and chess. Vladimir showed up around nine o'clock with a big cake and a few bottles of Coca-Cola®, which the teens devoured like a pack of hungry wolves.

At ten, David sent everyone to bed. "We've all had a long day. We'll see you tomorrow bright and early." He kissed Karina good night. "Rachael will show you your room," he said. "I'll lock up."

After completing his nightly rounds, David went upstairs. Hearing a muffled sob in Karina's room, he paused at the door and knocked.

"Come in."

As he stepped into the room, he saw Karina standing near the open window, her face red. A strong wind blew snow into the room. Though dressed in thick, flannel pajamas, she shivered violently.

David rushed to the window and slammed it shut. Pulling her against him, he cradled her against his chest.

"Why did you have the window open? It's freezing out there!"

Her teeth chattered as she spoke. "I need to see him."

"Who?"

"My father."

Wrapping her in a blanket, he laid her down on the bed. David eased himself onto the edge of the mattress. He held her close, willing for his warmth to seep into her frozen body.

"Karina," he said affectionately, "what are you talking about?"

"I can't forgive my father. I just want to kill him." She wept profusely. "I can't live like this. I was just so afraid . . . ." She clung to him, her fists gnarled in his shirt. "But I'm scared that if I don't forgive him, God won't forgive me."

"You'll forgive him. I know you will." He settled her down into bed like a child, smoothing the hair and tucking the blankets around her. "With God's help, all things are possible."

"I've tried to forgive him, but it isn't working. I want to see him and tell him face to face." Reaching up, she wiped the tears off her cheeks.

"If that's what you want, we'll try to find him. But it's late. Let's talk about it tomorrow."

Reaching up, she wrapped her arms around his neck and hugged him tight. "Thanks for being there for me."

"We'll find your father and everything will work out. You'll see." He kissed her on the cheek. "Be anxious for nothing."

CHAPTER TWENTY-SIX

Jared carried the small bag of clothes and shoes into the orphanage. He'd stayed behind in Russia for ten long, dreary days, visiting Yuri as much as possible. The language barrier made communication difficult, as Yuri didn't understand any English. But the waiting period was over, and they'd be going home.

Karina met him at the door. "Congratulations, Mr. Williams. You are the lucky parent of an even luckier boy. Yuri is in my office. He's been there since breakfast this morning. He refuses to do anything but wait for you."

Jared glanced at his watch. It was two thirty in the afternoon: Yuri had waited for six hours! When Jared and Karina entered the office, Yuri jumped off his chair and ran to Jared. "Papa! Papa!" He jabbered on in Russian.

"He says he wants to go home with you in the automobile," Karina translated.

"I'm glad he wants to come with me. I wasn't sure he'd want to leave," Jared said, relieved.

Karina kissed Yuri's cheek. "Be a good boy for your new papa and mama," she told him in Russian.

Yuri nodded. "I will."

"Paka, Yuri. Good bye."

"Paka." He took Jared's hand and followed him to the vehicle. Jared lifted Yuri into Sergei's van and closed the door. The little boy waved enthusiastically until the van disappeared out of sight.

Karina and David took the eleven o'clock flight to Moscow and then transferred planes en route to St. Petersburg. At the St. Petersburg airport David rented a car.

The little rust-brown car bounced along the rutted road to the outskirts of the city.

Karina shifted in the passenger seat, her gaze fixed out the window. Following her melt-down at the shelter, David had made arrangements for them to return to St. Petersburg. "I'm coming with you," he'd said. "No way will I let you go by yourself."

Now they were back in her old neighborhood. Rickety cottages lined the rutted road. Nothing had changed since she'd left thirteen years ago.

"Turn left at the next corner." They were close to her father's house. She plucked at the fringes of her scarf, her face toward the window.

"I'm here with you." David took her hand. "And God's with you."

She pointed to a dilapidated cottage. The fancy wood carvings around the doors and windows showed elegance from a bygone era. The windows and doors sagged from years of use and harsh elements. The wooden gate on the picket fence hung haphazardly on its hinges. A meager plume of smoke drifted out of the blackened chimney.

David parked the car on the opposite side of the street.

"Your dad may have moved during the last thirteen years," David cautioned.

"I know."

He placed his hand on her arm. "Before we go, I think we should pray." He took her hands in his. "Heavenly Father, please be with us. Give Karina the strength to face whatever is behind that door. Help her to forgive her father for the sins committed against her, as You have forgiven us. Amen."

"Amen." Karina lifted her eyes to his face. The thought of facing her father after so many years filled her with sheer fear. Seeing the cottage brought back a flood of terrible memories. But David's presence helped immensely.

Steadying herself, she opened the car door and walked up to the decrepit gate, her head held high. David followed close behind her.

A sloppily dressed woman in her fifties opened the door. Her faded dress stretched over her many rolls of fat, ending just above her crooked knees. Thick cords of varicose veins coursed down her legs to her holey sneakers. She wiped her runny nose on the grimy sleeve of her dress.

"Who are you?" she asked, her eyes suspicious.

"I'm Karina Gorsky." Karina held out her hand. "And this is my friend, David Valensky."

The woman harrumphed and crossed her arms over her chest, ignoring Karina's outstretched hand. "What do you want? Obviously not money cause I ain't got none, and by the looks of you, you don't need none."

"I'm here to inquire about my father, Ilya Gorsky. I haven't seen him for some time. Is he still around?"

"So you're the run-away who left her poor daddy to fend for himself, eh? I heard about you from the neighbors. Hope you're not looking for an inheritance," she cackled. "The old man had nothing but this miserable house, which had to be sold to pay for his debts. No money for a funeral even. The neighbors dumped him in a box and carted him off."

Karina shoved her shaking hands in her pockets. "When did he die?"

"About two years ago. I never knew him, but Lydia did." She pointed to the house next door.

Karina remembered the old spinster who'd lived beside them for several years prior to Karina's departure. She was more than likely the source behind this woman's in-depth knowledge of her life and family.

She swallowed hard. "I'm very sorry to hear that he's gone." With a simple "Thank you," she turned away from the door, shoulders drooping. Had she traveled this far only to have forgiveness and reconciliation elude her?

"I'd like to go to the graveyard where my parents are buried," she told David when they reached the car.

He started the engine. "Tell me how to get there."

They drove to the cemetery in silence. Long rows of gigantic crosses stretched out before them, adorned by urns filled with multi-colored, plastic flowers. Karina clung to David's hand as they walked across the snow-covered grass.

"They would've buried him next to my mom," she said, pointing to the far side of the graveyard. "Dad arranged for that when mom died. Why, I don't know. He didn't love her." He hadn't loved either one of them.

She slowed her step as they approached two small white-washed wooden crosses, side by side. The Cyrillic script on one of the crosses held a sharp contrast to the crude, uneven letters on the other.

"Mom's grave." Karina pointed to the tidy writing: *Svetlana Stefanova Gorsky, 1945–1988.* "I wrote that."

David stopped before the grave with the inscription: *Ilya Gregorovich Gorsky, 1942–2002.*

Karina pulled her hand out of his and hugged herself tightly. Where was her father now? Was he getting what he deserved? She clamped her lips. Anger, her bastion against pain, welled up in her heart.

And where would you be without God's forgiveness? Are you any better?

She bowed her head in shame. Without His grace she would've become nothing but a bitter old woman. She'd have died in her sins just like her father.

Pity filled her heart as she looked at the crosses. She'd stopped grieving over her mother years ago. And now, for reasons she could not explain, she grieved the loss of her father. Looking at the patch of dead, brown grass covered with a thin layer of snow, her anger seemed futile.

I wish I would have had the chance to tell you about God. I forgive you, Dad, for all the pain you caused me. I will not be angry anymore.

Kneeling, she placed her hands on her mother's grave. *I love you, Mom. I will embrace the past and walk through the pain with my head held high, just like you did. God has given me a wonderful man.* She closed her eyes. *Someday maybe David and I will have children. If we have a girl, I'd like to name her after you.* In the middle of her pain and sadness, joy crept into her heart.

Rising to her feet, she looked at the graves one last time. *I forgive you both. For everything.*

She held out her hand to David. "I'm ready to go. All is well."

With his arm around her waist, David led her off the graveyard.

⸺ ⧉ ⸺

Vanessa paced back and forth through the airport terminal. Jared and Yuri's plane had arrived an hour ago. Why were they not here yet? She hoped that Immigration Canada was not causing a serious delay. She squeezed Annie's hand. The little girl held a helium balloon and a large teddy bear, gifts for Yuri.

Straining her neck, Vanessa tried to peer over the heads of the travelers dispersing from the customs area. She saw Jared as soon as he came through the rotating doors, Yuri on his arm.

"There they are!" she exclaimed, gesturing toward two figures emerging through the glass door. Squeezing through the crowd, Jared and Yuri quickly approached Vanessa and Annie.

Vanessa flung her arms around Jared and Yuri. "You made it!"

"It's great to see you both!" Jared kissed Vanessa, beaming from ear to ear. "Hey, Annie, meet your new brother." He set Yuri down and lifted his daughter into his arms. Yuri stared at his shiny new shoes.

"He's shy," Jared said. "He doesn't speak any English yet, so this must be a scary world for him."

"How'd he do during the trip?" Vanessa couldn't keep her eyes off her son.

Jared laughed. "Just great. Candies are an amazing communication tool. I just point at whatever I want him to do, hold up a candy, and he does it."

Annie held out a huge teddy bear. "This is for you," she said to Yuri, "'cause you're my brother now."

"Spasiba," Yuri grinned, accepting the teddy bear.

Bending down, Vanessa hugged Yuri. "I like your shoes and coat," she said, pointing at his new garb.

Yuri pointed at Vanessa in return. "Mama," he said.

Tears formed in Vanessa's eyes and her throat tightened. God had been faithful, even through the hard times. Joy and healing coursed through her heart as she watched her family—Jared, Annie, and Yuri—step through the rotating airport doors and out into the clear daylight.

∞∞∞

Karina shrugged into her warmest winter coat and put on a traditional Russian fur hat with ear flaps.

"It looks like you're going to the North Pole," Hannah laughed, seeing Karina in the hallway.

"David told me to dress for the cold," Karina explained. "I don't want to take any chances." She'd caught a ride into Perm and was staying at Hannah's place for the weekend.

"Have a wonderful evening," Hannah waved, disappearing into the kitchen.

As Karina pulled her gloves on, she heard David's knock on the door.

"Ready to go?" he smiled and then kissed her. Pointing at the fur hat, he laughed. "You took me serious."

"Of course. I always take you serious." She'd learned throughout their brief courtship that David meant what he said.

As he opened the door, Karina saw a carriage, pulled by two horses waiting in front of the building. The driver sat on the box, huddled in a thick fur coat.

Karina clasped her hand over her mouth. "Oh, David!"

"Last week you mentioned that you wanted to ride in one of those carriages sometime."

"I didn't expect you to actually do it." His thoughtfulness touched her.

"Your wish is my command." David helped her into the carriage, hunkered down on the seat beside her, and wrapped a wool blanket around their legs.

"Where are we going?" Karina asked as the driver pulled onto the street.

"It's a surprise." He took her hand beneath the heavy blanket.

The driver cracked his whip and the horses broke into a trot. Their feet clip-clopped on the hard asphalt road. Soft snowflakes cascaded down into the carriage. Soon, they came to the bridge that connected the east side of Perm to the west side.

"We're going to the main shelter," Karina guessed as they reached the downtown boulevard.

"Oh, no, too many people there for a romantic evening for two."

"The Italian restaurant on Lenin Street, then."

Leaning over, he kissed her cheek. "Stop guessing. You'll soon find out."

The carriage pulled up in front of the day shelter.

"Your old apartment?" She didn't comprehend. Why would he be so excited about that? He hadn't lived here since his return to Russia.

David threw the blanket aside, hopped out of the carriage, and lifted her down. She followed him upstairs, a frown on her face.

By the door, David handed her the key. "Go ahead," he motioned to the door.

The key turned easily in the lock. Soft music played inside as she crossed the threshold.

"Come." Taking her hand, David led her into the open living area. The lights had been turned low. The table, set for two, held two candles on a white tablecloth. Sprigs of greenery had been arranged around the candles. Two napkins, shaped like a fan, were folded on each plate.

But besides the intimate dinner setting, she noticed that the walls now sported the same butterfly wall paper border as she had in her apartment. A new couch and two chairs stood against the wall, a potted palm beside the couch. A large, framed painting hung above the couch and a brightly colored rug lay on the linoleum floor.

"David?"

He stood to the side, observing her with a smile. Someone had taken great care in decorating the apartment, but why? Her heart beat faster.

CHAPTER TWENTY-SIX

Moving close, he placed his arm around her waist. "What do you think?"

"It's . . . beautiful. Are you moving back in?"

"Someday. But not yet. The board has given me permission to hire you to oversee the day shelter operations."

"What?" He'd never mentioned anything of the sort, although they'd discussed the possibility of her moving to Perm. He'd also told her that they needed a new coordinator for the day shelter now that he was overseeing the full-time shelter again.

"I don't like you being so far away, Karinka," he said, using the intimate diminutive of her name. "So I had to find a way to bring you closer." Taking her hand, he knelt down on one knee. "In fact, I'd like to have you much closer yet. Karina Gorsky, will you marry me?"

"Oh, David!" Looking at the man kneeling on the floor, she felt her throat constrict. "I could never have imagined . . . ."

"So you accept?"

"Yes, of course I will."

He stood and pulled a small box out of his pocket. Inside was a gold ring inlaid with tiny diamonds. David took it out of the velvet lining and slipped it on her finger. Holding her hand, he leaned forward and kissed her. For a moment he drew back, and then pulled her into his arms. "I love you, Karina Gorsky."

She savored his nearness, the gentleness of his touch. "And I love you, David Valensky."

"And the job offer? Will you accept that too?" He held her at arm's length and looked in her face.

She laughed. "Yes, that too. I wouldn't think of being far away from you if I don't have to. Never again. Besides, it sounds like we have a special event to prepare for."

David's eyes grew moist. "When I first met you I never thought it would lead to this," he said. "But God has ransomed you. You've been bought with a price."

Karina nodded, her throat tight. For the first time in her life, she knew what it was like to be truly loved. By David, but above all, by God.

To order additional copies of this title call:
1-877-421-READ (7323)
or please visit our Web site at
www.winepressbooks.com

If you enjoyed this quality custom-published book,
drop by our Web site for more books and information.

www.winepressgroup.com
"Your partner in custom publishing."